Circles & Squares

Also in the Tim Simpson series

A Back Room in Somers Town
The Godwin Sideboard
The Gwen John Sculpture
Whistler in the Dark
Gothic Pursuit
Mortal Ruin
The Wrong Impression
Sheep, Goats and Soap
A Deceptive Appearance
Burning Ground
Hung Over
Into the Vortex
Simpson's Homer

Circles & Squares

JOHN MALCOLM

First published in Great Britain in 2002 by
Allison & Busby Limited
Bon Marche Centre
241-251 Ferndale Road
Brixton, London SW9 8BJ
http://www.allisonandbusby.com

A catalogue record for this book is available from the British Library

ISBN 0 7490 0584 X

Printed and bound in Ebbw Vale,
by Creative Print & Design

JOHN MALCOLM is the author of thirteen previous Tim Simpson mysteries, as well as a number of books on art and antiques. A former Chairman of the Crime Writers Association, John Malcolm lives in a Sussex village with his wife.

Chapter One

It sounded more like a summons than an invitation. Chief Inspector Nobby Roberts is an old friend but the voice lacked warmth.

"Breakfast," it said sharply, on the telephone to my office, mid-afternoon. "Bit short notice. Tomorrow morning. Usual place. All right?"

"Fine," I responded, making a quick recovery. "What a pleasant surprise. I look forward to it. We haven't met for - "

"Usual time?" he interrupted. "I'm a bit busy just now, Tim."

"OK. Usual time, then. Is this for anything special?"

Silence. He had rung off. I stared at the dumb receiver in perplexity. Normally he would have at least one cheerful, bantering crack at me before he ended the interchange. And I would have one back. This was very clipped. But there you are; people in a hurry, or maybe people being overheard, do not dally with words. You have to make allowances. Besides, I always enjoy breakfast with him. I put his brevity down to pressure of work and went out the following morning in cheerful, innocent spirits.

We meet in a small Italian restaurant on Victoria Street. It does a good all-in English breakfast incorporating two fried eggs, rashers of bacon, tomato, mushrooms, sausages, fried bread, black pudding if you want it, baked beans and fried potatoes or American hash browns, all at a very reasonable price. The place is convenient for Nobby since his office in Scotland Yard is just down the road and I, having arrived from South Kensington, can nip into the Tube station at St James's in order to tunnel my way to the City via Monument. The menu may sound copious but it keeps a man going practically all day, which is some small compensation for this disgracefully lunchless, desk-bound, paper-cup coffee, business era.

Nobby had a preoccupied look and was quiet until we'd ordered and the plates arrived. Then the trouble began.

"I suppose," he said, spearing a section of bacon, egg and fried bread, "you must wonder why I suddenly instigated this meeting."

"I am all agog, Nobby."

"Your surprise is understandable." His voice went muffled for a moment as he masticated the assembly he had introduced into his mouth, then cleared again. "Usually it is you who initiates these things. For your own purposes. They bring memories of many events which professionally I would rather have avoided."

I frowned. "Really?"

"Yes, really." He paused as though to reflect for a moment before continuing. "You have, in the past, invited me here for discreditable reasons." A minatory fork, now empty, was pointed defensively at me as I opened my mouth to protest. "You have even convened a breakfast before you were indicted, interrogated or worse by one of my colleagues. Or to prevent other events overtaking you." He lowered the menacing tines. "In a sense, therefore, there has been a feeling of in some way being corrupted."

I gaped at him in consternation. He was dressed as ever in meticulous grey, the suit not too smooth but not too creased either. The jacket was open to reveal his quiet blue shirt and a sober tie with some sort of Divisional stripe to it. His gingery hair was clipped neatly, not too short, not too long, and his blue eyes had the healthy clarity of a fit man even though, nowadays, he walks with a limp. He is an inch or two taller than me but slimmer, as might a swift wing three-quarter compare to a front row forward, although the professional front row forwards playing rugby today would regard me as flimsier material than their battering-ram, bull-necked outlines require.

Moderating my surprise in order to assemble my most reproachful expression, I spoke. "I thought we were just having a chummy little get-together as old friends. I should have known better from the tone in which you called yesterday. Terse is hardly an adequate description; you were brusque." I leant back and narrowed my eyes at him accusingly. "You give past events a melancholy spin, considering how much they have benefited you. But there's no one to beat you when it comes to uninvited moral lectures, is there? "

"I am merely telling you how some previous meetings have struck me."

"Your recollections are defective. But never mind them." I speared a forkful of my own. "If those are your feelings why did you convene, as you put it, this particular reunion today? In such a hurry?" I gave him a probing stare. "My conscience is clear. You must have some misdemeanour of your own to confess, have you? That, or a favour to ask?"

It was his turn to frown. Then he compressed his lips, put down his implements and looked out of the window for a moment at the passing traffic. It seemed as though he was trying to see beyond our reflected images on the inner glass to a distant, desirable landscape before committing himself reluctantly to the start of something with unknown implications. After a few seconds he moved his stare back to focus on me and spoke. His tone was level and dispassionate, as he might use to someone under interrogation rather than an old friend.

"What does the name Bassington mean to you?"

"Bassington?"

"Yes. Bassington."

I thought for just a moment before responding. "Saki, I suppose. The pen name of H.H.Munro. He wrote *The Unbearable Bassington*. A famous story to addicts of polished prose."

"Who?"

"Saki. He was known for his epigrams. 'To have reached thirty is to have failed in life' comes from one of Saki's exquisite young men, Reginald by name I think. Which puts you and me in some sort of perspective, I'm afraid." I grinned at him. "What is this? A warm-up for a literary quiz game? Have the Met started a *Weakest Link* of their own?"

He closed his eyes briefly, then opened them again to give me the beginnings of a bilious stare. "No, we are not, I am happy to say, practising for a quiz game. There is no way I go in for quiz games and even if I did I would not consult you for answers."

"Nobby!" I was indignant. "You are thoroughly offensive today."

He ignored my response. "I will repeat: does the name, apart from snappy literary allusions, mean anything to you? Moira Bassington, to be precise about the full name. In a contemporary mode, rather than a dated, deliberately bookish one. Miss Moira Bassington? Ring any chimes?"

I shook my head confidently. "No, Nobby, it does not. Never touched the girl. Why should I know her?"

"Could I have a definitive answer, please?"

I considered briefly, looking at his still, solemn face under its gingery hair and resisted the temptation to bait him further. "An absolute blank. I do not know a Bassington of either gender. Is it a real name, from real life? Why do you ask?"

"I'm asking the questions, not you."

"Oh, really. There is no need to get pompous, Nobby."

"I won't. At least, I'll try not to. But I'd prefer you to answer me here, frankly and honestly, rather than down at a local nick."

I stopped eating. "Hey, wait a minute. This has suddenly become official, has it?"

"After a fashion, yes."

I gave him a bilious stare in return. "Well I can answer you, frankly and honestly, after a fashion, that the name Moira Bassington means bugger-all to me."

"Hmm."

"What do you mean, 'hmm'? Disbelief is a distressing trait, Nobby, when it comes to old friends. Do you think I am not telling you the truth?"

"I do not say that you are lying to me, no. But, from past experience, there are times when you have been economical with the actuality, as the late Alan Clark put it. You have not lied directly but have concealed certain facts from me in order to pursue your own devious and mercenary ends."

"This is sad and ungrateful stuff. Me?"

"It is, I should remind you, a serious offence to conceal relevant facts from a police officer during the course of his enquiries."

I put down my knife and fork and peered at him irritably. "Ho. Har. Now it comes out. Far from offering me a congenial and comradely breakfast as befits an old chum whose turn it is *to pay*, you are in fact conducting an unannounced interrogation during the pursuit of some squalid enquiry leading to the enhancement of your egocentric career. Not only that, you have clearly got out of bed on the wrong side this morning."

"What the hell do you mean, egocentric?"

"There is no need to be *aggressive*, Nobby. When I think of how many times I have helped you when you were utterly stymied, to put it mildly, and thus buttressed your reputation, I am distressed. Deception is not what I expect from you."

He sighed. "All right. I accept your assurance for the moment. But the Bassington question is important, so I will explain. Just listen to me and keep quiet until I've finished. Right?"

"If you insist, Chief Inspector."

"I do. Two days ago a woman called Moira Bassington was found dead. She had been murdered. A blow to the head, or maybe several blows, was the cause of death. It happened in an estate of flats in Pimlico, appropriately enough in that area behind what is now the Tate Britain gallery."

"Appropriately? What do you - "

"Shut up and listen! At first, it was considered to be a domestic matter or perhaps the act of a pick-up. Bassington, who was in her forties, was known to be a bit promiscuous."

13

I picked up my knife and fork again. "Ah. The bareable Bassington, was she?"

"Dear God. Will you never be serious? Try to resist flippancy, will you? Neighbours had heard shouting the night before. Naturally the local CID men pursued the normal line of enquiries. In going through her effects, they came up with a number of names written in a sort of diary or journal. One of these was the name Simpson."

He paused for effect. I blinked at him. "Common enough, surely - "

"The initial 'T' was next to it. Yesterday they ran the list of names through their computer records and guess what?"

"Oh, no. I really don't believe this. I really don't. Surely this is a joke? A poor joke? You've convened this breakfast interrogation on the basis of some ephemeral electronic rubbish?"

There is, in the records of the Metropolitan Police, or even police records countrywide for all I know, a little flag that leaps up whenever the name Tim Simpson is punched into the required box. The flag says 'refer to Chief Inspector Roberts, Scotland Yard' and that is what always happens. It comes of many past events upon which I prefer not to dwell.

"Well may you express disbelief. But I regret that it is not a joke. Right now I am in the middle of a very taxing and important line of enquiry which is no business of yours and from which I simply do not need to be diverted. I am damned busy. Another of your imbroglios is the last thing I want to get sucked into."

"Imbroglios? Me?"

"There has been a murder and your name has come up in the course of the investigation into it."

That did it. I slammed down my implements and opened my mouth, wide. But he beat me to the next line.

"All right! All right!" Mollifying hands fluttered in front of me. "Keep calm! Calm! I withdraw that statement. Your name has possibly come up in the course of it. I have agreed, despite being hard pressed, to question you on the matter as a

14

gesture of old friendship. I said I would see you before it might be necessary for the investigating team to give you the grilling you probably deserve." He leant forward to point at me with his fork once more. "So far, do you see, I'm protecting you."

"That," I responded with icy dignity, "is pretty British of you Nobby, dear boy. I am touched by your solicitude, even if this utter tripe stems from some ridiculous computer glitch. Your fears are groundless. I can assure you that this Bassington lady, however appropriate you may view her address behind the old Tate to be, is unknown to me. Absolutely unknown. In view of your remarks about her possibly immoral behaviour, I find the implied criticism of my character insulting. May I remind you that the name Simpson, with initial T, is not exactly the rarest in the telephone book? You can tell your computer-obsessed colleagues that there is, or rather was, no relationship of any kind with me."

"I am relieved to hear it." His expression relaxed a little. "You don't think she might, in any way, however remote it may seem, be likely to have crossed your path?"

"No, of course not. Why should she? Try, if you possibly can, to bring some objective logic, rather than entrenched prejudice, into your enquiries. I mean, what did she do, Nobby?"

He speared another piece of bacon and fried bread. "She was self employed."

"Doing what?"

"She was a researcher."

"A researcher?"

He replaced the fork on his plate and mumbled a simple affirmative. "Yes."

I gritted my teeth. This was like drawing blood from a stone. "Do I have to shout before you yield something useful about her occupation? What in hell did she research, damn it?"

His eyes came up from his plate to mine. "Calm. Keep calm, will you? She was a freelance and worked for certain TV producers."

A cold feeling went down the back of my neck. Why? Why all of a sudden did icy prickles tingle my spine? Why had my hands suddenly clenched in tension?

I kept my tone level. "What kind of research, Nobby? The word covers many activities."

He gestured vaguely. "Oh, the usual sort of thing, digging up material for programmes, particularly documentaries. Pretty much hack work. Back history, trawling out old still photographs and archive film footage from libraries. Background material and biographical facts. But images, mostly."

"Oh really?" The prickles had turned to huge icicles. Blood was draining out of my extremities, bringing on a sort of paralysis. It couldn't be, surely. It couldn't. Please not.

His ginger face went intent and his eyes locked onto mine. "Tim?"

"Er, what?"

"Why do you suddenly look as though you've just swallowed a wasp? You've gone pale and your eyes are bulging."

"Me? Wasp? You have much too lively an imagination for police work, Nobby. Bit too much pepper in the sausage, perhaps." I picked up my tea and took a swig of it. "Made my eyes water."

He shook his head. "You finished your sausages a while ago. You paled as soon as I mentioned still photographs and film footage. From libraries." He pointed a sticky knife at me with more than usual accusation. "Cough it up. There's definitely something bugging you. This Bassington woman is dead as a result of violence. Come on, put that tea down and start the explanations. Don't prevaricate in your usual, evasive fashion, either. Tell me now. Better to me now than to the murder team assembled at Chelsea nick."

"It - it must be pure coincidence. It must be. It must."

"Cough it up," he snapped. "And no funny business. You hear me? Now."

I coughed. For murder, I cough.

Chapter Two

It started, as these things so often do, at work. Nothing sinister, nothing creepy, just the underlying tension of yet another meeting at which results would be expected.

"The time has come," Jeremy White said, commanding close attention as his imperious gaze fell upon me, "to end all vacillation. We must get on."

He turned slightly and gestured at the grave figure beside him, causing a flash of gold to wink from his white cuff. "It appears that we have excess cash in hand. Interest rates are low. Time and tide wait for no man. A decision is required. Geoffrey and I are all agog." A wicked smile lit the patrician features under his blond mop of hair. "The floor is yours, so let us have it. Your unreserved and uncompromising recommendation, here and now, on the next work of art in which we should invest. At once. If you please."

He sat back, clearly content to have delivered this ultimatum of mixed, if still intelligible, syntax. But I resisted a temptation to point out that I could not, practically, let them have the floor even if, grammatically, that was what he had demanded.

The hot seat is no place for pedantry.

I braced myself carefully as I returned his gaze, then took a quick shufti at Geoffrey Price, seated beside him in calm, pinstriped, accountancy posture, like a Ming Dynasty mandarin setting new standards for impassivity. This was going to be tricky. The time comes when you have to face up to the flak your convictions will attract, but it is never pleasant. The face sets, the sinews stiffen. The eye has to meet the eye.

"I think," I said, firmly but I hope not in any way aggressively, placing my hands carefully on the cool mahogany surface of the Georgian table at which we sat, "that we should, without any doubt, buy a Nicholson."

Then I waited, with bated breath. Around us, the fine panelling of Jeremy White's office at White's Bank in Gracechurch Street looked down, as it so often did, with superior disdain for yet another scene charged with emotional static. Outside, the muffled sound of traffic passing by on its City of London business provided a dull mutter, as though providing the partisan murmur of a distant audience. On the cold, hard table, glinting against its dark red shine, stood the fine bone china of our coffee cups, offset by an even shinier Georgian silver coffee pot, only brought out for special occasions. In this case, the occasion was that of a board meeting of White's Art Investment Fund, of which we three were the prime, indeed the only, directors.

The silence which greeted my statement was nerve-racking. I much prefer Jeremy in explosive mode. It is, so often, easier to cope with him when he is going off like a box of rockets in all directions. He is my immediate employer and long-term associate in the operation of White's Art Fund, which we dreamed up together in order to satisfy those clients of the Bank wishing to invest in art without actually buying a Rembrandt or, more taxingly these days, a Van Gogh themselves. But the relationship has never been passive. Jeremy and I have been through too much together for it to be that.

His face lit up, as though sunshine had suddenly beamed in through the period panes of his shuttered sash windows. "What an excellent idea! Brilliant. I absolutely agree, Tim."

The words strayed into my disbelieving ears like the sonic fluttering of an incomprehensible foreign language.

"Eh?"

"First class. I've always admired his work."

"You have?"

"Of course." He gestured at the silver pot in front of him. "That still life in the Tate. Masterly use of paint. Those landscapes. The portraits. Didn't get a knighthood for nothing, did he?"

"Knighthood?" I frowned in recollection. "He turned the offer down, surely?"

"Nonsense." Jeremy shook his blond locks emphatically. "I'm surprised at you, Tim. Should have thought you'd have boned up properly, done your homework, before dishing up this one, even though I'm all for it. Sir William Nicholson? Excellent fellow. From the time he joined up with James Pryde and turned out those marvellous Beggarstaff posters - married Pryde's sister, didn't he? - then all that wonderful still life and landscape work, he was right on track. Even Whistler, a vinegar critic if ever there was one, praised him. That oil of the silver tea service. Superb. He was a Trustee of the Tate Gallery, you know. Rothenstein admired his work enormously. Called him a minor master." He paused, thoughtfully. "Bit condescending, that, I think. Mind you, Rothenstein wasn't exactly - wasn't always perhaps entirely - I say, what's the matter? You look as though you've swallowed a frog."

I gulped. Swallowing a frog would have been easy compared to the reversal of enthusiasm I was about to effect. I closed my eyes then had another go at getting through to him, clearly having fluffed the first shot by yards.

"I wasn't talking about William Nicholson, Jeremy. I was talking about Ben. His son, you know."

There was a silence. The panelling went back into suspense mode. Geoffrey Price, opposite, our excellent but conservative accountant, beside whom the prudent Scottish Chancellor, Gordon Brown, could produce budgets looking like the work of a rash spendthrift, let his jaw drop. His eyes widened and his breathing stopped, causing his pinstripes to swell just the slight swell allowed by the strict code of the Institute of Chartered Accountants regarding emotional display. Then the dam broke.

"What?" shouted Jeremy, causing a silver spoon among the bone china cups to rattle in its saucer.

"Ben," I said, firmly. "Ben Nicholson. The abstract artist. He - "

19

"*Ben? Ben Nicholson?* That - *that* - have you gone raving mad?"

"The most important," I kept it as smooth as possible, "abstract artist produced by this country in the twentieth century. Of international standing. The winner of more Biennale cups and prizes than his father got hot dinners from aristocratic clients. I - "

"Appalling. Dreadful. Circles and squares. Bits of white cardboard stuck on bigger bits of white cardboard. I'm not paying money for those."

"Reliefs, they're called, Jeremy, actually - "

"I don't care what they're called. They're no bloody good. I went to that retrospective of his work at the Tate in the winter of '93. It didn't impress me at all. Lot of dusty nonsense."

"The Tate, if I recall it correctly, said that he was one of the greatest English artists of the twentieth century. A pivotal figure in the Parisian and London avant garde of the 1930s."

"Avant garde? Pshaw. That tells you everything."

"'The primary force behind geometric abstraction in England, and its alliance with contemporary architecture in the 1950s' I think is the quote used on the catalogue. Although not all his work, by any means, is abstract."

"Contemporary architecture? Contemporary architecture? Well that damns the beggar for a start."

I raised my eyebrows. "I didn't know that you share Prince Charles's views on contemporary architecture, Jeremy."

He blinked and brushed aside wayward blond locks with an impatient gesture, causing another gold cufflink-flash from the snowy white sliver projecting from his charcoal sleeve. "There is no need," he snarled, between his teeth, "to be offensive. Absolutely no need whatsoever."

"I merely thought - "

"Oh no, you didn't. You were just being your usual, opprobrious self. I am not here to field insults by way of comparison with Prince Charles."

"Jeremy, really. The Prince's concern for artistic matters is, surely, well recorded." I sat back, with a bland smile. "He paints part-time, you know. Water-colours."

"You are a funny swine, aren't you? Really droll. I know what this is. You're just doing this to wind me up."

"No, no. I do assure you."

"Yes, yes. I know you too well." He shook his head as though to clear it, then employed a more wheedling tone. "Nicholson? Ben Nicholson? Come on, Tim. You don't really like his work, do you?"

I hesitated. The thing about Nicholson's work, I was beginning to find, was that some of it appealed to me powerfully and some seemed too trite for words. There was, to my eye, often a lack of power. Jeremy's adjective - dusty - was sometimes close to the mark. The problem with abstraction, for me as for many others, is its relation to the subconscious. The start of surrealism, you might say, and appeals to uncontrolled mental states.

"Ha!" He was on to my hesitation like a terrier. "You see? You don't."

I shook my head. "That is not the point, Jeremy. And actually, there is some of his work that I do like. It has an almost spiritual appeal. But my personal tastes are irrelevant."

He bridled. "Oh? Irrelevant? Are you not the effective executive director of the Art Fund? The man responsible for its investment policy and performance? Should our clients not be trusting your eye, as they might a suitable gallery owner's? As they have done," he gave me an emollient, oily smile "with success up to now?"

"No, they shouldn't. Not my eye. They should be trusting my view, my forward view that is, of the appreciation of the works of art acquired by the Fund. I use the word appreciation in its mercenary, rather than aesthetic sense of course."

Geoffrey Price cleared his throat. His expansion had abated. The pinstripes deflated marginally, back to normal volume. His expression moved somewhat off mandarin for a moment, showing a slightly interested cast.

21

Jeremy glared at him, as though this interruption by the scorer was spoiling the match.

"What, Geoffrey?"

"I have to say that I think Tim is right." Geoffrey, as befits a chartered accountant keen on cricket but encumbered with a Rover car and four children, cultivates the temperate tone of voice. "It is not a question of personal taste we are concerned with here. It is a matter of investment policy. Is this, in other words, the right time to acquire a Ben Nicholson painting? That is, surely, the key question?"

Jeremy cocked an eyebrow at me without comment, and waited.

"As a matter of fact, I think it is. Ben Nicholson's work became very expensive towards the end of his life - after decades of rejection commercially, of course - but since then he has somewhat declined. There was that chaos a year or two ago about a number of fakes, authenticated by unfortunate authorities on his work, which upset the market. Some critics of the 1993-4 retrospective were, a bit like you, Jeremy, rather condescending. Faint praise was in the air. Yet so many of his contemporaries, artists and architects, found him inspiring that he is bound to occupy a major place in the history of English art. And, I'm sure I don't have to remind you, it is the written policy of the Fund, set out in our prospectus and sent to all our investors, to acquire the very best examples of the work of British artists, or works relating to them, from the period of the last hundred and fifty years or so. One could be criticised for neglecting Nicholson."

Jeremy scowled. "As one might be criticised for neglecting his father."

"Indeed so." An idea, the spark of an inspiration, had suddenly come into my mind. Although precipitate, Jeremy is sometimes a useful marker of general public taste. I made my voice as mollifying as possible. "Indeed, Jeremy, indeed. How right you are. It might be a major coup, particularly at a time of uncertainty, to acquire the works of both father and son for the Fund. Simultaneously. That would cause amazing publicity. Wouldn't it?"

A look of the utmost suspicion crossed his face. "You are an absolute bastard, Tim. An utter shit. You've had one of each in view all along, haven't you?"

I shook my head self-deprecatingly. "No, no, not really. You, Jeremy, as ever, have been the catalyst, the spur, indeed the inspiration, behind my mere - "

"Oh, stop it. Cut it out. I don't believe you. However, I am prepared to agree, albeit reluctantly, to your exploring this - this regrettable concept but, and it is a big but."

"What?"

"Just tell me one thing." He held up a finger and levelled it until it was pointing at me like an accusing spear. "Is the town of Hastings in any way involved - any way at all - in this sudden conversion of yours?"

I swallowed. "It wasn't when we started this meeting, Jeremy. But now that you've insisted on Sir William Nicholson, it does just so happen that, perhaps in the near future, I might have to - "

"Oh God. Oh no. Not again. Not again." He threw his hands up in the air. "What dreadful, murderous genies are to be let out of their poisonous bottles if you visit Hastings once more? Eh? Eh?"

"Jeremy, *really*. You must control yourself. None at all. There is no danger of any kind. Get a grip, man."

"Of course there is. Danger is inevitable." He clutched at his head in mock horror. "It has never been otherwise."

"Many times it has. Many times, as you know full well. You are quite wrong, Jeremy."

I shook my head at him reprovingly as my mind started to take in the malevolent genies that might need to be released from bottles long stoppered if this project were to run to past form. Then I tried to block that line of thought. My denial had been instinctive but, as usual, Jeremy was almost certainly right. In the pause that followed my rebuttal I could see conflicting emotions chasing across his face. Jeremy is from a cadet branch of the White family but he has risen to its main board by dint of the application of a sharp brain and a risk-taking approach to most things. Like many of us, Jeremy is easily bored. He loves a flutter, something that will bring a bit of excitement into life. If its corollary is that some stress and anxiety accompany the excitement, that is all part of the cock-tail of stimulation. His philosophy is that Life is for Living with capital ells and the Devil take the hindermost. Our Art Fund was successful because of risks taken and events over-come. In this, Jeremy was more a creature of the eighteen-nineties than our own, risk-averse times.

"Damn it," he said, suddenly, his face breaking into a grin. "We're off again, aren't we?"

"If you say so, Jeremy."

"All right. Have a go. Nothing venture, nothing gain. Agreed, Geoffrey?"

Geoffrey Price, who understands perfectly that we are in the risk business, gave me a reproachful look, then nodded reluctantly. "One day," he rumbled, "one day you'll come horribly unstuck, you know."

"Fear nought! Tim is under starter's orders. The race is on. I loathe Ben Nicholson's work and love his father's. The Dismal Thirties compared with the Roaring Nineties. A joint acquisition, however, is a grand idea. It will be great publicity, I do believe."

"Splendid, Jeremy. I appreciate your support."

He gave me a quick, suspicious look, then glanced at his watch. "Well, that's that. I declare the meeting over. Mustn't make you late, must we?"

"Sorry? Late?"

"Ah! You thought perhaps I didn't know? About your meeting with Sir Hamish Lang in his lair in London Wall? This very morning? Not that you and he are great chums, are you? But Freddy seems convinced that you are the horse for the course on this one. And who am I to gainsay our respected

Chairman and Leader? Eh? I only hope this new caper leaves you time to slot in the Nicholsons."

"Jeremy - "

"Run along, dear boy, run along! Hamish is a demon for punctuality. As I'm sure you know."

I sat still. "I smell bloody conspiracy. I'm not sure I'm going, now."

"Tim! Such distrust. Such a scowl. I merely happened to bump into Freddy on his way to Cruft's and he mentioned he'd like to borrow you for a bit. On secondment, as it were. Quite apologetic, he was. I didn't know you'd impressed him so much. That business in Italy, he said, over poor old Richard. And the Art Fund. Excellent. Just the man."

"Oh, God."

"Stop moaning. On your bike. You have come to the favourable notice of Our Leader. Who am I to block the onward and upward sweep of your career?" He smiled another vulpine smile. "We shall watch your progress with interest. Intense interest. It is always a pleasure to see a true professional at work. Can you, by the way, work a Box Brownie? You may need to. Always a useful accomplishment, that, I fancy."

"You bastard," I said. "You utter bastard."

And left.

Chapter Three

"Amazing," I could hear Sir Hamish Lang saying as I approached his office from the corridor, "absolutely amazing. Huge sums. The Getty Foundation and Bill Gates, for instance. They are the two biggest investors, I understand."

There was a murmured reply, somewhat affirmative in its vague response, and then I was through the door, confronting three men.

"Ah, Simpson."

The white-haired figure in front of me was thin, spotlessly clean and tailored to a standard I'll never live to afford. Its sharp expression showed little warmth at my arrival. This was no surprise; Sir Hamish has never evinced the slightest enthusiasm for me. He glanced at his watch as he issued his perfunctory greeting, found nothing to complain of at a punctuality level, and held his hand out to shake mine, briefly. Sir Hamish is a crusty old trout who has always regarded me as too young, too poorly connected and certainly too irreverent to be considered seriously as a fully-blown member of the board of which he is Chairman and on which I sit as a non-executive director. It is one of many boards on which he sits throughout the City of London, whereas I sit on only two. His approach to my presence usually varies between superior condescension and downright disapproval. Today, he was in the former mode.

"Lord Harbledown insisted that you would be the right man for this matter," he said, disbelievingly, as though to explain an aberrant acceptance of my arrival in his City lair, "and as a result I've asked these gentlemen along to meet you." He gestured at the two men facing me. "May I introduce? Firstly, Mr Watson of Mangate Solutions Limited. Mr Watson, this is Mr Tim Simpson of White's Bank."

"What ho, Gerry," I said, holding out a hand, "how's life with the Champion?"

"Hi, Tim." Gerry Watson grinned at me as he gave me a firm shake. "Not too bad, not too bad at all. Glad to hear that Freddy Harbledown thinks you're still employable. One of his prize Old English Sheepdogs, eh? I guessed that you might be coming along today."

The elegant Gerry Watson left a very famous auction house a year or two back to run Mangate Solutions for an Anglo-French millionaire called Pierre Champion. According to its prospectus Mangate Solutions is a hire outfit, warehousing huge quantities of so-called antiques and art gear for rental to film and TV producers. In fact, I had a suspicion that Gerry was building up a prime collection for his boss, keeping as low a profile as possible. I couldn't see him spending his expert time invoicing some costume drama outfit for the hire of tin suits of armour and Jacobean oak buffets of dubious Belgian origin. Gerry is much too much of a specialist for that.

"You know each other, then." Sir Hamish Lang's impeccable accent - he was at Winchester and Trinity despite his West Highland ancestry - revealed little of the disappointment he undoubtedly felt. He likes to think of himself as an initiator. Gerry's irreverent reference to Freddy, Lord Harbledown, Chairman of the board of White's Bank, my supreme chief and enthusiastic breeder of Old English Sheepdogs, would not have met with approval, either. Sir Hamish has a strong sense of decorum, doubtless stemming from some innate Presbyterian instruction, and does not like to be upstaged.

"For some time, Sir Hamish," I replied respectfully. "Forgive me if I seemed to be jumping the gun. Our paths have crossed at various points."

"Indeed? How felicitous. Allow me, then, to introduce Mr Frank Cordwell, whom perhaps I do not think you will know." He gestured at the remaining figure in the room. "And who is crucial to the proposed scheme. Mr Cordwell, Mr Simpson."

"How do you do?" I reached forward once again to shake a hand. Cordwell was a bulky figure in his early forties, fairish in complexion behind horn-rimmed glasses which gave him a studious look. Like the rest of us he wore a suit, but the skill of his tailor and that of Sir Hamish were about as far apart as the Poles. It gathered round him in grey folds of worsted cloth unrelated to the form beneath, almost as though its designer had been intent on disguising the human outline in perplexing drapes. It occurred to me that perhaps he did not often wear it. He looked like an overweight librarian who has borrowed a corpulent uncle's outfit for a job interview.

"Pleased to meet you," he answered, thus condemning himself to Sir Hamish, who managed to control his usual grimace admirably despite this socially, to him, appalling response.

"Shall we sit down?" Sir Hamish indicated a boardroom-style table with a minor gesture, and we arranged ourselves around it obediently. "We are here," he continued, once we were all attention, "as a result of a discussion I had with Pierre Champion some days ago on the subject of film and photographic archives. This is a field into which he intends to expand, amongst his many other interests, and which ties in, one might put it, with the Mangate Solutions enterprise in that the principles and practices have parallels even if the markets are somewhat different."

What he means, I thought to myself, is that if you can rent out a Queen Anne bureau to the props department of a TV company, why shouldn't you rent out old footage of some past event to the features or documentary department as well?

"Mr Cordwell is an *archivist*," Sir Hamish put emphasis on this professional description as though the word was alien to him, "of considerable qualification and experience. It is he who will be assembling, for Pierre Champion, the extensive library of still photos and film footage which will constitute the stock-in-trade, as it were, of the new venture. Mangate Visual Records, I believe, is the company name chosen. Of course, such a collection will require financing, perhaps considerable financing, over a period. A long-term period in view of the nature of the business. This," he gave us all a thin smile, "is hardly a fast-food affair."

We all smiled back obediently.

"The finance," his stare was on me now, "will need to be tailored to the business's requirements. I need hardly say that Pierre Champion is not without his own resources and, indeed, backers only too willing to finance him. In view, however, of White's specialisation in certain fields, not least that of art and auctioneering, I was able to persuade Pierre, whom I have known for some time, to give White's a chance to look at this venture and make proposals for part of it if, of course, they feel it is within their ken. Hence this meeting and Mr Simpson's presence."

He maintained his steady stare but sat back slightly.

"Thank you, Sir Hamish." It was, clearly, time for little Timmy to pipe up. "We have, as I am sure Gerry will have told you, considerable financial interests in the art and auctioneering field as well as our other, industrial and commodity activities. I am fascinated to hear that you intend to set up a photographic archive. Is there any specialisation in view? I mean, many photo and film libraries do concentrate on particular subjects."

Cordwell cleared his throat and spoke, carefully. "Current affairs, I suppose, is the main interest, particularly political subjects. But frankly, acquiring photographic and film archive is a bit like antique dealing." He smiled at me. "You may have a set of principal objectives in mind, but you have to go for a bargain when you stumble over one."

"Of course. How historic is the collection likely to be?"

"Oh, as far back as possible. That's where the money is."

"So if you'd been set up already, you might have had a go at the Earl of Craven's family snaps?"

Gerry Watson grinned at this topical reference. An album containing a hundred or so albumen prints of Lord Craven's had recently been sold at Bearne's auction for half a million pounds.

"I think," Cordwell was again careful, speaking in a rather low voice, "we would try to acquire our collection at less cost than at widely-publicised sales like the William Craven material. Or that Julia Margaret Cameron portrait Sotheby's sold for a hundred and fifty-five thousand."

"So you have a budget and plan and so forth I could have a look at?"

"Of course. This preparatory meeting was on a purely exploratory basis. If White's are interested in funding the venture to some extent then we will get together on site."

"Where are you going to be located?"

"At the Hall, alongside Gerry here."

I gave Gerry a glance. His storage facilities were in a large old rambling mansion in the outer Essex village of Mangate, acquired by Champion cheaply some time ago. Various agricultural outbuildings had been supplemented by modern warehouses. The place was almost a mini industrial site on its own, quite convenient for Stansted Airport if not for Gerry's natural stamping ground of the West End.

"We'll have to convert buildings to climate control and so on," Gerry said, as if reading my thoughts. "You can't leave film archive to roast in the sun."

"No, of course not."

There was a brief silence while I mulled this over. Champion was a cunning man, brilliant and elusive, shunning publicity and using a French base to keep out of British press floodlights. He would be quite likely to pick off the best material for himself, for a private collection in the same way I was sure he was doing with Gerry Watson's art and antiques. Men like Champion sometimes have difficulty in distinguishing between what is private and what is company stock. Although they have no such difficulty when it comes to who is to benefit most.

"So," Sir Hamish Lang interrupted my thoughts. "You're confirming, then, Simpson, that White's are in the running?"

"Yes, Sir Hamish, we would be interested in assisting with finance. I'll need to see some figures of course, and discuss matters further when Mr Cordwell is ready."

"Whenever you like," Gerry Watson answered for him. "Come out to the Hall, Tim, and we'll give you the guided tour. I'll have a copy of the business plan sent to you beforehand."

"Fine." Gerry, clearly, was somehow involved in the new venture as well as Cordwell. "I'll look forward to that. I'll give you a ring as soon as I've had time to look through it. Then we can fix up a meeting."

"Great."

"I suppose," Sir Hamish smiled thinly in grudging acceptance as he gestured at me, "Simpson here is best suited to this sort of thing as far as White's are concerned. He has, after all, been responsible for assembling a collection himself for quite a few years. Not for rental, of course. For capital appreciation."

"Indeed." Gerry Watson gave me an emphatic nod. "White's Art Investment Fund. Celebrated in many circles. We've been in competition occasionally in the past, eh, Tim?"

"We certainly have. But there's no conflict of interest here, is there?"

"Oh, no. Not unless you're into old snaps as well, are you?"

"Indeed not. If you don't mind my saying so, there are quite a few archives already. As I heard Sir Hamish saying, the Getty Foundation and Bill Gates are two huge players in that game. Quite apart from a host of others."

"Sure. But we will have resources, Frank here has expertise, and there's tons of material waiting to be unearthed. It's a great new field for us. It's not so finite as art and antiques. Doesn't present the sort of problems that you, I imagine, have to contend with."

"No," I answered, "I suppose not."

"I mean," he smiled wickedly at me as he spoke, "deciding on which painter to invest in next must be quite a headache."

"Tell me about it," I said. "Oh, tell me about it."

Chapter Four

"I'm glad that you hadn't forgotten," Sue said, from the kitchen, "that Janet was bringing her new beau over tonight."

"No," I answered carefully, as I wrestled the end of a corkscrew into the cork of a bottle of claret, "I know my priorities. The entertainment of my wife's colleagues from the Tate, and their consorts, is of far greater importance than any old client or associate of White's."

"Tim! That's enough! I'm not letting you get away with that one. I've done my fair share of eyelid fluttering at boring old businessmen and bankers for you."

"You have indeed, Sue. And enjoyed their eager admiration."

"Rats to you, too."

I grinned to myself as the cork slid out of the bottle. "It's all right. I know my place. Grimy commerce must bow to pure curatorship. I shall expect erudite discussions on the latest aspects of the politically correct funding of - what is it? -'cultural diversity and social inclusiveness for art galleries'. And similarly high ideals. I shall keep quiet. I am merely the Bradley Hardacre of the art world. All Brass and mendacity. Do you want me to wear a waistcoat with an iron watch chain, as per Councillor Foodbotham of the Bradford City Tramways and Fine Arts Committee?"

"I said that's enough. Go and make sure William's still asleep."

I bowed obediently in the direction of the kitchen and sauntered quietly out of the living room, with its accumulated but modest paintings we had acquired separately and together, to the small bedroom where the Simpson sprog was beatifically smiling in cot-bound slumber. I gave him a wink and went back to the living room. Apart from the usual hustle and bustle of Bank shenanigans we were going through a calm patch. Sue was still working as a curator at the Tate Gallery, actually now called Tate Britain, but what I think of as the Old Tate on Millbank. The fact that her expertise is in French Impressionism was something of a paradox because Tate Modern at Bankside is where most of the French school was now centred. Somehow, within the Byzantine working of the Tate system, this was being accommodated, perhaps because she is no slouch on modern painting generally. For her it was not proving difficult to swing her expertise over to a field in which, to put it mildly, she had helped me considerably.

Perhaps part of the calm was due to a valuable inheritance, a painting which had come to me by pure good fortune and which I had sold to the Art Fund at Jeremy's insistence since the inheritance tax payable on it was out of my reach. After payment of death duties it had left us in a better financial position than we had ever experienced. The tranquility this had engendered had something of a phoney feel to it, as though a lull before another outbreak of tumultuous events, but we were enjoying it and making attempts to repair a social life disrupted by a period in which I had had to travel quite a bit.

Sue's friend and colleague Janet Heath at the Tate Gallery at Millbank was a specialist in miniatures. She had recently acquired a new boyfriend who Sue said sounded interesting. She said she was sure I'd like to meet him, in that way that wives have of suggesting new acquaintances who might keep a husband out of trouble. The new man - Janet had had one or two rather unfortunate affairs with academic sorts of chaps - was a curator at a South London public gallery and had, I gathered, a penchant for art biography which might correspond to my own. He was also something of a genealogy buff. All very different from my ex-rugger-playing chums who are less cerebral but usually a good deal more ebullient than museum and art gallery curators, and much thirstier.

As it happened it turned out that Janet's friend Jim Stockdale was a cheerful sort of bloke, around thirty, thin but wiry, who'd played fly-half for a reasonable Surrey side until crocked in one knee. Janet, who is rather intellectual, looked at him in surprise as we swapped rugger talk over a gin and tonic.

"Good heavens, Jim," she burbled. "I know you follow the international matches but I'd no idea you used to play regularly. I thought squash was your thing."

He smiled a slightly rueful smile. "It is now. Well, it always was. I didn't want to risk being lame for good so I gave up rugger and saved my knee for squash. It works quite well if I don't try any stupid stuff."

"Never thought of you as a muddied oaf. Oh, sorry, Tim."

"Don't mind me. I gave up playing a long time ago."

"But you were so distinguished." There was a slight mockery in her tone.

I shook my head at the gentle invitation to expound on past glories. "There's no old bore like an old sporting bore. Let's change the subject. I hear, Jim, that apart from an understandable professional interest in art biography, you're a genealogical buff."

"Heavens." He smiled modestly. "My CV has gone ahead of me, hasn't it? But yes; it is an interest. I used to cycle out in my schooldays and scratch round old churchyards. Gravestones and wall memorials have always fascinated me. My father thought it showed a moribund streak. Damned unhealthy, he used say. The boy's taken a morbid turn. But it's like biography really; fact, if you can get to it, is much more interesting than fiction."

"Some would say that biography is only another form of fiction."

He chuckled. "I wouldn't disagree too strongly. That's what makes it so fascinating. Trying to get to the truth, knowing that you'll never quite get there."

"My view entirely. Family trees and old buildings yield

some amazing surprises. And there's a new interest in it. Look at the TV programmes related to it nowadays. Lots of them. Even the Romans aren't far back enough. It does worry me a bit, this obsession with the past. As though the future can't be looked at. As if, unlike the Victorians, we're frightened of it. How many programmes do you see that are related to old houses, or prehistoric sites, or the wars, or history of some sort, even the creation of the planet and the dinosaurs? How many look forward to what life is going to be like? Maybe one for every twenty programmes about the past."

"That," said Jim Stockdale cheerfully, "is because you can get hold of lots of images about the past. From all sorts of sources. Archive footage is everywhere. But there's none available from the future."

I gave him a quick glance of surprise, suddenly visualising the wry face of Frank Cordwell, but his expression was humorous.

I smiled back. "Very true. All the same, Henry Ford had a point."

"Oh, no." Janet intervened with a proud note in her voice. "Don't say that. History's not bunk. Jim's actually doing a book based on one of his genealogical interests, aren't you, Jim?"

"Er, yes." Stockdale looked modestly into his glass, as though he'd rather Janet hadn't raised the subject.

She was looking expectant, however, so I obliged with the right question. "Oh, really? What on?"

"It's a history of the Finch-Hatton family," he murmured. "A bit abstruse, perhaps."

"Finch-Hatton? You mean the chap played by Robert Redford in *Out of Africa*?"

He nodded. "Denys was one of them, yes. Fascinating man. Everyone who met him was impressed." He smiled almost apologetically. "I'm afraid he wasn't as beautiful as Redford, though; his Africans called him Bedar, the balding one, and some other name I've forgotten for his ability to come out with put-downs. Film image and reality are never quite the same."

"It was a great film. Perhaps an example of how a bit of fiction makes a better biography."

"True."

"Jim says," Janet chipped in proprietorially, "that when he died in the plane crash, he wasn't with Karen Blixen at all. They'd broken up. The film's romantic but incorrect. Beryl Markham had taken him over. You know, the woman who first flew the Atlantic solo, east to west. She had a bit of a thing about pilots. And almost anything else in trousers, apparently."

"Oh. So it's to be a scandalous book, is it, Jim?"

Stockdale smiled. "The family - Earls of Winchilsea and Nottingham - is a very interesting one. Combination of the Finches, and the family of Sir Christopher Hatton, into which they married."

"Of Hatton Gardens, I suppose?"

"Exactly. There are connections all over. Car racing, aviation, you name it. Huge estates coming and going. They're a classic example of the decline of the aristocracy and the effect of the country's political and economic circumstances. Plus a deal of delightful eccentricity, of course." His eyes twinkled as he saw Janet's shining on him. "There's a wonderful story in a book by Wilfrid Blunt about Lady Muriel Finch-Hatton, or Lady Muriel Paget as she became after she married. Denys's cousin. Her mother Edith married Murray Finch-Hatton, the twelfth Earl of Winchilsea, and they inherited a huge Gothic pile called Haverholme Priory in Lincolnshire. Gone, now."

"It was a gloomy pile, apparently." Janet was still proprietorial.

"Anyway, Edith became a great hypochondriac once she'd had the regulation two children. Always in Bath chairs, complaining of mysterious illnesses, that sort of thing. One day she did seem worse than usual and her family got worried. They summoned one of her doctors to come urgently. He arrived but Edith sent him away. She said she was much too ill to see him."

When the laughter died away, I said, "Was that a book by the Wilfrid Blunt who was brother of the spy, Sir Anthony? Keeper of the Queen's pictures?"

Jim nodded. "The very same. In his book on Lady Muriel he mentions that he and his brother Anthony visited Russia together in 1938."

"Sounds like a bestseller you've got there."

He smiled again. "If I can ever get round to finishing it. It's very time-consuming in research terms."

"I'm sure. Wouldn't be my cup of tea at all, but good luck with it."

At that point, Sue came in from the kitchen with a snort of derision. "I've been listening to all this. You're a fine one to talk, Tim." She gestured at the bookcase along one wall. "What's all that but a preoccupation with the past? The art past maybe, but the past nonetheless."

I grinned and glanced briefly in the same direction. On the front shelf I could see the spines of the Tate Gallery catalogue for the 1993 Ben Nicholson Exhibition and Sarah Jane Checkland's recent biography. I made a mental note to keep them in a less prominent position. Even though the two guests were not in any way involved in commerce they were professionals in the art field. Discretion is vital when I am looking for a particular artist for investment purposes.

Too late.

"Gosh." Jim Stockdale had already moved over to the bookcase. "What a smashing library. The Pre-Raphaelites, of course. All the Impressionist stuff, masses of it - that's you, I'm sure, Sue - and here are all the Modern British. I can see you and I will have to get together, Tim. Wow. Biography and autobiography as well as criticism. The Rothensteins, father and son. That incredible crisis at the Tate with the villainous

South African, Leroux Smith Leroux, trying to chuck Rothenstein out. Leroux was an absolute Machiavelli, wasn't he? There's Richard Shone. Quite a bit of Sargent as well as Olson's - glossy stuff, that other stuff, isn't it? Sickert and Wendy Baron's Camden Town. Did you ever - oh yes, there it is, Sir Peter Napley's *Camden Town Murders*. I still think Robert Wood did it, don't you? Murder Emily Dimmock, I mean."

"Yes, probably."

"There's Holroyd's Augustus - old and new editions - and Susan Chitty's Gwen John. That old blowhard Nevinson's *Paint and Prejudice*. They say he was an awful bully at the Slade, turned little Stanley Spencer upside down in a sack and hung him up in the boiler room. Christ! The full Munnings in first edition, not to mention Jean Goodman and Jonathan Smith. Wyndham Lewis - you've got a lot of his. What a paranoic man that was. And there's Bruce Arnold's Orpen with two Ben Nicholsons, that was a great exhibition, and ha! Jack Skeaping's *Drawn From Life* - he was a boy, wasn't he? What talent, even if people thought him a bit slick. And a whole rank of Whistler stuff." He gave me a mischievous look. "Shall we bore the ladies?"

"No, you won't," Janet was quick to intervene. "Or we'll absolutely out-bore you, won't we, Sue?"

"You bet." Sue was incisive, as though reading my thoughts and wanting to divert their gazes from the serried titles. "Let's eat, shall we, before it all goes cold?"

Jim Stockdale put on a mock-disappointed expression. "Oh, but food is mere - "

And at that moment, from the depths of his cot, William let out a howl that went right through the flat.

"Excuse me." I put down my drink, ready to head off trouble. Seeing Sue's expression, there might be accusations of inadequate precaution earlier on. It might take a while to pacify William but I was sure the curatorial three could fend for themselves for however long it might take. Their shop talk wouldn't be anything like mine.

They grinned sympathetically and moved to the table as I left the room.

I know my place.

Chapter Five

"My goodness," Charles Massenaux smiled broadly as he took his polished black brogues off the top of his scratched oak desk and lowered his long pinstriped legs towards the floor, "we are honoured. Honoured indeed. Here is an amazing, and pleasant, surprise. The investment banker and fellow-director himself. To what do we owe this sudden descent from above?"

"Good morning, Charles. You look well."

He made a tugging motion at a non-existent forelock. His brow and hair are much too cultivated for forelocks to fall. "Thank you, guv'nor, thank you, thank you. So do you."

I smiled back at him as blandly, I hoped, as he did me. Charles is a smooth cove who works for Christerby's International Fine Art Auctioneers, in which the Bank has a stake and of which Sir Hamish Lang is Chairman. Charles is an expert on various matters, including Modern British painting and has, recently, taken to appearing on a TV antiques roadshow at key viewing times. This has enhanced his already glossy image no end. Although he might have a pinstripe suit in common with Geoffrey Price, our prudent accountant, there is nothing else by way of similarity. Charles affects the visually reassuring clothing of the financial sector but in slightly more florid form. His stripes are set a little wider and are somehow chalkier, the cut of his jib is more dashing in pinching of waist and slimness of leg, the tie bright mustard with blue spots, the Bengal-striped shirt capped by a snowy stiff collar just that edge higher than City men might sport. There was always a tendency towards the Mayfair car salesman about Charles's appearance, which television appearances have done nothing to diminish. His hair, always sleek, tamped down by an habitual sweep of the hand, still waved thickly away from his high, pale brow. His long nose, redolent of aristocratic Norman forebears, was dead straight. His blue eyes, set properly apart, gleamed under thick brows. His mouth, firm but full, smiled widely to reveal clean, even teeth. Charles has, I suspect, acquired a following of ardent ladies of certain age and aspiration since he took to the small screen.

"It's good to see you all so busy and well-occupied." I grinned at him. "But be at ease. My visit has no overtones, no purpose but to chat with your happy self."

Around us, the hushed premises dedicated to the disposal of valuable possessions were relatively quiet. In the old days, Charles had only a small glazed partition to separate him from the hurly-burly of brown-coated men who carry items ranging from frail glass to solid oak from room to room whilst indulging in cheerful banter or rumbled grousing. Now, his status as director, enhanced by his new-found public persona, has earned him a walled office, accessible to the main rooms and unprotected by a secretary, but much calmer in atmosphere. The same sagging shelves of reference works decorate one wall and a rank of old steel filing cabinets another, but his computer and attendant clutter stand clean on his old oak desk; interruptions are fewer.

"Chat?" A look of wry disbelief creased his face with a fleeting, humorous quirk. "You? Here? Just to chat? Tell me another. What do you want?"

"Charles, really. Can I not, as a non-executive director of this celebrated establishment, drop by for a friendly encounter, perhaps even an update of the current state of affairs, without rousing disbelief?"

"Of course you can. And are always welcome to do so. On the other hand, I know you of old. I can sense, before you even sit down on that fine, hard, office chair you so dislike, indeed by the very fact of your sitting on it, - yes, do be at ease, won't you? - that you are here for a purpose. What is it this time? Not Whistler, presumably, nor any of the others you have, so famously, or should I perhaps say notoriously, made a focus of your art investment programme, but someone new. Who is it to be?"

"Ah, Charles, to the point, eh? Always to the point. Tell me: how do you react to the name Nicholson?"

His eyes widened and he sat upright, sharply. His eyebrows flicked brow-wards for just a second before his face set, seriously. "Nicholson?"

His tone was slightly incredulous.

"Yes, Nicholson. How do you react to the name Nicholson, apart from looking and behaving as though I'd just goosed you?"

"With extreme caution," he snapped, staying upright and quite still.

"Oh? Why?"

"Dear Tim. My very dear Tim. You do sometimes have the most ingenuous way of hoisting great kites into the air, don't you?"

"Me?"

"Yes, you."

"Kites?"

"Kites. Come on: in return interrogation, what does the name John Drewe mean to you?"

"Ah," I nodded, approvingly. "A little skullduggery, perhaps?"

"Perhaps? Perhaps? A little, only? Look, Tim, eleven years ago a Ben Nicholson fetched over a million at auction. Even a year later one fetched three quarters of a million. It is said that a private sale went for over double that." He paused to let it sink in. "Two million jimmy o'goblins, dear boy. Two million."

"Pricey."

"Very pricey. But in the last nine years," he gestured at the shelves beside him, "if you consult the archives, there has been nothing sold at auction over about a hundred and seventy thousand. Or thereabouts. No, I tell a lie: *Wicca* was sold back in the '95 or '96 season for three hundred thousand. A

1923 job on masonite. But that was it. Nothing back in seven figures. Why not, I hear you ask; why not? Why has the Ben Nicholson *oeuvre* , in view of its prominence and importance, not been hitting the even higher spots like every one else?"

"Dear Charles. You are always so on the ball. The answer is John Drewe."

"Precisely. John Drewe, and his merry team, turned out fake Ben Nicholsons - and Graham Sutherlands - to God knows what tune during the late eighties and nineties. An estimated two million quids' worth, one policeman said, until Drewe was slammed in chokey back in 1999. About two hundred works, of which only sixty-odd have been recovered. Which has left a lot of private collections, and some distinguished public ones, looking with sick dread at the Nicholson purchases they made pre-1999. Do you wonder, therefore and forsooth, why I hear the name Nicholson with a certain reserve, if not scepticism, and extreme caution? Never mind sheer terror? The market has been buggered, dear boy, well and truly shafted."

"So I believe."

"And now, here into my dear little office, strides you, a man with an art investment history littered with violence, fraudulent deception and corpses, with your kite aloft, innocent expression fooling no one, asking blandly how I react to - *react to* - it's grotesque! White's Art Fund? Have you gone raving mad?"

"Precisely what Jeremy said, Charles. The exact words, actually."

His face changed. A nervous look came into it. "Oh? Did he? Jeremy? Are you sure?"

I chuckled. "Word for word. But for quite different reasons, Charles. He hates the painting, you see. Abstract art has a dire effect upon him. He loathes it. Ben Nicholson in particular. Calm yourself; it is not that you and he, suddenly, are on the same side."

"Oh, well, now look here, Tim, Jeremy's no fool you know,

I mean he and I might not see altogether eye to eye about certain things, but, after all - "

"Calm yourself, I said. I am aware of the effect on the market of the efforts of Mr John Drewe and his cohorts. Abstracts are much easier to fake than most types of painting. It was the false provenances he forged that upset the force. Rozzers will smile at fakery - *caveat emptor* and all that - but forgery now, that's serious."

"Very true. Quite apart from fraudulent documents, of course."

"Indeed."

He coughed, nervously. "But Nicholson, Tim? Really? Ben Nicholson? You're serious?"

"Never more so. He and Francis Bacon are the top British art bananas of the twentieth century, according to some."

"Who?"

"Well, Terence Conran, for one."

He made a dismissive gesture.

"I had no idea you based your Fund's policy on - "

"I don't. But Ben Nicholson is important. Isn't he? A major figure?"

"Granted."

"And right now, with the market down and in upheaval, like the stock market, should be a good time to buy. Shouldn't it?"

"Also granted. But - "

"But me no buts, Charles. Who dares wins, Rodney."

"Oh, God."

"What's the matter?"

"Nothing, nothing. Just that it's bad enough when you start with a calm scenario. Things always go downhill from there, with you. But when you start with a Ben Nicholson scene, God knows what will ensue. I mean, where will you start?"

"Any tips you can give will be gratefully received, Charles."

"I'm afraid I'm a bit out of the Ben Nicholson swim, right now, Tim."

"Pity. What about his Dad?"

His face cleared. "William? Sir William Nicholson? Ah, now there's a performer for you. Quite a different kettle of fish. Steady progression. The top numbers around a hundred and fifty thousand but plenty of good stuff, small still lives and those, from thirty to forty grand. Couldn't argue with a William Nicholson investment."

"Precisely what Jeremy said. You and he are chiming in nicely from the same hymn sheet these days."

"Damn it, Tim. You can be an absolute bastard sometimes."

I smiled cheerfully and got up. "Nice to see you, Charles, as ever. Actually, I bet you could fake a William Nicholson just as easy as a Ben."

"Oh, I don't know."

"Impressionism, of a Whistlerian tone? Can't be too difficult, surely. Ageing might be a problem, I agree."

"That's the thing, Tim. Those Ben Nicholsons, now, some of them are not too old, d'you see. Not so difficult to do. As you say, abstraction's easier than many other styles. You should get hold of one to study. Not that they're available off the shelf, as it were. But there's nothing like looking at fakes in the flesh. Haven't got hold of one, have you?"

"No," I answered. "But I know a man who has."

Chapter Six

Dorkie Collins was South African. Not Boer South African, long called Afrikaans, once a terror-figure and guttural Fascist to the entire world's media, nor African-South African, black and shiny, full of holy glory, martyrdom and rural, post-Mandela serenity.

He wasn't either of those.

Nor was Dorkie savage, violent, or corrupt, prone to toy-toying a murder-bent knees-up with axe or knobkerrie in hand. He didn't smell of cordite, raped women, sjambokked rioters, cocaine and pot, or whatever takes you for a whiff of that wide, handsome, lethal-robber country. He didn't play rugby because he wasn't much into head butts and cracked bones, but I met him at a rugger match, many years ago, because he liked to watch the game. I was still an active front row man then, before he went to live in Hastings.

He didn't play cricket either, not having the eye for a small, leatherbound cannonball approaching at ninety miles an hour, but he liked to watch that, too. People get enthusiastic about sports at which their countries are successful. It makes them feel better.

What he really loved was buck biltong, *boerewors* sausages, burnt beef and hot empty landscapes. I mean really empty landscapes, prickly ones too, with absolutely no one in them. He yearned for the solitude of those.

And he adored, was really besotted by, trading in artefacts, things that fascinated him.

Dorkie was an English-speaker from Eastern Cape Province. The Afrikaners would traditionally call him an *Engelsman* but he certainly wasn't English, or even really British, though he had come to live in England; he was South African. His speech, not guttural like an Afrikaner's, altogether lighter but still heavily accented, was peppered with strange words, some Xhosa, some Afrikaans, some God knew what. Somewhere, someone has published a dictionary of Eastern Cape English which, like so many overseas versions of our national tongue, developed its own, colloquial usage, casually picking up expressions more graphic to the locals than can be found in England. Sociable yet somehow solitary, Dorkie had something in common with his favourite bird: an ibis called a ha-de-da.

He was a relative of a chap who played front row with me at Cambridge, a graduate of St.Andrew's and Rhodes called Harry 'Alpie' Hannibal, who said that Dorkie was a relative of his by marriage, a step-uncle or maybe a much older second cousin, from the Bathurst district. Their families both had graveyard plots at the celebrated Settler Church, not more than a few yards from each other and within a number five iron shot from the Pig and Whistle. There was a joke, Alpie said, about it being easier, after death, to continue squabbles, jokes and borrowing money if you're buried near your *swaer* - brother-in-law to you and me.

Alpie Hannibal was short and stocky and dogged, his nickname coming from the famous elephant-crossing general of Roman times rather than his height, but he was a good tight head prop and, like me, occasional hooker. When our regular hooker was too damaged to play.

According to Alpie, everyone in the Eastern Cape seems to be related in some distant way or another. Everyone white, that is; they're not what you'd call very politically correct people. Maybe their interest in family is just a form of mutual bonding when faced with isolation, violence, dispossession and economic extinction. Anyway, Dorkie had been considered part of Alpie's family, and hence related to a multitude of Eastern Cape whites, as long as Alpie could remember.

Dorkie didn't fit the media's holiday image of floral Cape luxury, all swimming pools, chilled Chardonnay and refrigerated bungalows upholstered in cool imitation leather. Forget the images of rolling surf or safari sundowners when you think of Dorkie. Don't imagine plush game park visits either. His sort never was well off. He came, Alpie said, from a background of dusty but inexplicably damp verandahed shacks built on baked farm mud amongst flowering aloes in the tangled, rocky country leading to the Great Fish River. His was the frontier where, in 1820, the British Government played the dirtiest trick possible on its own settlers, putting them down like geese amongst impenetrable spiked thorn and prickly pear at the mercy of spear-throwing Xhosas who had to be driven out by musket. All this so that, after gory massacres on both sides, the settlers could try to eke out a living under corrugated iron roofs in conditions so primitive, hard, lonely and uncomfortable that they would upset the mildest trades union man from the unrestored back street of any impoverished Northern mill town. Most of the 1820 settler farms were simply chronic. You were better off growing oranges up the Sundays River.

At the time Alpie introduced him, however, Dorkie seemed reasonably well off to me. He came to a Blackheath match dressed in a tweed sports jacket and drove a smart, vintage Alvis Grey Lady saloon with chromed wire wheels. He joked that he'd spent some of his youth up in a *dorp* called Lady Grey and liked it. It was a lovely car with real leather upholstery, smelling of hot oil and tobacco just like a proper vintage vehicle. According to Alpie, Dorkie had become some sort of antique dealer doing a line in Boer War memorabilia and had never had it so good.

He had a habit of keeping up with me because we still met at some of the same rugger matches. I was always greeted with enthusiasm even though he was much older and Alpie was long gone back to the *blou water*. It was as though we were contemporaries; the age difference didn't seem to exist.

I couldn't help wondering about this curious interest of his in me as I drove down the familiar bad road to Hastings, the A21 that thinks that the world ends at Tunbridge Wells. After the Tunbridge Wells fork you're on your own, on a road that winds and stalls and jams with even minor traffic. On Bank Holidays, you can't get along at all quickly, which is a paradox; why do so many people want to go to Hastings on Bank Holidays, particularly bikers? Do they ever go back?

The medieval Old Town is very quaint in parts though, really picturesque. If the right people went there and spent the right sort of money, it could be a very expensive place. But they don't and it isn't. Dorkie had a tall, Regency house in a small shabby square crouched under the cliffs, a house which in any almost any other town would be a desirable period residence worth a lot of cash. He bought it for a song when the property market crashed ten years ago. The front gate had uncollected rubbish outside it and there was an old bicycle chained to the railings. Otherwise it was a bow-fronted, high town house of elegant shape, needing a lick of paint to its off-white, seagull-splattered frontage.

Not far behind me, over the tumbled rooftops, the clock on St.Clement's, the church where in 1860 Rossetti married Elizabeth Siddall in front of just one witness, chimed a single, mournful quarter almost like an echo as I rang a big brass bell.

The door opened almost immediately.

"Tim! My boy. How great to see you. This is a real pleasure."

He didn't look any different. Dorkie Collins seemed like sixty five the first time I saw him and he still looked the same age. He was tall and rangy. A dry, lined brown face with narrow-set bright blue eyes crinkled above a clean-shaven, easy smile. Thinning grey hair, going on white, was cut short round back and sides. His dark blue, v-neck pullover had a hole in one elbow but it was genuine cashmere. A khaki shirt underneath was open at the neck. Khaki trousers, slim cut, went down to sandy chukka boots; I supposed they'd be *veldtskoens*. He looked a bit like Denys Finch-Hatton might have looked if he'd survived another thirty years beyond *Out of Africa*. A long arm, reaching out to shake my hand firmly, showed no sign of incipient weakness.

"Hi, Dorkie. You're looking good."

"So are you, Tim. So are you. Come on in."

I stepped across the porch steps into a narrow hall. On my left, a long wall extending to the stairs was darkened by a big oak-framed steel engraving of Buller's troops crossing the Tugela, all horses, gun carriages and pith helmets, by Caton Woodville or Paget or one of those. On my right was a door into the front room, which was indicated by a sweeping gesture of welcome. I went obediently in.

"My showroom," said Dorkie, proudly. "Thought you might like to see it before we get to business. I don't have many visitors here, but I keep a bit of a display just in case. You never know when trade might turn up."

I grinned appreciatively around the room, taking it in slowly. Illustrations and prints were evidently a big line, especially some of the plentiful Dutch, French and German caricatures, their hostile propaganda portraying the British as nasty, oppressive, farm-burning crucifiers of gentle, enlightened Boers with saintly beards, standing next to matronly *vrous* in Dutch hats.

"They didn't like you then," said Dorkie with a wry smile as I winced at them, "before two world wars and the EEC made it even worse. Not even the Belgians. Can't think why anyone should believe they'll help you now. Or let you into their clever conspiracies, except to rob you."

I pulled a face at him. I wasn't going to get into a rant about Europe. It's too easy to find reasons to dislike people.

"Heard from Alpie lately?"' he asked, as I moved to a rank of Dutch jugs decorated with Steyn and Kruger's portraits, and a cup with a print of De Wet in slouch hat and ammunition belt next to a sauce boat with the Free State emblem on it.

"Nope."

"Nor have I. I suppose you boys are pretty cock-a-hoop about the last match against us though, eh?"

I grinned. "England have got a good side at present."

"We'll get you next time. We always do."

"Tell me," I gestured round the room, with its rather sepulchral memorabilia, "is there still a good market for this stuff?"

"You'd be surprised. It's a bit specialist, of course. But the past attracts all sorts, Tim."

"There are nuts everywhere, I suppose."

He chuckled. "More than you'd imagine. Wars have always fascinated people. I have to admit that the archive brings me my most steady income, though. Steadier than selling bits and pieces, even though they do bring a better margin when they go."

I stopped in my circumnavigation. "Archive?"

"Sure. I have a library of old magazines, illustrated contemporary magazines, books and photos. I buy any old Boer War photos. You'd be surprised how many people have got them, here and there. Family things, very often. I've even got some early film taken in the Cape and Natal at the time. Carefully preserved, of course. You'd be amazed what some of the magazine and TV companies will pay for the right images. Not to mention feature articles in papers and magazines now and then."

"You mean you've built up this - this library of images over a period and now it brings you income?"

"Sure. Now that South Africa's preoccupied with another history entirely it's been an unfashionable but for me fascinating business to collect up whatever I could find. There are people doing it all over South Africa, mind you. The Zulu War's another big puller. Chap called Rattray does a wonderful set of lectures and battlefield tours, that sort of thing. Not many photos of that about, mark you. The Boer War's got much more material; photography was really taking off then."

"Dorkie, could we talk about this another time? I've got another possible interest. I'd be grateful to chat to you about it."

"Sure, Tim. Sure. It'd be a pleasure. But business first, eh? Let's go upstairs."

We mounted a carpeted staircase with an old, polished mahogany rail up to a landing and then went into a handsome first floor room the width of the house, with a wide bay window letting in lots of light. The view was impressive: across the jumbled roofs you could see as far as the shore, with fishing boats drawn up beyond a litter of seaside arcades, ice cream stands and entertainment booths. The English Channel, beyond, was calm. A ketch, white sails up, slid gracefully through its surface. In the far distance a tanker plodded along the horizon.

"Nearly as good as Port Alfred," I said, with a smile.

He shook his head. "Not a chance. They've developed Port Alfred so that there's nothing left of the old days, now."

I turned to look back into the room, having had enough of the banalities, and froze.

"I was waiting to see when you'd notice," Dorkie said.

On the wall opposite was a painting. An abstract painting, not very big, perhaps twelve inches by eighteen, in horizontal form. The composition was set back in a rectangular wooden frame painted the same colour as the surrounding area to the inner design of whorled black, grey, puce and white shapes, vaguely cup or jug-like if you let your eye play loosely with the perspective. Next to it was a much less compromising painting, square, eighteen by eighteen, in which circles, squares and rhomboids overlapped in a variety of colours set off by one bit of bright yellow backdrop.

My jaw must have dropped. "Two?" I queried, incredulously. "You've got two of them?"

His pleasure was obvious. "I have. There were quite a few of them going around ten years or so ago. A local guy used to do them to order."

"The first is like a late one, Magenta Cup, or one of those. The geometric job looks earlier. Are these John Drewe versions?"

He shook his head. "Not as good as his. I couldn't have afforded them. His team used to use emulsion paint, lubricating jelly and dust to get the right finish on a fake Ben Nicholson. Then they'd forge provenances. No one knows how many they turned out; about two million quids' worth, the cops reckoned when they jugged Drewe, back in '99. Mind you, he did some good Graham Sutherlands as well."

I whistled softly. "These are not half bad."

"They wouldn't fool an expert. But John Drewe's did. They think there are still a lot in private collections, and some museums. Very embarrassing."

"And not good for the Ben Nicholson market, invested in quite heavily by some very top dealers."

"Quite so, Tim." He gave me a careful stare. "Which is now going to include White's?"

I bit my lip gently. "It might, Dorkie. Let's just say I'm interested. Not committed yet, but interested. The provenance would have to be impeccable, given this," - I indicated the fakes on the wall - "sort of activity. But that's not why I've come to see you."

"No, I know." He gave me an interested stare. "I must say I was surprised when you called."

"Oh? Why?"

He shrugged. "Sir William Nicholson? Ben's father? That's how he's known nowadays, isn't he? More as Ben's father than anything else, despite his own achievements. A minor master, Rothenstein said, not a great one. As little original as a man of high gifts and undeviating independence could well be. A dandy." He paused for a moment, as though recollecting. "The pioneer of the spotted collar worn with the spotted shirt. 'No one is interested in modest perfection now; the heroic failure is preferred to the completely achieved but minor success. That's why Van Gogh is today the most popular painter.' "

"I've read Rothenstein, too," I said. "And mostly agree. About what the market wants, I mean. William Nicholson was hard working, businesslike and knew his own limitations. The Newark engineering background had its effect.

The odd thing is that his father's life, with its children from different marriages, was mirrored by his own and his son's. The Nicholsons were all strung across their own generations."

"'Here comes Aunty, in her pram'?"

I smiled. "Right. That was a joke they could all share. It was a case of like father, like son. But never mind that. Why do you like him? All those Velasquez-inspired still lives and staid society portraits? Those bare minimalist landscapes? You've always had a thing about William Nicholson. I remember, you see. I remember a long and beery discussion after one of the matches when you beat us, England I mean, when it was still the usual thing. You said the Nicholsons were one of your many interests, especially William. Why?"

The reply came straight back, without hesitation. "Edie," he answered.

"Who?"

"Edie. Edie Nicholson. William's second wife. Stuart-Wortley that was. Phillips before that. She was South African, you see. That's where I started."

"You've lost me, a bit."

"Beautiful girl. Artistic. Painted as Elizabeth Drury. Women get used to different names and roles, don't they? Hard for us men, Tim. But women, you may say, live under pseudonyms - married pseudonyms - a lot of the time. Or other appearances. A man, when he gets up in the morning, doesn't disguise himself as something, as though he were going on stage. Women do. Every day. Dressing up, it's called when you're small. More serious, when you're older."

"Dorkie, this philosophical turn is leaving me behind. What has this Edie's name got to do with it?"

He grinned. "You must indulge an old man's fancy if you want his help. A man called Lionel Phillips is the start of it all. Jewish East Ender, like Barney Barnato. Went out to South Africa and made a fortune in diamonds. Hard life; his daughter Edith - Edie - was born and brought up in a tin shack. When she was six, her father went on the Jameson Raid and was captured. Had to pay Kruger's lot a fortune to get himself out from under a death sentence. He became an MP in Cape Town. Came back to England, launched Edie, was knighted. Sir Lionel, now. She was his only daughter. Worth a fortune. Could have her pick of the best men and the best boys. And there were some men after her, I can tell you. She met Ben Nicholson at the Slade; she wanted to be an artist. At that time, Ben was all over the place. She married a dashing officer, Jack Stuart-Wortley, a Fusilier then South Staffordshires. They had two children but he was killed in Ludendorff's offensive. March, 1918."

"Bad luck."

"Tragic. Ben began to fancy her. They saw a lot of each other. Considered themselves virtually engaged. But Mabel or rather Prydie, Ben's mother, died in the flu epidemic after seeing eldest son Tony off to his death at the Front. Father William already had a mistress or two - he was no slouch with women - but guess what? Once he'd recovered from the double blow?"

"Christ. Of course. He got Edie. Now I remember."

"Correct. Father William moved in, moved fast, and married young Edie, the rich heiress-widow. They had tragedy in common, after all. But tell it how you will, the father took the son's girl off him. Oedipus Rex or something, in reverse, isn't it? Especially as Ben had loved his mother devotedly."

"Never got on with his father much after that, did he?"

Dorkie shook his head. "Not much, no. It must have left quite a scar. There were reconciliations and Ben and Winifred - he eventually married into the Castle Howard family - often came to stay, but it was always edgy. There was a daughter by Edie called Liza, but the marriage didn't last. Affairs were on the go, both sides, by the end of the twenties. They went to South Africa in 1931, before they broke up. Marguerite Steen says the country didn't inspire William to paint but she was prejudiced; she was William's last resident mistress, of course. 1934 to the bitter end; Edie wouldn't divorce."

"So are there some William Nicholsons in South Africa?"

He grimaced. "Liza had a William Nicholson called *Hottentot Holland, Helderburg*. Others almost certainly exist outside of the well-known ones in Cape Town and Johannesburg official art galleries - which were endowed by Sir Lionel and Lady Florence Phillips, as it happened. They may still be there. There are a lot of British paintings in South Africa, Tim. Now that money's tight and black art is to the fore, numbers are starting to leak back here."

"Like people. I've never known so many South Africans over here as there are now."

He gave me a sharp glance. "Chickens come home to roost, eh?"

"You could say that. You still haven't explained why you're so keen on William Nicholson. Or buy fakes of his son's paintings."

"What starts any hobby, any fascination? I was in the Port Elizabeth art gallery when I was young and first saw a Nicholson still life. Fruit on a table. My dad said to me: 'He married a South African, you know, Sir William did: the Phillips girl. They were as rich as Croesus. Her father was head of the Witwatersrand Chamber of Mines. I saw her in Cape Town back in the thirties, my boy, at a reception. Look at that, how good it is. And he painted portraits of Jannie Smuts, too. He was a fine painter.' And there the still life was; and it was good. A boyhood thing, Tim. My dad, and associations with him, every time I look at a Nicholson. Later on, it came when I looked at a Ben, too. He was Edie's boyfriend once, after all. It's stuck in my mind; an image of my father in front of that painting, telling me about her but not knowing, not the background I got to know. I always wanted a William and a Ben Nicholson."

I nodded slowly. I have a thing like that about Orpen's mistress, Yvonne Aubicq, daughter of the Mayor of Lille. He painted her beautifully. Art is nothing if it's not personal, like music. As Charles Massenaux had said, the Orpens were friends of the Nicholsons; there was that family holiday together in Margate, four adults and six children.

"So what's the deal, Tim?"

Dorkie's voice cut through my thoughts. I banished them from my head, quickly; it's too easy to get side-tracked.

"A purchase or a finder's fee," I answered. "Whichever you like. There's a risk if you purchase; we may not buy the item off you. If, on the other hand, you put us on to a painting we subsequently buy, we give you a finder's fee. Two and a half percent."

"Three. I'd want three."

"Two and a half is the going rate."

"For a good William Nicholson painting, good provenance, I think three is right. I wouldn't *verneuk* you, you know that."

"Where are we talking about? Location, I mean?"

"No, Tim, no start, not even the area, until we've agreed on a fee. Not that I don't trust you."

I sighed reluctantly, thinking. Then he played his best card.

"It should be worth three, shouldn't it, if you get both father and son together?"

"Eh? You mean you know where there's a William and a Ben available for sale together?"

He smiled and put a finger to his nose. "I thought so. I thought you might want to pull off a double."

"Why? What on earth gave you that idea?"

"I know you, Tim. I've watched you. You go for things so cleverly. Buying when the profile's low, when the market's attention is elsewhere. It would be a boost to both of them. And the association is such a good story. The story's more important than the art; isn't it?"

"Like Van Gogh, you mean?"

"Precisely. And it might help if the Tate Gallery's embarrassment was attenuated by White's rehabilitation of the market for Nicholsons, mightn't it?"

I stared at him, a bit perplexed, until he let a slight smile come back to his lips.

"I appreciate, Tim, that you have your very own personal lines of communication to the Tate."

I pursed my lips. "Maybe I have. But never mind that. Business before pleasure, as always. This is very confidential, Dorkie. Really confidential. I don't want my interest getting known."

"Of course, Tim, of course. Mum's the word. You can rely on me. Absolutely stumm. I can be as clandestine as the next man. Or woman. Odd, isn't it, how they can do it? Live different lives, I mean. Edith Phillips, Edie Stuart-Wortley, Edie Nicholson, Elizabeth Drury; they were all one and the same woman. I wonder how you get used to changing your name like that?"

I looked at him with a tolerant smile. A straight fellow, colonial, straight shooter, straight bat, stuck on old values and virtues; the transparent emotions, art could read the mind's construction in the face. Was that Dorkie?

He was looking at me anxiously, waiting. "How about a compromise, Tim? Two and three quarters percent?"

"All right," I said. "Two and three quarters percent. Done." We shook hands.

And let the genies out of their bottles.

Chapter Seven

"So." Nobby had finished his breakfast while I went through the events of the last few days and now sat in front of a clean plate. He signalled the waitress to bring him more coffee during my peroration. I still had the remains of a pot of tea. "Let me see if I've got this right. You have been engaged to look into the investment, by Pierre Champion no less, of substantial funds into a film library. Correction: a still photo and film library. An archive, no less. Up in Essex. Essentially for rental purposes, like his furniture business. And this comes from a connection of Sir Hamish Lang's. Yes?"

"Yes."

"I am right, am I, in using the word substantial in relation to funds?"

"Could be, Nobby, could be."

"You don't know yet, though, do you?'

"No."

"On the other hand, one does not engage the services of a merchant bank, even a small merchant bank, in order to borrow a fiver."

"No."

"And from what you have said there could be big prices to pay. The Craven material you mentioned; half a million? Just for one album?"

"Yes. Although that would be more of a collector's investment than a film library job. There's some enormous money going into nineteenth century photographs. And, let it be said, twentieth century ones of certain kinds."

"I know. But we have one possible connection with you from this angle. Moira Bassington worked in this field. That's what turned you white at the gills."

"It seems incredibly remote, Nobby, but I hate coincidence. I mean, no one could have known about my nomination for the job except Freddy Harbledown, Jeremy, and Sir Hamish Lang. Yet it is the same field."

"An eminently respectable trio," he said, drily. "I doubt if they visit Pimlico much. The investment does seem to be a logical extension of Champion's prop hire business, it has to be said. Let us therefore examine the art angle for a moment."

"Just because she lived behind the Tate - "

He held up a hand. "I know. I know. Nevertheless, we must look at all possibilities. You say the only investment you have on hand is this Nicholson idea?"

"Right."

"Which you started when?"

"At our meeting at the Bank. Well, I thought about the Ben part of it before, of course. Mugged up some research, naturally."

"Who knew?"

"To start with, Sue. About Ben, that is."

He looked thoughtful. Nobby has long had a strong admiration for Sue's character, often making offensive remarks about how lucky I am, what on earth she could see in me, and similar insults. I, reciprocally, am equally admiring about his wife Gillian, who is a close friend of us both. There was no way Nobby would see Sue as a source of suspicion.

"Well I'm sure Sue's security is tight. You haven't really started on this yet?"

"Just off. Apart from my own reading. Research. Whatever you want to call it."

"But you talked to Charles Massenaux. Apart from getting far too flash on telly these days, I suppose Charles is pretty sound."

"He'll be delighted to hear of your approval."

"This Dorkie Collins, now. He's a relative of that awful yarpie front row man, Alpie Hannibal?"

"Nobby, really. How politically incorrect. Alpie's no yarpie. He's not a Boer. He's from Eastern Cape."

"Hm. Brought me down just short of the line once. I was going flat out. Nearly broke my leg."

"You were on the wrong side, that day."

"I remember Collins, I think. Still a South African supporter. Drives an old grey Alvis saloon, doesn't he? Saw it at Blackheath once. Nice car."

"That's your man."

"Lives in Hastings, you say?"

"Yes."

"Well that makes him suspect, for a start. Next thing to Brighton for crime, only cheaper."

"Nobby! These regional prejudices must cease, you know, they really must."

"He's got an archive of some sort, too, you say."

"Very specialised. Boer War only. Not exactly Pierre Champion territory."

"You never know. I seem to recall that the Oppenheimers have a huge archive of South African historical photographs. So far there are two strands to all this and, knowing you, the Art Fund is, from past experience, the prime suspect. Big sums of money in small, portable pictures are so attractive to the criminal. Hiding a painting is one thing. Hiding a great unwieldy archive of lower-value individual items is quite another. As you've said, quite a bit of hoo-hah, wasn't there, a few years back, about fake Nicholsons?"

Nobby worked, years ago, in the Art Fraud Squad. He doesn't now, but he keeps his eye in.

"Yes."

"Fellow called John Drewe, eh?"

"Correct, Nobby."

"But he's still inside. I think. I'll look into it."

"Good. But I don't believe the Nicholsons have anything to do with this Bassington affair. The Pimlico proximity is purely coincidental."

He sighed. "You're sure, absolutely sure, that she - no, no, don't look at me like that - never contacted you or any associate that you know of?"

"Certain."

"Hm."

I gritted my teeth. "I wish you wouldn't say 'hm' like that. It really gets under my skin."

"You've always been a bad-tempered bugger. Lash out like a Prescott, don't you, at the slightest provocation."

"Nobby - "

"All I'm saying is keep your hair on. I'll tell the local CID what you've told me. I can't see the connection either. Needs thinking about. There may not be one. It's amazing how often coincidence fogs an enquiry. But - " he held up another of his infuriating warning fingers - "if anything does come up, anything at all, connected however remotely with the Bassington woman, you are to tell me. You may well remember something later on."

"Which may be used in evidence?"

"Just try to remember. And tell me. Clear?"

"Of course."

"Don't say 'of course' in that weary, resigned tone, as though it's all such a bore. I mean it. You tell me at once. And no going off on your own little wild goose chases or amateur sleuthing codswallop. I know you. None of it. Right?"

"Right."

He paused, looking a bit irresolute. Then a decision expression crossed his face. Don't ask how I can recognise a decision expression in Nobby; I've known him a long time. "Now that you've promised," he said, "although from past experience your promises are worthless, I think you might look at some material for us. I'll arrange to get it to you."

"What sort of material?"

"Some pictures. Photos. They seem to be the in-subject at the moment, don't they?"

"Nobby - "

But he was looking at his watch. "Good God! The time! I

63

must go. I've told you what to do." He got to his feet. "Have a quick shufti at what I send you. Just in case. You know where to get hold of me. Now I'll let you get on with the mendacious City life you love to lead."

It was useless to protest. His changes of direction can be very irritating. There's only one way to deal with them and that is to ignore them or to emulate them. "As a matter of fact," I answered, pushing my cup to one side, "I think I'll head elsewhere this morning. I need to pace myself."

But he had already gone. I looked up to see only the waitress, standing beside the table.

Holding the bill.

Chapter Eight

Men are seldom so innocently employed as when among books. The celebrated second-hand emporium of Mr Goodston's on Praed Street is one of my favourites and Mr Goodston, although not normally an early riser unless off to the races, is always pleased to open up for me.

After my distressing breakfast with Nobby, I needed space in which to think and time in which to act. His warnings on carrying out my own investigations were standard stuff to which, I'm sure he knew, I would pay no attention. The police have no time in which to pry into the sorts of crannies we citizens can find. Their computers simply do not contain the information.

Who on earth could this Moira Bassington really be? Why was my name on her list? What research could possibly have dredged me out of the entire population of London?

If it was me.

Whilst musing agitatedly on Nobby's alarming presentation, however, I had new research of my own to do.

My tap on the bookshop door soon brought a response from the dusty depths within.

"My very dear Mr Simpson! What a pleasant surprise! How fit you look! It is indeed a pleasure, on such a fine day, to find you on my humble doorstep first thing. Come in, come in. You look, if I may say so, a little preoccupied. What can I do to alleviate your concern?"

Mr Goodston is a cautious, fat man of great professionalism who I suspect flatters me because members of the younger generation are not prominent amongst his clientele. The newspapers' obituary columns absorb him because, from time to time, he muses gloomily on a future in which his current customer list has died off. He is, additionally, a serious addict of the Turf and most of his profits are lost on the fleeting backs of horses less swift than his hopes embrace. The day is spent, nonetheless, perusing the sporting pages of the papers with rapt attention whilst, in his dingy shop, time and events seem to pass silently and uneventfully by.

He preceded me into the shelved room, crowded with sub-fusc bindings and teetering stacks of books arranged in some idiosyncratic order only intelligible to himself, to sit down behind his densely-heaped desk with a gesture of goodwill.

"Have a seat, my dear sir. This is indeed an honour and a pleasure. You are the only rugby blue amongst my clientele. I have admirals, generals, even masters of foxhounds aplenty, knights of distant shires as it were, and many actors and actresses, bless them, but of rugby blues only one: your good self."

"How are things, Mr Goodston?"

He smiled modestly as he took off his half-moon glasses to polish them on a yellow duster. "One survives. One must not complain. Yesterday, at Catterick, a complete no-hoper on which I had received inner intelligence," he placed a savvy finger against the side of his nose as he put his glasses back on, "came in at eighty to one. Eighty to one, my dear boy. Odds to warm the cockles of an old heart like mine. Compared with a celebrated winner like Galileo, first past the English and Irish Derby posts but at ridiculous odds-on terms, an unknown Catterick nag at eighty to one sparkles like a star."

"And the books?"

"Oh, the books! The *books*." The lightness which had infused his countenance at the memory of the horse at Catterick was replaced by shade. "Books! No one reads books any more, dear boy. Second-hand videos would provide a bet-ter trade. They watch images all the time, thinking that pic-tures are reality. No, I exaggerate; people do read books, but only utter trash. Nowadays the books that sell are written by fertile young women with no shame about their private behaviour. But it will not last; it can not. The wheel will turn, dear boy, the moving hand will write and, having writ, will move on. Things must get better, they must. Somewhere, somehow, scholarship will rise again."

"People are collecting books, though. The prices of modern first editions are a scandal."

"A scandal! Indeed, a scandal! How well you put it. No one is going to read books at those prices. They will moulder on shelves. Museum pieces, they will become."

"The title of a book by James Laver, I recall."

He beamed at me. "Indeed! Indeed! *Museum Piece*. Did you buy it off me?"

"Of course. I bought it from you at the same time as his delightful but inaccurate essay on James Tissot, *Vulgar Society*."

"Dear boy! Of course you did! Laver falls into the theatrical category of my modest range." He waved grandiloquently at his stock. "You know me: sporting, military and thespian specialities. Into which art, the omnipresent aspect of culture, always intrudes. I have just acquired a rare copy of Laver's *Portraits in Oil and in Vinegar* if you're interested? Published in 1925 by a man called Partington of The Bookman's Journal, who thought up the title before the existence of the book. Full of excellent illustrations by the artists of your Fund's attentions?"

"Possibly, Mr Goodston, possibly. Actually, there is an account in the book - *Museum Piece*, I mean - of an elderly Sir William Nicholson and Marguerite Steen, staying at Milton Waldman's house, the old rectory at Fen Ditton outside Cambridge, during the 'forties. Nicholson is one of the portraits in Laver's 1925 book. Laver, being head of a department at the V & A which had a huge collection of posters, was a great admirer of Nicholson. Said that he'd invented poster art in this country."

Mr Goodston's expression had sharpened. "I take it that Nicholson is the object of your attentions just now? The cause of your preoccupation?"

"He and his son, Mr Goodston."

"Ben?" He pulled a face. "Really? Sir William meets with my entire approval, dear sir, but I can exude no enthusiasm for Ben."

"I understand. I am not here to ask you to furnish me with material on Ben. I did not expect to find him in your distinguished repertoire."

"No, he isn't. Sir William now, that's a good line for you to follow. My thespian side perks up. Many of his friends were thespians. He designed the costumes for the first production of J.M.Barrie's *Peter Pan* at The Duke of York's Theatre in December 1904, you know."

"No, I didn't."

"There was always an air of theatricality about Nicholson. His dandified clothes, his mannered manner. A façade to hide the man beneath. A pose, almost a disguise. Bit like his friend Orpen, eh?"

"My thoughts entirely, Mr Goodston."

He heaved himself to his feet. "He did other theatrical work. Not always with success, but he was splendid. A character of the sort produced by the eighteen nineties and which we sadly lack now. I do have a copy of his grandchildren's book, a biggish monograph on him, excellently illustrated, published by DLM de la Mare, that is."

"I'll take it."

"Thank you, kind sir. I regret that it does not illustrate *The Marquis Wellington Jug*, one of his best according to Rothenstein, and which I seem to recall from my thespian memories is, or rather was, in the possession of Vivien Leigh. Lady Olivier, as she was. But the book has much to commend it. And then there is also, somewhere over here," he mused to himself as he moved to the back of the shop, "a copy of Marguerite Steen's 1943 book on him, published by Collins, when he didn't have long to go. Ah, here we are. Jacket a bit ragged but a good reading copy nonetheless."

"I'll take that, too."

"You are too kind." He came back, grunting, to his desk. "Sir John Gielgud had one of his, you know. A still life. Sold recently amongst his effects."

"I expect you were at the sale? For his books?"

He smiled modestly. "I venture forth so little these days. Sir John was a kind, and discriminating, client. He loved Nicholson's work. There was a meticulousness about him, even in minor things, like painting paper butterflies, which Sir John admired."

"Butterflies?"

Mr Goodston nodded, indicating the larger of the two books on his desk. "You will find therein a charming account by his daughter Liza - the one by the South African lady - of how, when he was in the garden, butterflies would settle on him. She says that it was, perhaps, his characteristic smell, blended of turpentine, bay rum and Balkan Sobranies, which attracted them." He took off his glasses reflectively. "One can not help but warm to man who loved children and would allow the very butterflies to settle on him."

"Heavens. He had more in common with Whistier than I thought."

Mr Goodston smiled at me fondly. "I'm afraid I have no other works on him here just now. I shall try to locate Marguerite Steen's other autobiographical writings if you're interested?'"

"Please do, Mr Goodston." I stood up. "I must be off. For the moment, this is excellent. Business calls. Let me settle up with you."

"Thank you my dear sir. Thank you. And the Laver *Portraits in Oil and in Vinegar?* The vinegar is reserved only for Sir Frank Dicksee, President of the Royal Academy at the time."

"I'll take it."

"You are a scholar and a gentleman, my dear sir." He smiled benignly as he made out an invoice by hand. "A scholar and a gentleman." He peered at me over his half-moons.

69

"Do take good care of yourself, won't you, during the chase you will, once again, doubtless be pursuing? I should hate to lose your custom. Especially for the sake of a Ben Nicholson, of all things."

Chapter Nine

"What I didn't quite understand," I said to Sue, that evening, "is why Dorkie Collins talked of the Tate Gallery's embarrassment. And we saving it by rehabilitating Ben Nicholson - commercially, that is."

I was standing under the big Clarkson Stanfield marine painting which hangs over the mantelpiece, a soothing drink in hand. Sue was sitting on the settee, similarly provisioned, and William was fast asleep.

She looked up at me with an amused expression.

"Come on, Tim, you're supposed to have done your research. It's a reference to Alan Bowness, obviously."

I nodded gloomily. Sir Alan Bowness, as he became, married Ben Nicholson's daughter Sarah, one of the Barbara Hepworth triplets. He was an art lecturer, Courtauld no less, and career committee man according to all accounts, who succeeded Norman Reid as Director of the Tate Gallery. He and Ben were not on good terms due to an article he wrote on Sir William to which Ben, defensive of his father's reputation, objected. The unfortunate Sir Alan, considering himself an expert on his father-in-law's paintings, had authenticated a number of John Drewe's fakes. The provenance documents and Drewe's smooth talk convinced him, as he frankly admitted in a Channel 4 news interview after Drewe's conviction.

To have the Director of the Tate Gallery no less, son-in-law of the artist and familiar with nearly a lifetime's output, authenticate some of Drewe's work at the height of the Ben Nicholson boom was unfortunate, to put it mildly. Punters, dealers and public galleries had suffered.

"Could have happened to anyone I suppose," I muttered. "But Dorkie seems to be letting me know that he is well aware of the background and that he's operating all above board."

"You've set yourself quite a task, Tim. A William Nicholson

painting will be much easier than Ben's. To authenticate, I mean."

"Maybe. To get two together would be quite something. I believe that we'll have to find each one separately, though."

"You don't think that Dorkie will come up with the goods?"

"He might. The chance would be that one might be a good example but not the other. In the meantime, I'll do some digging of my own."

She gave me an old fashioned look. "Hastings. A controversial acquisition. Skulduggery in the background. This has all the makings of one of your classic imbroglios, Tim."

I frowned. "You haven't been meeting Nobby secretly by any chance have you? Imbroglio is the word he used this morning."

Her face changed. "Oh did he? That's interesting. I wonder why." Her tone changed to a deceptive, lightweight-interest, curious pitch. Always a bad sign. "You haven't told me how your breakfast went, by the way. I was a bit surprised that he called you to meet him just now."

"Why?"

"Because Gillian says he's very busy and their social life is suffering. It seemed odd that he had time to natter over old times with you."

"Oh, you know Nobby. Needed a break from the pressure, I expect."

"Then why did he use the word imbroglio?"

Women are unbelievable. You can't let your guard down for a minute. The slightest slip of a word and they're after you, burrowing like terriers smelling a warren full of soft, floppy bunnies.

"In relation to past events, you know, Sue. Just a casual reference to old times."

"Oh? Which past event in particular?"

"I, um, I can't remember which one. Italy, perhaps."

She put her glass down with a firm clink onto the table beside her.

"I don't believe a word you're saying. Nobby is harassed to death with some big criminal project according to Gilly and he meets you to chatter over old imbroglios? Never. That's not Nobby; he's much too focused for that. You've hardly started on a new acquisition for the Art Fund and Nobby's called you in already. Why? It's too much of a coincidence." Her eyes had narrowed at me. "You're hiding something."

I sighed. "There are times when you remind me of Miss Prendergast, my old school matron. Gormengast, we called her. She had an obsession about clean sheets. And bowels: her questions about bowels were deeply distressing."

"Never mind the boarding school memoirs. I've no doubt she had a terrible time with you all. What was your meeting about? Cough it up!"

"When you don't remind me of Nobby, that is. You're wasted on art connoisseurship, you know. Imbroglios and coughing seem to be the in-words for the fuzz just now. You should have joined the Force."

"Tim!"

"Have you ever heard of a woman called Moira Bassington?"

She frowned. "Who?"

"Moira Bassington. Lived in one of the Pimlico estates behind the Gallery. Fortyish. A researcher for TV companies. Library work. A bit of a goer, apparently."

"No I haven't." Her voice went a shade lower in tone, suspicion trickling into it like warm dirty water into an old jam jar. "Why, should I?"

"No, not necessarily."

"So - "

"Someone bumped her off a few days ago. Blow or blows to the head, according to Nobby."

"And what has that - "

"The name Simpson, T., was found written down amongst other details in her diary."

"*What?*"

73

"There is no reason to suppose that it referred to me. Particularly. On the other hand, the Metropolitan Police computer has a penchant for, is partial to, pointing its greasy finger in my direction whenever that surname, appended to the initial T, comes up. It's absurd. Insulting, really."

"So Nobby - "

"So Nobby, as you correctly surmise, was doing a little probing *ex officio*, as it were."

Her expression went all knowing. "And doubtless, as one lad to another, being discreet about what might be an embarrassing connection? With - how did you put it? *A bit of a goer?*"

"Sue, really! This is unworthy of you. My private life will bear the most scrupulous examination. As well you know."

"Hmm."

"What do you mean, hmm?"

"Your private life, I am willing to concede, just might - although I am ever vigilant, after the way you behaved with that Wilson girl at the last party we went to - but your professional life won't. You've hardly started and an unfortunate woman has been erased already."

"Just because she lived behind your blessed place of work does not mean - "

"Hang on! Researcher for a TV company, you said. That means photo and film archives, doesn't it?"

"Yes it does."

"And you've just started with this Pierre Champion business?"

"I have agreed to look into the financing of a film and photo archive, yes."

"Dear God."

"There are probably hundreds, if not more, Simpson, Ts in this city and even more in the country. Let alone worldwide. We Simpsons are prolific. There is no reason to suppose that this Bassington woman, with whom I may hardly need to add, I have had no *connections*, as you call them, of any sort, was referring to me. Researchers must have many contacts."

"Now you're getting pompous."

"As well I might, grilled by you. The thought of the archive possibility did occur, disturbingly, to me. I have been absolutely open and above board about it with Nobby. As I am with you."

"After I had to quiz you about your breakfast."

"I was waiting for the right moment to advise you. In the past, you have over-reacted to these things."

"With every justification."

"Not so."

"Tim, I can't stop you getting into these imbroglios, I've long realised that. Despite my natural reactions, I am willing to stifle my alarm. Just remember that you are now a father and have a responsibility over and above minor matters like me and our future."

"Sue, really, now who's getting pompous?"

"And that I shall expect to be consulted. All the time."

"Of course. Don't I always?"

"I mean all the time. Not just when guilt overtakes you. I want to be involved. Fully involved."

"You shall be. You shall."

"You promise?"

"I promise. I mean, how else will I reassure myself about a possible Ben Nicholson painting?" I promise. I mean, how else will I reassure myself about a possible Ben Nicholson painting? A Tate Gallery expert will be essentian, won't it?" I smiled meaningfully. "For elimination purposes, if nothing else."

For a moment, she clenched her glass in preparation for its use as a missile. Fortunately, the Clarkson Stanfiele marine was behind me and Sue knows she can not shy objects with any accuracy.

Not for the first time, a painting came to my rescue.

Chapter Ten

"Nobby Roberts said," Sam Johnson looked with satisfied eye at the remains of his Ploughman's Lunch as he spoke, "that I was to show you these photos. But - and it is a big but - he says you are not to try any funny tricks. This is strictly off the record, this is."

He grinned at me slyly, sort of sideways. Sam Johnson is a CID Inspector at the Chelsea station and we have been involved together before. At the beginning things were awkward, but we overcame various difficulties to become good friends. I am sure that he takes the view, privately and without telling me, that if an amateur wants to go careering off like a loose cannon it is OK with him providing the results are satisfactory and credit accrues to his career account. Like many policemen, Sam is only too glad to save legwork if someone else will do it. He is a good sort, with neat brown hair, a distressing disregard for sartorial appearances in the form of wearing brown ties, and a liking for pub lunches, providing they are paid for by someone else. Like most CID men he drinks whisky for preference but today, going cautiously, he had joined me in a pint of bitter at the City pub where we had met by prior arrangement.

"Funny tricks? Me? A strange admonition. What can he mean?"

Sam chuckled and fished around in his pockets to produce a manila envelope of more or less A5 or octavo size, with a stiffened backing for the protection of contents. Glancing round quickly to make sure we were not overlooked, he pulled out a pack of small, card-like illustrations and put them down on the table.

A selection of photos met my eye. The top one was a portrait black-and-white, about four inches by six, the sort of semi-passport, semi-studio type, taken with careful lighting, at an angle. It showed a youngish, attractive woman with dark hair. Her eyes were wide under large swept brows, the nose unremarkable, the lips full. The jaw line was clean and her skin was clear.

"Moira Bassington," said Sam, with evident satisfaction. "Taken about ten years ago, we reckon.

"Good looker, wasn't she?"

"Not half bad. Nice face. She'd be about thirty, then. Still doesn't strike a bell, though?"

I shook my head. "I'm afraid not."

He pushed the portrait to one side and presented me with a few more snaps, some colour, some rather old-fashioned in black and white, all much smaller. They were of the same woman, now with a slight fold at the plumper jaw, older, eyes a bit narrower, not portraits but standing in various locations. In some she was smiling, broadening the face to a round, fatter look. In others, she was serious, the mouth slightly sullen. Her figure, whether in dress or trousers, was full, her calves, when visible, sturdy. There was a poignancy about these snapped moments, these frozen instants, of a kind which always unnerves me when looking at old photographs. Here is the fleeting moment in someone's life, its surrounding circumstances unknown to the viewer but having, for its owner, an enormous memorial penumbra like a huge, magnetic field stretching out all round the circumstances of that instant into lives, events, emotions and lost meanings. Whenever I see old family photograph albums for sale in auction rooms, I tend to shiver and move on. I feel I have no right to acquire such tragic relics, to peer into the lovingly-assembled record of someone else's private past.

In one photo she was outdoors somewhere, in sunglasses beside the door of an old sports car parked on grass, its bonnet invisible. A man in a blazer and flannels stood beside her, his back to the camera. She had a wine glass in her hand.

I glanced quickly at Sam as the significance hit me. "No blokes?" I queried.

He shook his head sadly. "No blokes, Tim. You've put your finger on it. If there were any with blokes, they've gone. Just the back of this guy. These came from a secret drawer in the dressing chest in her bedroom. She had a desk in the main room but there were no photos in that."

"Mm. But there was a diary?"

"Sort of. More a notebook than a diary. Only a few pages had been used. Odd jottings, reminders, that sort of thing."

"Including Simpson, T.?"

He smiled again. "Yes."

"Other names?"

He frowned. "Not really. Just initials. Like it was people she knew well and couldn't be bothered to write the full name. G or J or D or P, or two together like AF and PC."

"Odd."

"Odd?"

"Well, she writes down my name, or someone with a similar name, by the surname, but no one else?"

"Not in the notebook we've got."

"Almost as though she's protecting the other names."

"That thought occurred to me, too."

"Was this notebook confined to a specific subject, d'you think? A particular project, perhaps?"

"Could be."

"Come on, Sam! What else is in it? Addresses, references, phone numbers, assignations?"

He shook his head.

"What then?"

"Numbers. Dates. What could be sums of money or index references. Almost a sort of code. I've got a couple of experts looking to decipher them. If they are decipherable."

"You mean her desk is clean apart from this?"

"I didn't say this was in her desk, Tim. It wasn't. It was in her mattress."

"Eh?"

"In her mattress. Not under it. In a place accessible by a

thin slit at one end. If anyone searched her place quickly, they'd be bound to look under the mattress. We found nothing there. Whoever killed her seems to have cleaned the place out."

"Family?"

He shook his head. "None. Bassington is not that common a name. We've checked. No Bassington in Britain claims to be related to her. She had a bank account and the usual bills, all in the name Bassington, but no driving licence, passport, nothing like that."

"Is that her real name, then?"

He shrugged. "There's no marriage certificate. Or other documents of that sort. Not in that flat, anyway. I was away when the body was found. I only came in on this case a day or two ago." He compressed his lips. "Just my luck to be handed it as soon as I got back."

"I was thinking that it was nice of Nobby - and you - to see me privately. In fact, you're the Torquemada on this one, are you?"

"I am the Inquisitor, yes. For my sins."

I picked up the little pack of photographs to glance through them again, quickly. There was one in a village, at a farm gate with a church tower behind. Then a seaside sweep of grass with caravans and a tall church, maybe the same one, with the woman standing smiling rather shyly in front. Now there was a promenade and a bay behind her, not Hastings, Jeremy, I thought quickly, certainly not Hastings, the bay is curved and the surf-laden sea more contained. Now a town shot, on a pavement with railings and a terrace of houses behind. Another, less like a city, more suburban. Then one at a gate with a severe house with what looked like a weathervane on it. In each of them she stood self-consciously smiling, holding herself erect but diffidently, as though this was not a pose to flatter herself but rather to record the moment or the place.

"The question is," I said, still leafing through, "who took them?"

"Right. Recognise any of the locations?"

I shook my head. "Sorry. Not a clue. Look like they could be anywhere. Holidays of some sort, I imagine." I looked at another one, where she stood beside a bush with little pale yellow flowers, shielding another tall, rather exotic plant with red blooms. Here her blouse was almost strapless and shapely bare shoulders were square to the viewer whilst her arms went down into the side pockets of a pleated cotton skirt which ended at the knee. Her feet were in skimpy sandals. "Looks like it was warm that day. Must be holidays, don't you think? Memories of some outing of some sort."

"Or outings." Sam leant forward to point at one of the snaps. "I think there's time elapsed between these. Her face has changed a bit from one to another. And the clothes; this one in town, on the pavement, she's got a coat on. The weather's cooler, even cold. The light's quite different. Could be London somewhere."

"That's true."

"Look here," he fished around at the bottom of the pack and pulled out a colour shot. "This one's obviously London."

Now she stood smiling in front of Wheeler's Oyster Restaurant in Duke of York Street in St James, just off Jermyn Street. Of the various Wheeler's fish restaurants it's the one that's on a corner and goes up in four diminutive floors. The shot had been taken from across the road, probably outside what used to be La Colombina, the Italian restaurant which offered a rather good grilled Dover sole at much less cost than the more famous establishment opposite. Behind her was the green signage of the restaurant and the alley which goes down the side. I stared at the photograph in fascination as the start of an idea, a pattern, started to come into my mind, an idea which started those icy prickles, the ones that Nobby had instigated, to come up on the back of my neck and down my spine.

"What's up?" Sam asked.

"Oh, nothing." I made as quick a recovery as I could. "I

was thinking that at least she must have had a well-to-do boyfriend if he could take her to Wheeler's for lunch."

He nodded vigorously. "That's what I thought, too. Although maybe they didn't go in. Maybe it's just a sort of tourist photo."

"It would be an odd memento if they didn't go in."

"You're right. I'll get the lads to take a photo round and ask them. Someone might remember her, and her friend, if they went in."

"Good idea. Are there any other photos in her flat?"

He shook his head. "None that we've found."

"I'm sorry Sam. I still can't say that I recognise her. Would it be possible to have copies? Just in case something occurs to me?"

He frowned slightly. "These are official evidence, you know. Why do you want them?"

I shook my head as I chose my words carefully. "I can't explain. I'd just like to brood on them for a bit. There may be some pattern to them that will occur to me if I can take a bit of time."

He smiled. "You say you've never seen her but you want to brood over her private snaps? For pattern purposes?"

I shrugged casually. "It's supposed to be my name in the diary. In my own defence I should be able to have access to all the prosecution's evidence. Shouldn't I?"

There was a slow nod of acceptance. "Nobby wouldn't like it. But I'll get them copied on the new colour photocopier we've just been allowed to use. You can have those copies. OK?"

"You're a hero, Sam."

"I'll probably rue the day. In the meantime we're covering all the sorts of studios, producers and editors she might have worked for. Three have recognised her already. Nothing to report. They say she was good, did the job thoroughly, kept her private self private, no histrionics but then what they asked her to do was pretty straightforward. Paid via an invoice, no fiddles, no names, no pack drill."

"No sort of relationship with the producers?"

"All three are women." He gave me a meaning glance. "No, don't think she was that way inclined, nor them. It was all professional."

"Any contact with Frank Cordwell?"

He shook his head. "Nope. One of my colleagues called him at the number you gave Nobby, out in Essex isn't it, yesterday afternoon, and made a point of quizzing him. No knowledge of any researcher called Bassington."

"Odd."

"Why odd?"

"I would have thought, in that industry, names got around. Maybe there's a bit of secrecy between producers and archive libraries and researchers. Like antique dealers not giving away their sources."

"There's a lot of them, Tim. Researchers and libraries, I mean. Bloody dozens of them. Lots of legwork for us to do." He sighed. "And damned few people to do it."

"What about her neighbours? Sorry, not trying to teach you your trade, Sam."

"Feel free. Her neighbours say she brought blokes to the flat from time to time. My guys seized on that to start with, but it's leading nowhere. In that estate people keep pretty much to themselves and at the local pubs we've so far drawn a blank. This is London, not Little Chattering in the Marsh. Actually, I'm inclined to believe that she didn't live there full time."

"Oh? Why?"

"The flat has a - how should I put it - partly-used feel to me. Slightly neglected. Not treated with affection, like a woman usually dillies up a place of her own."

"An assignation place?"

"No, not quite that. But slightly that way. As though she had somewhere else where she did her real living. Out of town, maybe."

"She must have travelled about to do her research."

"That might be it. One of the neighbours thought she was away quite a bit. Even so, if this was the place she came home to, she'd surely have made it more personal. It was a work place all right, with an answering machine and all that, but not much else. That aspect needs working on." He looked at his watch. "Oh God. I have to go. There is just never enough time in the day. I'll get these copies to you. You will let me know, won't you, if you have any real info? Immediately?"

"I promised Nobby," I answered. "And I promise you."

"Good. Thanks for the lunch."

"My pleasure. We citizens have a duty to keep our guardians victualled."

"That's what I like about you. The strong sense of public duty. Nobby's always remarked on it."

"Nice to see you again, Sam."

"And you, Tim. No good my advising you to stay out of trouble, I know that. But nice to see you, all the same. However briefly." He paused, looking thoughtful as he scanned my face. "You're sure these photos don't strike a chord?"

"Not right now. But they might, if I can brood on them."

He held up a warning finger. "I'll send you the copies. I don't know why, but I will. Past experience, I think. As long as you tell me, the first inkling you get."

"You may depend upon it, as the late Duke of Wellington used to say." I paused for thought. "Even whilst he was still a Marquis."

"What does that mean?"

"Nothing. Just an expression. I'm into Sir William Nicholson's paintings just now, and he did a still life of a moulded lustre jug with the Marquis Wellington, as he then was, depicted on one side. Staffordshire, it was. Vivien Leigh bought the painting, I'm told."

He shook his head sadly. "You're an odd fellow, Tim. I hope that somewhere in that crowded brain's collection of idiosyncratic esoterica some inkling of what these photos mean will come to light. That's why I'm willing to send you the copies."

I grinned as he put the snaps back in the envelope and took himself off with a cheerful wave. An inkling, as he put it, was starting to trickle round my mind, just the glimmer of what might be a mad idea based on dimly-remembered gleanings. The icy prickles were subsiding, letting me start to think analytically, but it was much too early to voice the concept that was forming, to express it in words.

One of the photos had been taken in St. Ives. I was sure of that from the sweep of the bay and the church tower in the distance. I'd been there with Sue to the Tate. That was where Ben Nicholson and Barbara Hepworth lived, loved and held court until he went off to Switzerland with another lady. Hepworth's studio house is open to the public. I had a feeling, too, that another church in the photos was that of Happisburgh, on the Norfolk coast where, one famous holiday with Henry Moore and Ivon Hitchens, Ben Nicholson took the sculptor Jack Skeaping's first wife, Barbara Hepworth, off him.

Then there was the shot in Duke of York Street. The alley down the side of Wheeler's is called Apple Tree Yard. It is where William Nicholson had his studio for many years. It is the place from which his daughter Nancy went forth to marry the poet Robert Graves in January 1918. The studio doesn't exist now but that blind alley was once a Nicholson centre, teeming with life and painting. I didn't recognise the other places but something whispered to me that it might be worth checking to see if they had Nicholson connections, too.

Why? Why take photos at such sites? Was it pure coincidence? Like Simpson, T., written down in a notebook?

I hate coincidences.

There was no point in alerting Sam and Nobby just yet, though. Inklings like mine need work doing on them before they can be brought to light.

Chapter Eleven

The village of Mangate is out beyond Great Dunmow, well into rural Essex but not too far from the A120 for access to Stansted. Agricultural country surrounds it in that low-lying, laboured way which characterises a lot of the Eastern Midlands, as though preparing you for the wide plains of Lincoln, Suffolk and Norfolk. The skies are not as big as the spacious East Anglian canopy and the ground goes into rolling mode from time to time, as though fed up with its own hedged and treed clutter around wide-open expanses of rich, arable earth. The clustered architecture of pretty hamlets and small towns varies from pargetted stucco under thatch to fully-beamed Tudor and fine red brick as well as much indiscriminate, later construction. There is a misleadingly uneventful look about the land behind the cow-parsleyed verges which belies its heavy use as a productive resource, pressed by heavy machinery and bedewed by many chemicals.

At one end of the village, beyond a dull terrace of brick Victorian cottages, a pair of white barred gates flanked the entrance to the Hall, with a gravel drive leading to the front door. Behind the four-square, Georgian brick house with later additions rose the extensive corrugated outlines of farm buildings, silos and grey barns set in wide concrete yards where big lorries and perhaps tankers could manoeuvre. This was agro-industry in its full business sense, with hoppers and vibrating conveyors and cyclones above pipework connecting process to process. I parked my Jaguar in one of the bays marked 'Visitors', next to a varied rank of dusty executive and secretarial vehicles which were outshone by a gleaming blue Aston Martin DB7 before striding in through a pillared portico, stuck on to the double front door in a recent, expensive attempt to add importance to the facade.

"Tim." After a brief wait and a call from a smart

receptionist, Gerry Watson, suited and stylish as ever, came into the foyer with outstretched hand. He looked as far removed from agri-business as it is possible for a dedicated townee to be. "Nice to see you again. Thanks for coming along. You got the business plan all right, obviously."

"I did."

"Frank's waiting for us. And Pierre's here today, but he's down the yard right now."

"That's his DB7?"

"It is." Gerry grinned. "All one hundred and sixty thousand pounds' worth of it. Just for UK driving, of course. He keeps a Lamborghini in France. He'll see you later. Let's go through."

We walked out of the foyer into a brief passage and then turned into a room set up for meetings. Here the style was modern, with a light wood conference table, chairs, a video set-up, presentation board, overhead projector and screen. All the paraphernalia of the bullshit brigade used, presumably, to impress visiting media executives and even humble researchers. The windows were fitted with white vertical slatted blinds, reflecting sunny light from outside but capable of cutting off anything too brilliant if required. In one corner, stooping over a coffee machine, was Frank Cordwell.

In the time that had passed since my meeting with Sam Johnson I had prepared myself carefully for this. Stumm, was my strategy, absolutely stumm about a possible Bassington connection. Let Sam and his men pursue the dogged paths of enquiry at which they were so professional. There was no need to let Cordwell know that I had passed his name to the police; that would not help my relationship with him in any way. If by extraordinary coincidence he was somehow guilty, the chance was, if I really was the Simpson,T., of Moira Bassington's jottings, that he'd have guessed. If not, no point in mentioning it. He'd denied any knowledge of the woman, according to Sam; nothing I could add would make any difference.

There was no ill-fitting suit this time. He was in a blue cotton shirt, grey lightweight trousers and spongy suede shoes. The casual gear suited him, if that's not too bad a pun, much better than the outfit he'd worn at Hamish Lang's. He still looked bulky, but relaxed and alert. I noted, now, that his hair was almost blond and that behind the horn-rimmed glasses his eyes were blue. The face, though fleshy, was smooth and youngish for a man in his forties. He gave me a friendly smile as we shook hands.

"Hi, Tim. Coffee?"

"Please."

"Good trip up?"

"No problems."

"Good. Help yourself to milk and sugar."

The coffee was in a china cup, no paper or plastic, and tasted good. We sat down round the table and I got out my documents. Cordwell gestured at them.

"Plan strike you as reasonable?"

"Eminently. As a plan, it holds together well. For a banker, the assumptions about cash flow are the key to it all, of course. But if the size of acquisitions you're going to make stays within the figures, and if the rentals don't start too far away from the time scale, and if they are of the scale used, I suppose it should all run reasonably within the figures you've set. It all depends on sales, as usual."

Gerry Watson grinned. "From my experience, those ifs are big ifs."

"I'm sure. At the moment, it's all just arithmetic."

"Maybe before we get too enmeshed in figures, you'd like to look round? When you've finished your coffee?"

"Great."

After a few pleasantries over coffee we left the room and passed through an open-plan office before going upstairs. Here there were individual offices and tiers of shelves full of files.

"Come and meet Jessica," Frank Cordwell said.

I was presented to a dark-haired, serious lady of about fifty, who rose from behind the rather clogged surfaces of a big desk to greet me with a smile.

"Tim, this is my assistant, Jessica Browne. Jessica, this is Tim Simpson of White's Bank."

"Hello, Tim." Her voice was low and pleasant. "What a pleasure. I've always wanted to meet you."

"Me?"

I looked at her in surprise as the other two stood back slightly, waiting. She was neatly dressed, wearing a dark blue, long-sleeved top and slender, subfusc trousers. Her face was clear-skinned, with no make-up. It was smooth and untroubled, as though she was a health-food freak but relaxed about it rather than dogmatic. Her eyes were shrewd and intelligent. She didn't look like someone who'd lecture you on diet.

She shook hands firmly. There was no wedding ring on the other hand.

"You indeed. I know all about White's Art Fund. You found that big missing painting of Wyndham Lewis's. *Kermesse*. In a farm barn near Leighton Buzzard, wasn't it?"

"Potterspury, actually. Stony Stratford way."

"That's it. Brilliant work. And you got a sketch of Iris Barry, too. A study for *Praxitella*, wasn't it? I read all about it at the time. Whenever I'm in Leeds I go to look at that painting."

"Really? Are you a Wyndham Lewis fan?"

She shook her head emphatically. "No, indeed not. Iris Barry."

"Why - oh, I get it. She was a film buff, wasn't she?"

Iris Barry, an early mistress of Wyndham Lewis's, bore him two children before his paranoid character and unabashed grapplings with Nancy Cunard and others drove them apart.

"An absolute expert. After Lewis ditched her, horrible man."

I thought back, quickly. "As I recall, her career took off once she'd left him. Novels, poetry and then the founding of the Film Society."

Her smile broadened. "Well done! She was marvellous. Just marvellous. My heroine. Film critic for the *Daily Mail* before she went to America. Hollywood, then the Film Library at the Museum of Modern Art in New York. What she knew about the films of the thirties! She was wonderful, way ahead of her time. Someone should write a book on her. Alistair Cooke would have been a good candidate."

"She died rather poor, growing plants for perfume in Grasse though, didn't she?"

There was a nod and a knowing smile. "A bad chooser of men. There were quite a few. Pierre Kerroux, the last one, did at least stay for twenty years. He was much younger than her, of course. An olive oil smuggler she met at the Cannes Film Festival." She made wry expression. "Oh dear, I'm sorry, you're here to talk archive finance business and here am I, off on one of my hobby horses. Sorry."

I grinned at her. "Not at all. I could talk about Iris Barry and Wyndham Lewis until the cows come home. Unfortunately, today's not the day." I turned to the others, who were standing listening intently. "Sorry, Frank. Sorry, Gerry."

"No problem." Frank Cordwell chuckled. "I'm glad you've hit it off. We'll let you two swap Iris Barry talk some other time. Jessica is my invaluable aide and knows more about film than has ever been recorded. She's practically a walking Halliwell, only much deeper."

She smiled at this reference to *Halliwell's Film Guide*, a standard reference work listing the innumerable films made over God knows how long, as I asked, "Are you the film, rather than the still photograph, archivist?"

She shook her head. "Both. Well, don't let Frank fool you. He's no slouch. We've assembled some marvellous things together. There's a terrific market opening up and the CD storage technology is changing everything. With this new interest of Pierre Champion's the future looks marvellous."

"Great. I hope I'll be back to talk Iris Barry with you sometime."

"That's something to look forward to."

We gave each other a cheerful smile and I moved on to pass through cool offices full of filed reference material, stored videos, computer diskettes and CDs. It was far removed from the standard image of a library, without gloom or hush or academic illusion. I always think of libraries as being in towns, with congested streets outside, so it was very different to look out of windows that provided clear country light and rural skies.

Soon however, we were outside, in a vast modern barn full of Gerry's furniture and period decorative gear. There was everything from Elizabeth the First to Elizabeth the Second, every style you can think of, under high skylighted roofing but arranged on a floor plan in careful blocks separated by aisles to enable fork-lift trucks to move swiftly between. Around the sides were steel structured racks for smaller items and even elaborate china, so as to save space.

"Christ," I said, looking round at the pieces near me, which included a huge French Provincial library bookcase and a whole rank and file of repro Queen Anne chairs under dangling elaborate chandeliers. "This reminds me of the old days at Austin's of Peckham Rye, only ten times more."

Gerry grinned. "I suppose you think this is a very rural site to hold material like this. But most of our customers are in studios all over the place, not just London. This is a very economic distribution site."

"You're not located here yourself, are you, Gerry?"

"Of course not. This is just where the material is stored. I come up here from time to time. My office is in Hammersmith. Almost every item in our stock has been digitally photographed and is on CD. I can send an image, by e-mail, to anyone who's interested, in a flash. Pictures of whole rooms, if necessary. Frank here will have an internet site like mine for browsers and much more on other records."

I turned to Frank Cordwell. "You'll be in Hammersmith, too?"

"Partly. I'll divide my time between there and here, with Jessica, until we work out the best arrangements. Jessica likes it up here, she's bought a bungalow nearby already. We'll both have to travel round quite a bit you know, sourcing material."

"Of course."

A bit like me, I thought, except that the Art Fund only needs part of my time because it's not used for hire or demonstration except on the odd occasions when we have a new acquisition to show off, or a loan exhibition for promotional purposes. And it's not bulky like furniture, suits of armour and great bogus libraries of books. For people who show interest we too have CD and internet site viewing facilities. The stock is well documented, most of it, most of the time. There were parallels with this operation everywhere in the Art Fund.

"Showing the banker our prize possessions?"

The sharp voice, completely unaccented and English, which cut into my thoughts, came from behind me. I turned to see a short, stocky man in a mid-grey suit, blue shirt and silk tie striding towards me, hand held out to shake. I recognised him at once. It was Pierre Champion, pepper-and salt stiff hair cut *en brosse*, smiling broadly but blue eyes keenly narrowed to take stock. I turned to meet him head-on as my mind adjusted to coping with one of the current City legends, a baron who bestrode the Channel with a range of British and French operations, and who I was to court as a customer without ruining the Bank or disappointing Hamish Lang.

His hand was firm. He looked as though he might have been a scrum-half, years ago, and still kept himself fit. Or maybe a rider, legs muscular, but too big for jockey. His black leather shoes were dusty from grain, presumably the result of a tour of the arable empire around us.

"Mr Champion." I was respectful as the other two stood back to let him greet me. "This is a pleasure."

"Me too. The famous Tim Simpson. Wanted to meet you for a long time."

"Oh?"

He nodded emphatically as he let go of my hand. "I've told Gerry and Frank already. Your Art Fund is a kind of model for this sort of operation. For capital appreciation, of course." He cocked his head to one side as he kept my eye. "The Whistler of the Thames and a Monet of the same. The Camden Town paintings. Munnings - that whole Crockingham Collection. Wyndham Lewis - that was a hell of a find. A Norman Shaw bureau bookcase. You're a shrewd operator, Tim. The appreciation of the Art Fund units has been very satisfactory. Couldn't have done better myself."

Light dawned. "You're an investor."

I made it a statement, not a question. He knew it all, obviously. Yet I was certain I hadn't seen his name on our records of unit purchasers.

He put a finger alongside his nose. "Not me personally."

"A nominee, eh?"

He smiled again. "Let's just say one of my interests does it for me. I need to spread my portfolio, my broker has always said. Not that I pay him too much attention. He's much too cautious."

I can imagine, I thought, what problems a broker would have with you. If you really need a broker; men like you make their own decisions. The idea made me uncomfortable; to have the intrusive Pierre Champion in bed with the Art Fund, even as an investor, gave me immediate food for thought.

"You going to lend us some money?" The question was challengingly put.

"I don't see why not. I need to talk it through with Frank here, of course."

"Of course." He smiled at Cordwell. "I hire the best, Tim, and Frank here is one of the best. Like Gerry in his field. Mangate Visual Records has a huge future. My advice to White's is to get in on it as early as possible." He cocked his head to one side. "Although that may go against your well-known corporate reputation for caution. Your French associate is still Maucourt Freres, is it?"

"That's right." I put aside a response to the crack about White's caution.

"I've met Eugène Maucourt, the PDG." He smiled meaningfully. "Something of a traditional fellow, ain't he?"

I smiled back. I am not one of the glacial, Gaullist, elderly Eugène Maucourt's favourite people, being regarded by him as an Anglo-Saxon of the worst sort, definitely not *comme il faut* and generally behaving in a way which humorous English diplomats call *au-dessus de sa gare*. Eugene is a stuffy old bugger.

"Yes, I think Eugène is rather one of the old school." I kept a pleasant demeanour. "His brother Charles was much more dynamic and Christian, the grandson, who's a personal friend, is definitely the up-and-coming force in that outfit."

Champion nodded approvingly. "I've only met Christian briefly but I've heard that what you say is correct. Do you get over to Paris often?"

"From time to time," I answered, cautiously. "I'm responsible for quite a bit of co-ordination between White's and Maucourt's." I didn't want to tell him that the circumstances under which I have been to Paris, in the past, have been rather fraught ones.

"Good. You speak French, then?"

"Yes. *On peut continuer en français, si vous voulez, Mr Champion.*"

"No need. But I see quite a lot of opportunities in France for Mangate."

"That's very good, I'm sure."

"We have to be able to seize opportunities all over Europe, but Britain and France will do for starters."

"Indeed. The trick, as I understand it, is to find the material before others get to it. As well as your intention to buy up existing archives before someone else does. So much has been bagged already, hasn't it? Bit like the antique trade, I think."

He nodded sagely. "It takes one to recognise one. You in particular, eh?" He stroked his jaw with what I afterwards found to be an habitual gesture of thought which had the added merit of concealing his expression. "I mean, deciding which artist to go for next for the Art Fund must be crucial, eh?"

Et tu Brute, I nearly said. I glanced at Gerry Watson, thinking of his identical remark in front of Sir Hamish Lang, but his face was expressionless.

"Yes, it is, apart from buying better examples of the existing ones when they come up at auction."

"There are risks to that too, of course. An artist can go out of fashion, can't he? Or she?"

"Of course. There's a book - "

"*The Economics of Taste* by Gerald Reitlinger." He was nodding emphatically as he interrupted me. "I know it well. Charts the rise and fall of many painters. And their rise again. Used to be my bible. It's well out of date now."

"Maybe someone should write a new one."

His shrewd eyes still rested keenly on mine. "No one who's making the grade has time. Or wants to give the game away in a mere book. Fashion's a funny business. If someone knew which artist White's were going for next, they might make a windfall, mightn't they? By getting in before you? Just like the stock market."

"The very same."

"Your decision on who to buy next must be quite a headache in that respect, eh, Tim?"

"Tell me about it," I said. "Just tell me about it." I found this repeated pressure on the subject a bit suspicious.

He grunted. "Not me. I wouldn't presume. But maybe, if we collaborate on Mangate Visual Records, we could set up an art archive that would redo Reitlinger in pictures. Press a button and an artist's record could be played back on a wide screen, in ragtime. With the evidence of each painting in front of you. Reading some dusty tome's no good; you need to see the pictures, don't you?"

I smiled carefully. "There speaks a man dedicated to the visual future."

"Right. Absolutely right. Excellent. Books are finished. Pictures have only just started." He bared his even white teeth at me in an approving grimace. "I think we're going to get on well." He turned his gaze back to his two managers and made it commanding. "Gerry, Frank. Look after this man. Show him everything he wants to see. But make him talk turkey when you're back in the office." He stuck his hand out at me. The encounter was obviously over. "Pleasure to meet you, Tim. I look forward to doing business with you."

"Me too," I said, as he strode off.

I can, as Nobby said, be economical with the actuality.

Chapter Twelve

"Ah. Here he is. Splendid. Do sit down, won't you? Jeremy said you'd take coffee, so we took the liberty of putting one out for you. Welcome to the den, as it were."

The burly figure of Frederick White, Lord Harbledown, smiled diffidently at me across his desk. Beside him, Jeremy White produced a significant roll of eye. In response to a summons, I was back at the Bank, attending Our Chairman in person in his own panelled lair. There used to be an advertisement for business courses entitled 'Do you Call or are you Called For?' propounding the virtues of higher education courses and hence, apparently, elevation to the Boss Class. I went to Cambridge; ask me to which category I belong?

So far, however, my reception had been favourable. Harbledown was smartly suited, white shirted and foulard tied in traditional bankers' armour but his face had gratifyingly lit up at the sight of me. He hadn't said 'Ah, Simpson' in the disdainful manner of Sir Hamish Lang. His manner was openly pleasant as he waved at a bone china pot of coffee, set on a small tray with matching Worcester cup, jug of milk and sugar bowl beside it on the table in front of me.

"Thank you," I said, cautiously, not having had time to consult with Jeremy about what this meeting was for, but guessing all the same.

"Do you mind very much if we use Christian names? We've met before, of course, but don't seem to have had much time together, have we? Which I regret. I'm Freddy. May I call you Tim?"

"Of course."

"Much easier, these days, the way things are done. Used to be the most frightful protocols. Never could stand it." He grinned at me significantly, as though letting me in on the myth that he had been part of some past structure I knew he must be too young to have joined. Freddy Harbledown, for all that he occasionally adopts mannerisms associated with English aristocrats in Hollywood fantasies, is not yet fifty, extremely astute, and naturally bereft of the style a Lord Emsworth might portray even if hinting at it in a form of diffident verbal smoke screen. His love of Old English Sheepdogs is only marginally to be compared with Emsworth's dotty passion for the sow, Empress of Blandings. In this he reminded me of the Lancashire mill owner Jack Ashworth with whom we had dealings, a man who gave the impression that he was a raw small-town textile magnate from Darwen whilst concealing a sharp international mind. Freddy Harbledown had no easy patch to hoe, keeping one of the last British merchant banks afloat whilst the storms of international finance and contractions due to market rationalisations and globalisations bobbed our little ark from side to side. To mix a few metaphors.

"I've never really thanked you enough for your role in Richard's Italian affair," he said, as I helped myself to coffee and milk. "Saved our bacon in many ways. Tragic about Richard but thank God we dished that criminal Bertrasconi."

"Indeed."

"Might have destroyed us entirely."

"That was the plan, I'm afraid."

He was referring to an unpleasant recent episode in which the Bank had nearly suffered a hostile and disastrous take-over by a predator who had not stopped at murder, including that of Freddy's relative, and Jeremy's uncle, Sir Richard White.

"I was very pleased that you came out of it with a bit of a bonus of your own. Apart from ours, I mean."

Ha, I thought to myself, ha, Jeremy, you've been telling tales, obviously, about my fortuitous inheritance and the Art Fund's gain by buying it off me. I gave him a quick glance but his expression had gone impenetrable.

Freddy Harbledown was giving me an open look of approval, however. "I know it's not the fashionable thing, but a measure of financial independence is, in my view, a great help to cool, objective thought."

I grinned at that. "Me too," I said.

He smiled back. "Good. So, now down to business. I hear you've met the famous Pierre Champion."

"Indeed I have."

"He's told Hamish that he's impressed. Phoned yesterday, apparently. Well done. What did you think of him?"

"He's a tiger. Utterly predatory. Shere Khan in person. Smooth, beautifully striped, claws as sharp as knives under pads sheathed in Dralon."

Freddy Harbledown laughed. It was a rich sound from a strong frame. "Well put. I must say Hamish holds him in awe. You know Hamish pretty well, don't you? Sit on the board of Christerby's as one of his non-execs?"

"Yes, I know him well."

There was a fractional pause. For a moment I thought the subject of Sir Hamish Lang's view of me might come up, but Freddy Harbledown was too tactful for that. At the same time, the pause let me know that he knew.

"So are we going to finance this tiger? What's your feeling?'

I left my coffee to stand for the moment. I needed to compose my thoughts. "It's a business with great potential. There's a lot of competition, though. Big names like Gates and the Getty Foundation have been buying up archives all over. The French are no slouches, either. It seems to be growing exponentially. I remember the stir when someone bought up Ronnie Lee's big library of photos of antiques - Time Life I think it was - for a six-figure sum. Everyone thought it was a fantastic return, then, for the simple assembly and filing of adverts and photos. Small beer, now. Have you seen the recent series, *Jazz*, on the BBC? Six years of putting together old film, and not such old film, of jazz performances. A fantastic piece of work, impossible without archive footage. Then there's all the war and politics and slums and ecology and the rest. Not to mention sport."

"So one needs to concentrate? To specialise?"

"Look, there are innumerable archives already in official hands, like museums and art galleries and TV or media companies. Outside those, it's a great speculative long-term business for people with quantities of spare cash. Hence Gates and Getty, who hardly know what to do with their unallocated income because they've got so much of it. It's a flier, a rich man's flutter, like putting together a collection of French furniture or art. Got to be long term, or at least medium term unless you've stumbled on a cheap, innocent source. It's like antique dealing - you go out to buy a walnut bureau and while you're there you stumble over a pottery group by Obadiah Sherratt or a Barye bronze. You have to think laterally and store facts mentally like a megabyte computer. An eternal game of Pelmanism in which you turn one card over and remember another one, way off, that will match it and make three out of two. It's also like horse racing or gold mining or growing eucalyptus in Bahia. Or merchant banking."

"Or running an art fund?" Harbledown grinned at me.

Jeremy chuckled in unison with him. "We've financed gamblers before, Tim. Including ourselves."

"Sure. All I'm saying is that it's only got a certain amount in common with industry, trading, bonds, futures, currencies or the stock market."

"It's not in the realm of our bread and butter, in other words." Freddy Harbledown gave me a chance to sip at my coffee. "But it is akin to the many higher-risk things we provide for our more sporting clients. And the returns are higher than the bread and butter lines, with which we are in competition with great thundering hordes."

I nodded. "That's true. In this case, we would be the sporting clients. Although, to be fair, we would be providing cash facilities against the security of the stock. Which brings up the question: how do you value the stock? And, more important, how do you know that the best bits of stock aren't being quietly slipped away into the proprietor's personal collection?

Just like an antique dealer might put away the best bits for his personal pension fund?"

"You don't," said Jeremy. "But provided there's plenty of equity in the stock and you're well covered, you're just like any bank facility."

"Yes."

"Who financed the furniture hire business?"

"Champion set it up himself. It's a sideline, really. A smokescreen, under which, though I can't prove it, I think he's collecting choice antiques. Now he says he wants to do the Visual Records company but that may need more than he's got in his piggy bank under the bed. Hence the approach to us. Via Sir Hamish, who put him together with Frank Cordwell."

"Are we being offered equity in the business?"

"That's for us to stipulate."

There was a pause. Jeremy and Freddy Harbledown looked at each other enquiringly. Then Jeremy said: "What's your feeling, Tim?"

"The market research consultant in me wants to know things like market sizes, shares, the usual measurement criteria. There don't seem to be any but I'm not sure that it matters. A while ago the *Antiques Trade Gazette* produced a fine report that said that art and antiques are a business worth over two billion a year in this country. Interesting, but not necessarily the basis for a business strategy. It's the segments that matter. Sometimes you just have to know that your segment is big enough, that's all."

"So what do we do?"

"Champion's a fast horse. If we're betting on horses, which we do, it's no good going for the slow ones, is it? If we can make sure we're properly covered, and that some controls are in place, then it's not that much different from any other risk business. There is one thing that worries me a bit though."

"What?"

"He's into the Art Fund. Through a nominee of his own.

We'll have to get Geoffrey to check. He knows all about us. He's checked over Eugène Maucourt and our French end."

"That's a compliment, isn't it?"

"In a way. I think I was able to convince him that we can cover France too, if necessary, and that Eugène, who is an old fogey to put it mildly, isn't the only man on our Paris scene."

"Good. Well done. If we take equity, we'll need a man of our own on his board." Freddy Harbledown leant forward towards me. "Would you be prepared to take that on? You're obviously the best placed. From what he's said to Hamish, he'd accept you."

"If you want me to, sure."

"That's rather a laconic answer. Would you not relish the thought?"

I smiled. "Sorry if I don't naturally react with boyish enthusiasm. I'm a bit cautious about people like Champion. I remember Piers Hargreaves at Christerby's, you see, and others like him. As a film director said of Sam Goldwyn: as long as you've got a bentwood chair and a twelve-foot lash, you can deal with him, no problems. It's the ones that try to be friendly and say they want to work with you that you have to watch out for. They get you alongside and then all of a sudden you find that they've boarded you. Besides, if I reacted with too much enthusiasm, you'd have a worry; I might get too close to the client. Identify too much with the business. There'd be a danger of my going native."

Jeremy, who had gone a bit watchful, starting nodding vigorously. "Very true, very true. I'm sure we can take it, Freddy, that Tim's natural scepticism, allied with his unswerving loyalty, would make him an excellent choice for the task. Apart, of course," he gave me a huge, synthetic, bare-toothed beam, "from his absolutely perfect professional qualifications. This is a venture entirely in sympathy with what we do. I'm sure Tim is the man for it."

You oily bastard, I nearly muttered, why this sudden encomium? But didn't. Instead, I said, "I think I need to talk, off the record, with Gerry Watson for a bit, before we set out our stall. Buy him lunch and chat him up about Mangate Solutions. It would be useful background."

"Good idea." Freddy Harbledown looked at his watch. "Let's settle for that, then, for now. Champion will expect a brisk response, from what I gather of him. Can we meet again, soon? Is this Gerry Watson available quickly?"

"I'll get on to it right away," I said, standing up. "Then come back to you."

"Good." He nodded approvingly. "I think this is an exciting venture. Or, at least, has the potential to be one. Thank you, Tim. Thank you, Jeremy; can you hang on for another matter I want to discuss? Tim, we'll see you again soon."

"Fine," I said, taking my leave.

I know my place. The ball was in my court and results were expected. To phone Gerry it was only a hop skip and a jump back down a few passages to my office.

Where, on my answering machine, there was a message.

"Tim? Dorkie here. Sorry I haven't contacted you sooner but there's been a slight *komplikasie*. A bit of a *gemors*. Things are clear now. Can you come down to see me as soon as possible? I'm at home for the next few days. I think I've got the right goods for you."

Then there was a click. No other messages.

I picked up the phone and started dialling.

Chapter Thirteen

The small shabby square of Regency and earlier houses still crouched under Hastings cliffs. The clock on St.Clement's Church was, for the moment, silent. They had collected the rubbish from outside the front gate but a bicycle was still chained to the railings.

So far my arrangements were working well. Dorkie was expecting me and I was pretty much on time despite traffic jams on the way. I was to have lunch with Gerry Watson the next day, so the Bank couldn't complain that I was dragging my heels on its important project. Gerry had sounded pleased to be asked but not surprised, which made me think a little. Was he expecting me to make an approach? Or was this his expectation of collaboration to come?

Anyway, *more is nog een dag* as Dorkie would say, or tomorrow is another day, in the Biblical sense of sufficient unto the day be the evil thereof. Here I was and inside, presumably, was Dorkie, with details of paintings by the Nicholsons, father and son, or even the paintings themselves, which was exciting. Even Sue, when I told her what was going on, had started to sparkle.

"Oh, Tim, that sounds terrific! Hell, I wish I could come with you but we've got another of our eternal budget meetings and I daren't let some new, underhand cut get through by default."

So I was alone, and excited. I had parked round the corner and now, as I strode up the pavement, I glanced up at the house as I reached its frontage. The big bay window above me on the first floor, from which I had admired the passing ketch out on the Channel, had its curtains drawn. So had the downstairs ground floor window, presumably the showroom I'd been proudly taken in to see.

Which was odd for nearly midday. I could understand the

lower window being curtained to prevent curious peepers, but the main room?

Suddenly I felt apprehensive.

As I put out my hand to ring the big brass bell at the front door, I heard a distant, but distinct, cry and a thump from within. Then another cry, rather muffled, but still a cry.

The bell was left alone. I went round the side of the house at a fast trot via an alleyway between it and the next building, an alleyway that led to one of the narrow public paths known as twittens with which Hastings Old Town is criss-crossed. Through a side gate, across a back yard up to the back door, I never deviated. Adrenalin was starting to surge through my system, shocked and anticipatory adrenalin, roused from previous experience. I went in to Dorkie's kitchen easily because the back door was shut but I gave it one swift kick and the retaining bolt yielded. The main lock looked damaged.

As I strode in, the first thing I saw was a solid man wearing a Balaclava helmet over his head. It left only his mouth and eyes free. He was heating something up on a cooker gas ring and there was a nasty smell of hot metal and singed material in the room. He had turned towards the doorway, and me, in surprise.

He threw the article he was holding on the stove - an aluminium pan, smoking with heat - straight at me and then lunged towards me, leaving the gas-ring jets burning at maximum setting.

I was moving forward, so had no time to do anything but knock the flying pan out of the air with a wince as my hand brushed its hot surface, then hit him hard, straight in the mouth. This checked my forward rush and enabled me to set myself up for his counter, which was a wild swipe at my head then a rush to grapple and try to pin my arms to my side. Neither of us, so far, had spoken. There seemed to be no need.

I hate fighting in constricted circumstances. The kitchen was small, with a four-seater pine table with bare chairs under it in the middle of the floor and working surfaces with cupboards below set round the walls. There were hanging cupboards with shelves between, peppered with pot hooks with various receptacles and implements hanging on them. I noticed some nice blue and white striped pottery before getting into the fray.

As the intruder tried to close I pulled a chair out from under the table and he tangled with it, checking himself. He shoved it away, gave a shout and hit at me again, a sort of right hook from close, aiming at the solar plexus. I swayed back to let that whoosh upwards past my nose, trod hard on his foot and hooked him under the chin. Pinning the foot prevents the victim from moving back to ride the punch and, with any luck, damages the foot tendons as well. There was a gratifyingly wet grunt from inside the wool helmet and he staggered. I stepped off his foot. Then I crouched, got my shoulder down and rammed him back against the stove so that, as he was arched over, the gas burner jets played nicely on his sweatered back. He shouted again, a small spray of blood coming from the woollen mouth opening as he squirmed to avoid the heat.

From inside came the sound of heavy footsteps clumping down the stairway from the first floor sitting room, the one with the view. Reinforcements were arriving. There was no time to lose. I stepped back and pulled a heavy pottery rolling pin off the wall, one with handles, and brought it down on his head with all the force I could muster.

It snapped off at the handle. Cornish Ware, I suddenly realised, by T G Green, like the rest of the pottery, rather nice, pity to have broken it.

I took a stride across the floor, seized a doorknob, and swung the inner door, which led to the hall, open. I was in time to see another Balaclava helmeted figure running away towards the front door, past the big print of Buller's troops crossing the Tugela river.

"Oy!" I shouted, and moved to start after him.

Which is when the first one, on whom I'd just ruined a

good T G Green pottery rolling pin, must have hit me from behind. Over the head. With something heavy, like a cast iron frying pan.

My knees buckled and I had to grab at the banisters for support. For a moment the hallway went dark. There was a nasty, suspenseful silence as I braced myself to receive another blow of some kind, or worse, putting up my free arm to ward it off.

It never came.

By the time my head cleared, there was no one about. Both front and back door were open and I was alone in a draughty hallway, leaning groggily against the polished mahogany rail I'd admired on my last visit.

From upstairs came a nasty gurgling sound.

I stumbled up as quickly as my legs would let me, into the big room, still curtained, where the two fake Ben Nicholsons still hung on the wall. Dorkie Collins was tied to a wooden chair in the middle of the room, tied much too tight, and badly battered about the head. Blood ran from over one eye. He let out a hoarse noise as I came in, then his head rolled back and sideways. His eyes closed, then tried to open again. One side of his face looked frozen.

A stroke, I thought, oh Christ, he's having a stroke, what I do? Looking round, I saw a telephone on a side table and snatched at it.

There was no tone. My horrified gaze took in the wire pulled out from the wall before panic subsided a fraction and reason returned.

I pulled my mobile out from my inner pocket and dialled like mad for assistance. Then I took out my penknife and started to cut through the tight, cruel ropes that held a silent, tortured Dorkie Collins to the chair.

Chapter Fourteen

"So," Nobby Roberts spoke with satisfaction as a steaming breakfast plate was put down in front of him, "to concur with Foster of the Hastings CID, Tim has run to form yet again."

"Quite like old times, he said it was," nodded Sam Johnson cheerfully as a similar platter arrived on his side of the table. "Hastings Old Town, a dealer in dire straits, Tim bashing out at all and sundry. Foster was sounding pretty chuffed when we spoke on the phone." He gave Nobby a deferential glance. "I must say I am honoured to be invited to one of these breakfasts of yours. Quite a pleasure it is, for an outsider like me to be included at one of your private festivities."

"Not at all," Nobby picked up his knife and fork. "I thought it entirely appropriate that you, too, should be stood breakfast on this occasion. In view of the disgraceful circumstances we both find ourselves having to encompass. I knew, of course, knew it was a stone cold racing certainty that nothing would really get going until Tim was in a bundle."

I glared at them across the table. "When you have quite finished this smug, self-congratulatory preamble, may I remind you that it is your turn, Nobby, to pay. As it was last time. And Inspector Foster of the Hastings CID, who we all know from previous experience, was extremely polite and pleased if surprised to see me. My survival appears to astonish him. I was gratified that he complimented me on the way in which I had prevented the possible murder of one of his parishioners. Or whatever you call those unfortunate enough to be exposed to your local, non-existent protection."

Nobby frowned. "There is no need to be offensive, Tim. No need at all. The public receive excellent protection and the enforcement of law entirely appropriate to the resources and dedication of the Force."

"Hear, hear," said Sam Johnson, picking up a cup of tea.

"Codswallop. Anyone would think that you had made progress on the Bassington murder, which clearly you haven't. And poor Dorkie Collins would have been battered to bits or fried alive if I hadn't turned up."

"And why, one has to ask, did you turn up? How is it that a busy banker, addicted to mendacious practices in the City, commissioned to carry out a major investment review, has time to go slumming in Hastings Old Town? Without, despite repeated promises, advising me or, more importantly, Sam here?"

I shook my head firmly. "There was absolutely no need to advise you, or Sam. This was an exploratory matter relating to a possible Art Fund acquisition which, I hardly need remind you, it is both my business and responsibility to prosecute."

"Alas we both do know that, all too well."

I ignored the dig, even if it irritated. "Dorkie Collins indicated that he had found Nicholson works for which, in accordance with a commercial agreement, I would pay him commission if they proved suitable for acquisition. As I had already explained to you. I merely went down to look at them or illustrations of them and to discuss their provenance. You knew all about him already and neither you nor any of your abundant resources did anything to contact him or question him about your investigation. You can't deny your neglect of duty because he said nothing to me on the phone and Foster said it was the first he'd heard of the whole business."

Nobby drew his mouth into a line. "Sam has been following up all sorts of enquiries here in London. We have a lot on our plates, both of us. Foster is not involved in this investigation, which is entirely the responsibility of the Metropolitan Police. Spreading the net down to Hastings would have had to come at a later stage and only if nothing came to light here."

"So much for all your grilling me last time. You're a parochial crowd, you lot, aren't you? Stuck to London, are you? Last time you spoke as if Hastings was the centre of all criminal activity."

"I was speaking figuratively. This was an entirely Metropolitan enquiry. Until your careerings came into it. Can we return to the new, typical, violent and disgraceful episode in hand? The sort of thing with which, all too often, I associate you? And which you consistently deny? Where are these Nicholson works, as you call them?"

I shrugged. "Search me. Poor Dorkie is still unconscious and the Conquest Hospital confirm that he has suffered a stroke. The extent to which he will be affected is not yet known. Nowadays strokes respond to treatment much better than of yore. They will advise Foster and his merry men as soon as there is any improvement or possibility of questioning him. I have played the game with an absolutely straight bat, giving every assistance to the fuzz."

"Oh, have you? Yet there is much to uncover in this matter. Who do you think his assailants were, and what were they looking for?"

"How the hell should I know? I assume they were after the same paintings, although I don't know that for certain. They are not in the house. I checked. Dorkie is a canny fellow. If he's hidden them, he's done it well. The chances are that they are located somewhere else, possibly even as far away as South Africa, and he has photos of them he was going to show me. I have not found those, either. It is quite idle for me to specu- late. They could be after his Boer War memorabilia."

His archive, I suddenly thought, has this something to do with his archive? My head throbbed unsympathetically as I tried to cope with that idea.

"Clearly, he has some knowledge which these thugs were trying to prise out of him. It is an unusually violent incident. Maybe he has come across yet more fakes and the fraudsters wish to suppress the knowledge."

"John Drewe?"

"He can be ruled out."

I sighed, picked up my own implements, and started on my breakfast. I had a palpable lump on the back of my head. I had trouble with Sue, despite my assurance that it had all been a minor incident. She had sprung an outing on me for that very evening, insisting that as a penance I should take her to the opening of a contemporary flower painting exhibition at Jim Stockdale's gallery. Janet was looking for support and we were to be part of it. In the circumstances I couldn't refuse.

I would almost certainly have trouble with Jeremy, who was still in blissful ignorance of all these events. I was due to meet Gerry Watson for lunch and I was not feeling like it. I had spent hours at a police station in Hastings the day before, explaining myself *ad nauseam* to deliberately dumb rozzers who made me repeat myself. I was worried stiff about Dorkie. There was a pattern to the Bassington woman's photos I still had to figure out. There was a nagging feeling in my mind that both Gerry Watson and his boss, Pierre Champion, were trying to pre-guess my next acquisition. I didn't like Champion's close interest in the Art Fund. I had taken aspirins that morning but my headache was coming back, in spades.

"Sam says," Nobby Roberts's voice, breaking my concentration, was deceptively casual, "that you looked at all those photos of the Bassington woman's without coming up with anything."

"Yes."

"But you asked for copies, all the same."

I gave Sam Johnson a reproachful glance but he didn't respond. His face was impassive. I supposed that since the Hastings outbreak he had no option but to tell Nobby everything. "Yes."

"And you've got them? The copies?"

"Yes. They arrived yesterday."

"So: any ideas?"

"For God's sake! I haven't had time to go through them

110

again. What with being bashed over the head by burglars and one thing and another, like spending hours and hours at Hastings police station answering deliberately thickhead questions by suspicious rozzers and making unendingly tedious statements in quintuplicate, any ideas, as you put it, have not yet surfaced."

"Now you know why police work suppresses creativity. What sort of pattern, may one ask, will you be looking for? Once you deign to take another look at them? Is there a maze for which you have the key?"

His voice sounded hectoring. He and Sam were tucking into their food with relish as they fixed their eyes on me, waiting for a response. At the counter, the waitress I had had to pay last time was writing items down onto a bill, doubtless our bill. Suddenly, I felt even more off colour. I closed my eyes to try and reduce the headache as I replied.

"A pattern that might suggest any association, however remote, with any recent events involving myself or my activities."

"So despite your initial reaction and protestations, you have not ruled out some connection, as it were, between yourself and the Bassington woman?" Nobby gave Sam Johnson a significant leer. "You may come out and admit that there could be one, as I suspected when we first met?"

That did it. My headache moved forward to a hot band behind my eyes as a red mist formed. I put down my knife and fork. Then I stood up, leaving my breakfast on the table.

They gaped at me in surprise.

I picked up my briefcase. "Bugger you lot and your interrogations," I said. "I'm pissed off with your bloody stupid, offensive questioning. I'm not going through all this again. I haven't asked you what the hell you've achieved so far with your useless routine enquiries and I don't suppose you'd tell me if I asked, you miserable, self-satisfied, incompetent sods. You're not getting anywhere, either of you, and I'm taking the flak. As usual. You haven't even got the decency to say please or thank you or how are you feeling. Bugger this; you don't deserve my help or my ideas. I've got a splitting headache and I've got work to do. It's your case, so you get on with it. I'm off."

"Hey, Tim, steady on, wait a minute - "

But I was beckoning to the waitress.

"He," I said to her querying expression, between my teeth, loudly, pointing at Nobby, "will pay."

Then I left.

Chapter Fifteen

"Can't see no number thirty-eight, guv'nor," the cabby said, as we cruised round Mecklenburgh Square. "There's a whole block under number twenty-six over there, though. Are you sure there's a number thirty-eight still going? Looks to me like a lot of the numbers have been dropped."

"I'll soon find out. You can leave me there on the corner, thanks," I answered.

It was still quite early. I had plenty of time before I was expected at the Bank. Mecklenburgh Square is in Bloomsbury, well into that bland area east of Russell Square where everything seems to be part of London University or similar seats of learning. Staid ranks of long sash windows and grey Georgian facades conceal the suspended lives of readers of and writers on esoteric and cogent aspects of this world's lofty knowledge. Creepy graduate students of all races gumshoe sparsely about, singly or more often in ill-assorted pairs, doubtless discussing advanced thought on academic subjects whilst clinging dutifully to some protuberance or another of their partner's. The high canopy of huge old plane trees in the central garden of the square rustled softly as I paid off the cabby and looked around me to get my bearings.

Fresh air soothed my nostrils and cooled my aching head. I was starting to feel better. The scene I was looking at is no longer architecturally intact but it still has stretches of Georgian terraces of grander proportions than, say, Islington and Canonbury can boast. The necessity for efficient studious accommodation has driven new quasi-Georgian blocks, vaguely windowed and proportioned to style but not identical, into the original spacious architecture. Handsome period houses with big front doorways capped by fanlights still remain amongst the intrusive misalignments, though.

Of number 38 there was no sign.

I thought: they've probably changed the numbering since 1906, anyway.

By stalking around carefully I managed to find that number 38 was probably on the north side, where number 43 starts the remains of an original terrace. Next to it, number 35-40 is now a long, 1957 modern Georgian block called William Goodenough House - hostel, residence, dormitory, college, whatever - in bright stock brick with GLC Georgian sash windows and a wide, speaker-controlled main doorway. There is a more traditional, black-panelled door further towards the corner of the square, with radially-spoked fanlight but no sign of usage as an entrance. As in the rest of the area, spiked black iron railings are set along the pavement in front of the facade, having apparently survived any long-forgotten wartime enthusiasm to render them down to tanks or cannon shells.

I stood back to gaze for a moment and take in the ambience.

It was in a house here, rented by William Nicholson around 1906/7, that William Orpen, who is something of a fixation of mine, painted the group called *A Bloomsbury Family*. It is now in the Scottish National Gallery of Modern Art in Edinburgh, despite being a painting by a famous Irishman of an English artist's family in a picture-hung London room. I suppose the Scots have it in their foreign section, although there is a Scotswoman in the painting.

Orpen and Nicholson were close friends and so were their wives but *A Bloomsbury Family* comes out as an odd composition. Nicholson *père* sits armchaired in his spotted silk dressing gown beside the dining table, so that you see him from the side, in profile. Around the scene range his children. Christopher, known as Kit, who was to become an architect and die in a glider crash, stands awkwardly at the front, in the sort of girl's dress fledgling boys then had to endure until they were older. The eldest boy Ben is severe in counterpose to his father, seated at the head of the table. Tony, the charming favourite, destined to fall in October 1918, sits next to his sister Nancy, both of them facing you. She was to marry the poet

Robert Graves long before Laura Riding-Reichenthal-Gottschalk-Jackson, another four-surnamed talent, got her grisly hooks into him. Nancy looks serious, which she was; there is a scurrilous story that when she and Robert Graves lived near Oxford, where they ran a village shop and struggled to cope with four children and poetry, he tried to kill her.

Oddly, the children's feather-bonneted mother Mabel stands at the back, moved from Orpen's original intended placement of her beside Kit on the right. She seems to withdraw from this posed tableau and look on her husband and brood with the detached, remote expression of someone dressed to leave. She was not pleased with the appellation Bloomsbury due its literary connotations and was happier when they moved to Chelsea, with its Whistler-painter reputation.

Mabel, known as Prydie from her maiden name, was superior Edinburgh in attitude if not with justification, seeing the manufacturing background of the Nicholsons as "trade". Although she was an artist herself, motherhood seems to have distanced her from William and the male artistic coterie, with all its louche, promiscuous, model-mongering to which he belonged.

She doted on Ben, but didn't prevent his early dispatch to boarding schools. He had something of a rum youth, dispatched hither and yon in strange attempts to develop him whilst being allowed to spend periods of time back in the bosom of the family, like a pup half in a pack, half out of it. Like Orpen and his father, he became an obsessively acrobatical sports performer, lashing out with bats, racquets and balls to defeat opponents as though to release a volcanic inner tension. The curve of flight, the line of trajectory, played an important part in his art.

Contrary to what Marguerite Steen says in her book on William, the studio he then shared with Orpen, finding the top room here in Mecklenburgh Square an unsuitable reception place for the portraiture essential to economic survival, was not paid for by William. It was temporarily the Orpen studio in South Bolton Gardens, later made famous by the queue of Rolls Royces outside, their owners waiting to have themselves painted by, vying with Sargent, the most success-ful portraitist of his day. Orpen did not give *A Bloomsbury Family* to Nicholson for rent as Steen avers; it was sold at the New English Art Club for £60 and a Colonel Walker Brown of Renfrew presented it to the Scottish National.

You have to be careful about biographies, especially those written by family, friends and mistresses. Little things can mean a lot. Partisan lovers write their own versions, like Marguerite Steen and Laura Riding who, even her most ardent supporters agreed, was guilty of 'retrospective falsifi-cation'.

I took the copied photographs out from my briefcase and stared at the one where Moira Bassington stood by the rail-ings of what I had taken to be a London house. My heart start-ed to race as I took in the standing figure, erect and posed, the chin up, the mouth drawn firm and unsmiling. It was in front of the smaller door in the façade of number 35-40, William Goodenough House; there was no doubt that it was here. In the background the arched entrance stood black and still, unused, as it did now. Why? Why did she look as though this one was so important, her expression fixed, almost severe? Why come here, of all places, to have this photo taken? And who by?

In the book edited by Andrew Nicholson there is a photo of the Nicholson children, Nancy, Tony, Kit and Ben, on the pavement outside their Mecklenburgh Square house, taken in 1906. The children are in a row, Nancy conventionally dressed and the two older boys holding each hand of their little broth-er Kit. The future architect-glider is still in a frock. To this house came Orpen and Paul Nash and doubtless many others now artistically celebrated, like Augustus John, who painted William and generously gave him half the fee the Fitzwilliam sent years later.

Why? Why was she here? The Nicholsons used the house as a London base until sometime around 1916, when William acquired Apple Tree Yard.

I stood irresolute, staring at the façade. A neatly-dressed African came out of the main door and walked past me without showing the slightest curiosity. A few people were moving briskly along the further pavements as though animated by the cool start of what looked to be a promising day.

There was nothing else to be seen here; no blue plaque to Nicholson, father or son, adorned these walls. But Moira Bassington had carefully posed herself, right here, in front of this building.

I walked away down Doughty Street towards the Grays Inn Road and found a café. Going in, I ordered a limited breakfast to replace the one I'd precipitately left with Nobby and Sam, and spread the coloured photocopy sheets upon the table while I waited. Slowly, carefully, I took their images in.

Here was St.Ives, no doubt of that. So Ben was the subject, was he? The houses he lived in with Barbara Hepworth, I remembered vaguely, changed as the years went by and she was replaced by Felicitas Vogel, his third wife. Moira Bassington was standing on the sea front with the town, or part of it, a backdrop to her. She looked a little windblown and distracted.

Next, the church scene was Happisburgh, I was fairly sure of it, once a Norfolk village set back from crumbling cliffs, now, someone had told me, caravan parked, hutted and dismal, with a long, intrusive timber barrier to slow erosion. In 1931 the beach was the source of wonderful, sea-smoothed pebbles and stones, which Henry Moore collected and retained for sculptural inspiration. I remembered reading somewhere that he liked to use stone with fossils in it, to give his work historical depth. Here Jack Skeaping had left the holiday in rented Church Farm early to return to London and a torrid affair. His wife, Barbara, then took a passionate shine to Ben whilst in turn his wife Winifred was way up north with their children. So this was about Ben, too.

Here was Apple Tree Yard, though, down the side of Wheeler's. That was surely William, not Ben. And here was a shot with what looked like bare Sussex downs behind it. That would be William too, for his celebrated paintings around Rottingdean.

The severe house with a weathervane: wasn't that Great Shelford, with the flying fox motif Ben adopted? He was old, then, his third marriage over, and he was intruding on a Cambridge don's family.

Outside, in sunglasses, beside an old sports car parked on grass. The bonnet invisible but the side of the car distinctive, with the man in blazer and flannels beside it too, his back maddeningly to the camera. Why?

A shot in what might be Hampstead. Ben, again. Then the shapely bare shoulders in front of the pale yellow-flowered bushes and the exotic red blooms. Where was that? Kew? Some Devonian garden? Or could it be Spain, where William spent so much time with Marguerite Steen?

Here Moira Bassington was, now, in front of a strange red brick complex like a shopping centre with an impressive, mansard-roofed, pillared and arcaded building in the middle. There was a river - of course! Newark! It was the remains of the Nicholson's Trent Ironworks in Newark, now unproductively adapted to a shopping centre. This was William's birth and burial town, his birthplace on the London Road dutifully plaqued. The Nicholsons were prolific and the house was in fact two houses with an internal connecting door and common back garden. Sons from different marriages with children, half-siblings and cousins, mingled together. What affinity could Moira Bassington have with this?

Here comes Aunty, in her pram?

I wasn't sure of the next one. She stood on a gravel drive, looking rather diffident and nervous, with trees to one side and a sweep of grass to the left. In the distance was what looked like part of a long stone manor house - could that be Sutton Veny in Wiltshire? It was painted white by William and Edie after the house was bought for them as a wedding present by Sir Lionel Phillips. This didn't look like a white house. On the other hand, a long Gothic window somehow looked familiar and the paint could have been cleaned, or weathered off in the last seventy-odd years. If it was Sutton Veny this would be William again, although Ben and Winifred came there, as did Kit, and Nancy with Robert Graves and their four children. William and Edie's child Liza, and Edie's two by the previous marriage, John and Anne Stuart-Wortley, were often together at the house. A happy place, full of children, which William said gave him twelve wonderful years.

A place where the garden butterflies settled on a man smelling of turpentine, bay rum and Balkan Sobranies.

What on earth was she after?

What was the pattern of these photos? What was missing? The photographer, certainly. Never a sign of him. Or them. What else? Places like Blewbury and Switzerland and Dieppe or La Rochelle or Harlech. That house up North on Hadrian's Wall, called Banks Head or something like it. Such places were all part of the Nicholson tableau, whether for residence or just for painting. Had she just not got round to them or were they not important?

Why my name? What did we have in common?

The connection was becoming evident, slowly, remorselessly. Moira Bassington had some sort of interest in both William and Ben Nicholson. Dorkie Collins was trying to put together paintings by William and Ben Nicholson.

I was in the market for work by the same two.

Moira Bassington was dead.

Dorkie had been nearly dead. Might still be.

I was alive. My head hurt, but I was alive, and I was steadily getting better.

The waitress put bacon and eggs in front of me and I ate them quickly, hungrily, before heading for the Bank.

Chapter Sixteen

Back at the Bank, a little peace would have been too much to expect. One again I was Called For.

"My dear Tim. I have to say I was just a trifle disappointed."

Jeremy had evidently decided upon a reproachful tone rather than the fireworks. *Nanny is not angry with little Timmy, she just feels very let down.* I hate that sort of approach. Enjoying the session beside me, seated in a similar chair to mine, an equally summoned Geoffrey Price was, as usual, fairly impassive, just giving me supercilious sideways glances from time to time.

Both of them were getting on my nerves.

"Disappointed? Why?"

"I really do think you could have shown a little more enthusiasm in front of Freddy, you know," Jeremy fluted, getting into a sort of stride. "He didn't actually say it, but I could tell that he wasn't too happy about your rather glum reaction to his rather flattering offer to propose you for Champion's board. There aren't many he'd have offered the post, even if you'll say your French co-ordination role makes you the prime candidate. He does set great store by signs of willingness in the staff. I'm used to you, of course, can see the signs, my God, I've certainly got used to your truculence, but for Freddy, rising cheerfully to the challenge should be part of our ethos."

"What?"

"There's no need to snap at me! My goodness, you're in an irritable mood this morning. Like a bear with a sore head." His eyes whitened slightly. "In fact, you have got a sore head, haven't you? You've put your hand to the back of it twice so far and winced each time you touched it. At the top." His expression changed to one of horror. "Oh God! It's just occurred to me! Where were you yesterday?"

"In Hastings."

That did it. He leapt out from behind his desk like a scalded Saluki and charged round to stand in front of me, blond hair in a tangle.

"Hastings! I should have guessed! You've been to Hastings! Again! My warnings mean nothing to you! And you've been injured! Oh Lord! Oh heavens! Violence again! Let's have the worst: who is dead?"

"No one in Hastings. So far."

"So far! *So far*?" His hair fell straight down over his eyes. "You mean there is a possibility?"

"Yes. Unfortunately. But there are grounds for cautious optimism down there."

"Dear God! And elsewhere?"

"A woman called Bassington, I'm afraid."

"*What*? A woman is dead?"

"Yes. She was murdered a few days ago. By a person or persons unknown. In Pimlico."

He positively capered in agitation as he tried to restore order to his hair and his clothes. "Bassington? Pimlico? Who in heaven's name is this woman Bassington?"

"I've no idea. Look here, Jeremy, it's all very well you going on and on about my showing enthusiasm in front of Freddy Harbledown, like some keen young subaltern being sent to scour the Boers out of a *koppie* back in 1901. Oh yes sir, jolly good, sir, we'll be over the top at oh-five-thirty or whatever, and rout the frightful blighters out, sir, leave it to me and my chaps and all that twaddle before getting shot to bloody ribbons."

"Off," said Geoffrey, suddenly.

"Eh?"

"Off, not out. A koppie is a hill. One would clear the blighters off a *koppie*. One would clear them out of a *bos*, which is a wood."

"How the blazes do you know that?"

"I have played cricket in South Africa."

"Really? I bet you lost."

"Not at all. Squared the series, actually. Queenstown, it was. Rather a triumph. I got fifty-three not out."

"Well, never mind that. You pedantic person. A *koppie* might have a *bos* on it."

"Not if it's like Majuba. Or Spion Kop." He grinned at me. I grinned back.

Jeremy made a wild gesture. "Can we, for God's sake, leave these appallingly sad anorak exchanges and get *back to the point?*"

"Certainly." I looked him straight in the eye. "'It's not you and Freddy Harbledown who are going to deal with Champion and take the rap when things go wrong, are you? It's all very well for you sit here and send me off into the blue to wrestle with a tiger. You're not exposed. I know what'll happen if anything goes wrong. There'll be Hamish Lang clucking his dour Caledonian tongue and moaning *there what did I say about Simpson* and *oh dear another opportunity lost by the Bank*. Or grinding on that the Bank is taking risks that it shouldn't or that it'll lose money. You and Freddy will be sipping coffee from best bone Worcester and I'll be the sitting duck for target practice. Try being enthusiastic about that. And by the way, talking of the honour of being invited to join a board, look at that bugger Hargreaves you and Hamish Lang landed me with at Christerby's. Sheer disaster. I don't hear you talking much about him nowadays, do I? Or the female dragon, Shauna Spring, taken onto the Bank's very Board itself, with whom I so memorably had to deal. Where were you and Lord Freddy then? Not up on the *koppie* or down in the *bos*, not you, you're much too fly for that."

He did a sort of half-strut up and down his carpet in frenzied agitation. "That's irrelevant! In the past! Never mind the Champion project for the moment! I deeply resent the idea that I, or Freddy, would be so meretricious as to duck our responsibilities and fail to support you, as I always have. You ingrate! Stick to the point! This Bassington affair is obviously another Art Fund disaster! What in hell have you been up to in Hastings and Pimlico? What did you do to the woman?"

"Nothing. So far. Sit down calmly, Jeremy, and I'll tell you all about it."

Which I did. Or at least, an edited version of it. I wasn't going to tell Jeremy what I was starting to think about Moira Bassington's holiday snaps; it was too early for that, not to mention implications which would add to his anxiety.

He clutched at his head. A sort of moan came from him. Then he stared at me.

"You're not suffering from concussion, are you?"

I was about to give him a sharp retort when, across the desk at which he had reseated himself, I saw genuine anxiety in his face. Jeremy and I may make sparks but his heart is always in the right place.

"Thank you, Jeremy, for your kind concern. I don't think so. My mind is quite clear."

"Have you had that injury looked at?"

His face was still creased. Suddenly, I felt like a real shit. A real, bad-tempered, miserable, ancient fart. "A doctor would do nothing. Just tell me to stay at home, in bed. Which is impossible. Look Jeremy, I must apologise for my truculent remarks just now. I'm a bit out of sorts. Bad headache and all that. I withdraw my grouses unreservedly. They were completely uncalled for. It's a stimulating project and you've never failed to back me. Never. I'm really sorry. Put it down to a concussive hangover."

His face cleared from a dark clouded countenance to one of sunny, clear pleasure. "Dear boy! I understand perfectly. Think no more of the matter. The hurly burly of our activities has always made sparks fly and you have had a dreadful knock. I could see when you came in that you were not your normal, robust self. You must be careful, you know. You must take more care. You can not continue to take these impacts indefinitely."

"It's only his head, you know. Nothing serious for a front row man."

Geoffrey, like any Englishman faced with embarrassing expressions of remorse and heartfelt emotion, was trying to be humorous. Never a good idea for an accountant. Jeremy frowned at him.

"Geoffrey, really. That's not funny." He gestured at me. "It's Tim's head we need, not his burly frame."

"Eh?"

"This matter and the Champion business need absolute concentration. Complete commitment. You must be focused, Tim. These are desperate times for merchant banking. Everyone here, and I mean everyone, has to be on top form. I suppose there is nothing one can do about this Bassington affair, which has occurred at a really appalling time. From past experience, I can only watch helplessly while events take their inexorable course. The police, you say, have the matter in hand. Not a reassuring prospect." He leant over the desk to fix me with an appealing stare. "I beseech you to leave it to them."

"Very good, Jeremy."

"A smart answer, which I will not take for a yes. Never mind. Under your aegis, the Art Fund has ever been a wild card." He straightened up. "Let us look at something we can control. We must move on. There are very, very important implications in this proposed venture. Geoffrey: tell us what you have found out about Champion."

"His investment in the Art Fund is quite substantial." Geoffrey shuffled a few papers on his lap. "Held by a management company based abroad. Not France, Switzerland, and from there way back offshore. It seems to be a sort of personal investment company tracking a portfolio of pension-type investments for growth rather than income. Which fits. More importantly, yet another company of his, more of an industrial investment outfit, has been buying shares in this Bank. Nothing too serious at this stage, but it might bear watching. I

124

don't have to remind you that we have a bunch of minority shareholders who are, to put it mildly, fickle?"

"He's getting all the information about us that he needs then," I said. "I wonder; there's more than one French billionaire been snapping up the big auction houses. Bonhams and Phillips have just merged, with French involvement. Could he be prowling around Christerby's?"

"Yes. He has been buying there, too. Both shares in the company and articles in the rooms. The latter ostensibly for his hire company."

"I must talk to Charles."

Jeremy nodded briskly. "Good idea. Gerry Watson first, though, eh? Are you fit enough today?"

"I'm OK."

"You need to be on top form! I remember Watson as a sharp fellow. Expert on furniture, isn't he?"

"Furniture, Continental and English, yes. Plus a good eye for porcelain."

"There you are, then. Perhaps you should postpone until you are less, how dare I say it: distrait?"

I stood up. "I am not distrait. I shall be focused. I have dealt with the Gerry Watsons of this world before."

Geoffrey Price looked up at me. "He's more of a man for a *bos* than a *koppie*, Tim. Like his employer. Camouflage is all with that mob. Their movements are carefully concealed."

"Excellent!" Jeremy gave me a synthetic beam. "It will be one careful concealer talking to another, then."

I scowled at him. And left.

Chapter Seventeen

I picked what in business terms looked like neutral ground. A restaurant that could be said to be halfway between the City and Hammersmith, so that Gerry Watson and I could approach and meet from equal distances, so to speak.

You've probably guessed: it was a *trattoria Toscana* in South Kensington, anonymous but good quality, so that I could stroll home to Onslow Gardens afterwards and have a little fatherly time with the sprog William. And a rest for the sore head, which was still throbbing.

"This is very pleasant, Tim." Gerry looked down with approval as his starter of melon and *prosciutto* was served. "I really feel that it ought to be Frank Cordwell here in my place, but he's up country looking at a collection of fashion stuff. And I suppose it has long been time that you and I got together. We've been working similar patches, in our own ways." He looked up from his plate to meet my eye. "Converging, in a sense, aren't we? Steadily converging. You've become a non-executive director of an auctioneer's and I'm a financial manager. Soon we may even merge. Meld. Blend. Whatever." He grinned mischievously. "How's your man Charles these days?"

"Charles Massenaux?" I nodded approvingly at my *frutos di mare*. "Very well. TV has changed his perspective enormously."

"Always liked old Charles. I have to say I admire his style on that antiques roadshow. Very smooth. He and I worked together at one time, you know. Youth, oh youth; Barnwells of Notting Hill, a dreadful old set of brown-boarded rooms, long gone now. In those days we did everything from tea cosies to Piero Della Francesca. God, what drudgery it was. All that cataloguing work; frayed basketwork chairs from Lloyd Loom and old po cupboards still smelling of pee. Awful prints. Always on edge in case you missed something vital. Christ, you had to be quick on your feet. And not very well paid; it's amazing what slavery auctioneers get away with as far as expert staff are concerned. Even in the West End."

"Prestige, Gerry. There's the prestige. The imperturbable expert image of the auctioneer is much more prestigious than anything the poor old dealers have managed to convey."

He snorted cheerfully. "Prestige butters no parsnips, Tim. None at all. Dealers can make good money. Prestige is not the world we live in, these days. One slip and you're gone. You and I know, personally, more than one really good auction expert who's been blown out of the water by some trickster or another recently. Those fake Chippendale chairs, made to deceive, that got Sotheby's into hot water. Really cunning. I'm damned glad I'm out of it. Much as I liked where I was."

He smiled as he picked up his implements. A sort of contentment emanated from him, not exactly a self-satisfied one, but something very close to it. He was well dressed, clean, urbane. Yes, that was it; here was an urban, urbane man, who belonged to the rooms, the galleries and the pavements of London's antique trading scene. An eye trained to scan mountains of junk for nuggets, as a magpie walks a hedge for fledglings. Values would match through his mind, sticking to objects like tags at a tailor's. It was as though life's slings and arrows could be dealt with impenetrably by Gerry, as though something was putting him out beyond normal vulnerabilities. He gave the impression that he had a Star Wars shield of his own.

"I thought that you were looking pretty chipper," I said. "The Pierre Champion set-up seems to suit you well."

"God. It was a lifesaver, Tim. He's a tough cookie but he knows what's what and he pays well."

"How did you meet him? Forgive me, but how did he come to pick you?"

Gerry chuckled. "You mean of all the guys in all the auction joints across Europe, how come he chose me? I'm not offended. Ruhlmann's your answer. You know I was into French modern furniture a long while back. I made a speciality out of Ruhlmann's work."

"That's quite a tall order, considering how long a period and how many designers it covers. 1910 onwards, isn't it?"

"Indeed it is from thereabouts. Anyway, one of Champion's friends put a piece into our rooms thinking it was just another Art Deco article he wanted to get rid of. I identified it as Ruhlmann but finished in collaboration with Dunand. The Swiss designer." He smiled modestly. "I was into lacquer in those days. Anyway, we got him a really good price for it. Way over the top. Champagne flowed. He told Pierre and Pierre came to see me. He said there weren't that many people good on French work as well as the normal run of things in London. He had this idea for a hire company run by someone who really knew his styles and who wouldn't foul up when a producer wanted something a bit esoteric. Who could put the stock together at the right price. He offered a good salary and a piece of the action. It would have been years before I got offered a partnership or anything like it where I was. And with all these amalgamations going on, it was a knife-edge whether I survived at all. I jumped at Pierre's offer, even though a lot of friends said I was going up a cul-de-sac and I'd never get back into the normal trade once I'd gone."

"That's surely not true."

"No, it isn't but I don't care anyway. I won't be going back. Mangate offers a much wider future."

"So that long apprenticeship at Barnwell's and after has stood you in good stead? You can move round the rooms and stock Mangate's with all the styles needed, knowing prices of the real thing by heart."

"That's it."

"And you can do it at low cost, or at least at wholesale, using repros quite a bit, I imagine."

"Correct."

"And if, as may happen from time to time, you come across

the odd Ruhlmann, or some English or American equivalent, which the auctioneer's eye hasn't seen, and the trade not sussed out, so much the better for Mangate. Or Pierre. Or you. Opportunities for all, eh?"

His eyes went cautious. "I'm not quite with you, Tim. As I said, I have a piece of the action. Mangate's gain is my gain."

I nodded understandingly. It would be a precaution of Champion's to make sure his managers didn't trade on the side on their own account. "Let me put it another way. A while ago it was all the thing in the City to have a Georgian mahogany partners' desk. Big pedestal jobs. Lawyers, bankers, company directors, you name it, all wanted one. A really good one might be in five figures."

He nodded. "Six, some of them. Even the better repros are fetching big dosh."

"Exactly. But the desk goes into the books as an office desk. The guy is working in an office, after all. He needs a good desk to impress his clients. And office furniture can be written down. Twenty percent a year. After five years it's in the books at zero pounds, zero pence. The partner, director, whatever, retires. What a nice little non-taxable present there is, right there in his office, to take with him. Or maybe not even on retirement. Just buy it off the company for a nominal sum once it's written off. Quite a perk. On the books, a desk is just a desk. The possibilities seem endless, to me."

His eyes were still cautious but he still didn't look too perturbed. "I hear you, Tim. I hear you. It's a question of stock valuation, isn't it? If your stock is your work-in-trade, there are laws about how you treat it. And you have to satisfy auditors, of course. But remember: who paid for the thing in the first place?" He leant forward earnestly. "And made enough money, all taxable, to cover the stock write-off? It's all very well for people to get het up about paying tax on profits. They're damned quiet about compensation for losses. You've read Reitlinger; art and antiques can go down, as well as up.

Just like shares and the Equitable Life Assurance Society, they're not plumb certs."

"Pierre collects both art and antiques, doesn't he? For himself, I mean."

"Enthusiastically." He sat back as a waiter took his empty plate off him. "He's a man with a very low opinion of money, Tim. Sorry to say that to a banker but then you're not exactly a conventional banker, are you? Your Art Fund is something Pierre really admires. He hates cash and he's deeply suspicious of stock markets, you see. The American influence is his great bête noir. And Japan. New York and Tokyo are very unpopular with Pierre. He says that he wants his money in things, not cash, and in things he can control, not shares and currencies manipulated by a greedy bunch of Yanks and Japs. Quite apart from your City in-crowd dealers."

"Understandable. Although he's not exactly an outsider."

"He thinks of himself as one. And wants to act like one. That way he can keep ahead. Once you think like the thundering herd, you're finished."

I waited while our second course was served. Veal for him, lamb for me. There were parallels between Pierre Champion and the late Jimmy Goldsmith, although I hadn't heard that Champion was quite as encumbered with families. That way of having a foot in both countries, though. Houses here and there. Swift predatory raids on sleepy companies and, almost exactly the opposite: steady, lethal consumption of well-aware, wide-awake grandiose ones, swallowed almost like hypnotised rabbits by a steadily devouring snake. Offshore funds and careful trusts completed his armoury. There were others like him but somehow they were less clandestine, less resentful of stock market operations. It would suit the character of Pierre Champion to put together a valuable collection of art and antiques using Gerry's expertise and the subterfuge of what was supposed to be a warehouse of hireable props for film scenes.

And yet, and yet; one of the well-known pop groups, years

ago, was percipient enough to put a big investment into rock concert paraphernalia, mobile stages, audio equipment, lighting, amplifiers of all sorts, flashing lights, stage smoke generators, all for concert hire. They are said to have made big money from it. Why should Champion not apply the same thinking to TV and film operations? If you are a performer, why not hire out the stage props as well?

Once we'd got our dishes served, I looked at Gerry steadily. "I was leafing through one of the big Tate catalogues the other day. An old one of Sue's. It listed twenty public collections and fifteen private ones from which the paintings were lent, but over a hundred sources for the photographic credits. The archive business is not exactly under-supplied, is it?"

He paused to think briefly before replying. "In one way it is. In another it's like land, a finite resource, even though there's a lot of it. It's a contradiction, but some areas are very finite - the nineteenth century, for instance, is heavily researched and documented even if some great finds will still be made. But the twentieth is expanding territory and, as long as the number of TV channels continues to increase, and publishers still produce books, nothing will stop it. Why do you think the Getty Foundation and Gates have gone into it? There's some marvellous stuff lying out there somewhere. I was all for it when Pierre mooted the idea. It's a logical step. He has interests in a media channel and in magazines. He's seen the business from a customer's angle. He researches many things that way."

"I saw that you're on the board of Mangate Visual Solutions. If we're helping with finance, you're going to be an executive director we deal with, too?"

"You bet."

"'Valuable connections with the media, programme producers and designers' I think was listed in your CV in the business plan."

"That's me. Actually, I seem to recall that you're a bit of a film buff, Tim."

"I was, yes. I don't have much time to go to a film club these days. Are you, too?"

"You bet. That's why I really like this project. I've been keen for a long time. We do all sorts of film analysis at our club over in Stockwell, technical stuff, that sort of thing. I'm a whizz with a camcorder, I can tell you."

"Frank Cordwell isn't exactly lacking in that direction, is he? The media contacts as well as the technical side?"

"He's got his contacts, sure." Gerry looked thoughtful. "But Frank is enraptured by his material. He's a mad keen archive trawler rather than a technician. Get him watching some stills or a can of old film, and he's off in a world of his own. Pierre has no doubts about his expertise with the archive but there's just a hint of the nerd about Frank. He really impressed Sir Hamish Lang with some marvellous old footage of golf at St. Andrew's. Way back stuff he'd picked up from a Scottish source along with a mountain of stills. That's how the contact came about. Apart from the car racing material. Pierre is a motor racing maniac and Frank sourced some early Le Mans races and Montlhéry speed record attempts. Terrific. Pierre was a goner once he saw those."

"Didn't know Pierre was a racing car fan."

"You bet. None of that horse nonsense, like so many. He's a real Grand Prix buff. He's got a collection of vintage cars, over in France. Not like the Schlumpf brothers, with a hundred Bugattis, that would attract trouble. But a nicely-chosen small selection. There's a superb Delaunay-Belleville he gave three of us a ride in to Beaulieu." A thoughtful look came to his face. "Tell you what: Frank's going to Weybridge this week, to look at a whole library some Brooklands enthusiast put together over the years between the wars. The son's around seventy now; wants to retire and is selling his old house for development. The archive won't go into a smaller place. Pierre's asked Frank to mosey along and have a look. He's had a first recce now he's going along with Jessica to talk turkey. Why don't you go, too? It'll give you maybe a bit of a feel for things. See how we will operate. Get a look in at ground level."

I smiled. "You seem sure we're going to get together."

His face went serious. "I certainly hope so. I'm committed to this new venture and to Pierre. I admire the way you've pitched into Christerby's. I don't think White's would have done it without you. Why not us? You're the ideal man, Tim. I can tell you: Pierre thinks that a close mesh with White's is a logical step. He's only held off starting his own Art Fund because he admires yours so much. Not that he's any slouch when it comes to investing in art personally."

"Oh? What's his collection like?"

"You must let him show it to you. French Impressionists, of course. He likes an Anglo-French connection, like Sisley. That's why your London Monet made him green with envy. Braque. Picasso. Mondrian. But quite a lot of English artists. Moderns as well as older ones. From Turner to Victor Pasmore, you might say."

"A catholic taste. From realism to abstraction."

"More like a real sense of money than an abstract, conceptual one. Nothing subconscious about Pierre. It's no different in principle from your Fund. Or putting old footage away for appreciation as well as, even better, rental income. We live in an age of ephemeral dot-com chimera, Tim, as far as shares are concerned. Pierre hates that. Assets are his big interest. Oh, he's got property companies; they are necessary but they bore him. Things don't. Things of quality, rarity and provenance; they can't go wrong."

His voice had risen. Not enough to attract attention from other lunchers but enough to tell me that this was a polemic, Gerry was a believer, here was a gospel. Suddenly, I knew, something extra was going to come out. He'd been working himself up to it and now he had arrived at the point.

He put his knife and fork down. His eyes fixed themselves on mine. "I don't know how White's will react, Tim. From what I've heard, they're a pretty stuffy lot. It makes me wonder, sometimes, how you fit in." He held up a hand as I opened my mouth. "Sorry, don't mean to pry. All I can say is that if ever things don't work out, Pierre is one of your greatest admirers. He'd love you to set up an Art Fund for him. Amongst other things. But in the long run, he's hoping that White's and Champion will become much closer. Possibly even some share swapping. Or something like that." He grinned suddenly, a vulpine, meaningful grin. "After all, someone like Pierre is bound, some day, to own his own bank."

Absorbing this, I considered his face as he considered mine, intently, while the half-humour sank into my mind.

"That's his strategy?" I asked.

"Oh, he's not one for written strategies, mission statements, that sort of crap. Pierre's a marketplace animal. It makes sense, though."

"And an auctioneer's? Would that make sense too?"

"He has shares in Christerby's already. If there's an accommodation with White's, who are heavily involved, the bonds will be even stronger. Why not?"

"Hmm."

He leant forward and dropped his voice. "This is just between us, Tim. You and me. I'm an ex-auctioneer and you're a banker. With overlaps. Think about it. Think what operations we could both get to run. We wouldn't clash; there'd be mutual agreements over territories. No need for more at this stage but Pierre is a horse worth backing. Why not have a discussion with him? Brainstorm a bit? He's told me he'd like to talk to you less formally. We can get together with him when he gets back."

"Back?"

"He's off to buy a painting. Down in the West Country. I can't say more but I think you'll be surprised once he's completed the deal. Pierre is nothing if not courageous."

"Is it an English artist?"

He put a finger on his nose. A smile full of, to me,

unpleasant meaning twisted his lips, almost like the smile of triumph you see on winners of satirical television competitions. "My lips are sealed. But he says that one of this one's went for a million, once."

Chapter Eighteen

"I'm glad you and William got time together today," Sue said, as we set out for South London. "It's nice to know that you're turning into a dutiful Dad."

I ignored the tinge of banter in her voice. I had been pleased to caper about with our son and make him giggle. After my lunch I needed something distracting and William had taken my mind off matters that were building up into a mental storm. For the moment I was letting it hang over me like a great black cumulus but soon, I knew, something would burst.

"It's a poor world if you can't work an afternoon off with an offspring," I answered, amiably. "I've been lucky not to have to travel too much recently."

"No. And I was glad that you didn't let any work problems intrude on home life, did you?"

"No."

"At least, not this afternoon anyway. Have you had any news from Hastings?"

"No."

"Did you see anyone about your head this morning?" She smiled. "Anyone medical, I mean?"

"Very funny. No."

There was a silence. I was tempted, if this interrogation continued, to borrow a line from Lewis Carroll and say 'I have answered three questions and that is enough' but that would imply that I was Old Father William rather than the old-feeling father of William. And it would not have gone down at all well: *women and elephants never forget an injury.* That's Saki, Hector H. Munro himself, who kept creeping insidiously back into my mind.

Why Bassington?

"Gillian phoned me today," Sue announced, breaking my disturbing thought train as we crossed Battersea Bridge.

"Oh? How is she?"

"She is fine. She was asking after you, actually."

"Me?"

"Yes, you. She asked if you'd seen a doctor."

"Me? How extraordinary. Why?"

"She seemed to think that you might be suffering from aggravated concussion."

"Oh God. I know what's coming next."

She twisted in her seat to peer at me. "Tim, she says Nobby phoned her in a great bate. He says you behaved like an enraged bear at a dog-baiting session over breakfast this morning. Went barking mad. In front of a colleague he'd asked along specially, apparently. You said terrible things to them. Gilly says you walked out in a fury. Leaving your breakfast untouched. Did you?"

"Yes, I did."

"Why?"

"I was pissed off."

Silence for a moment. Then: "He's very worried about you. He thinks you're badly concussed."

"That's the version he's given Gillian, is it? Brilliant but indefensible. Nobby has never worried about me."

"That's not true."

"All right, he may have. Now and again. In the past. He was damned rude this morning, so yes, I walked out."

"What sort of way is that to behave? To your oldest friend? Are you *sure* you're all right?"

Three questions, I thought, that's three more questions. None of them anything but pejorative.

"I am fine. I have a sore patch on the back of my head, but it is no more than a bruise."

"I think you should see a doctor."

"Well, I don't. Nor do I think I should sit and listen to nasty, sneering allegations about me and the Bassington woman."

She sat up straighter. "Allegations? What sort of allegations?"

"You know the sort of thing. Inferences that there might be

more to this than meets the eye, nudge, nudge, wink, wink to Sam Johnson, and would I like to think again carefully about my denials over this woman, and all that sort of low-grade, locker-room banter, with a degree of genuine accusation thrown in."

"But you've no need to be defensive about it. You've nothing to hide. Have you?"

"No! Don't you start, Sue."

"Then why the outburst?"

"Because I was pissed off, that's why. There they go, great clodhopping rozzers, smug as smug can be, getting nowhere but making nasty remarks to me and not a word of apology for not checking on poor Dorkie. Then expecting me, me of all people, to come up with the full Moira Bassington story, nice and easy and all tied up for them, after I've been taking bashes on the head with a frying pan while they fartarse about, prancing round Pimlico like a bunch of prize pansies. I'm not putting up with it. I'm not. Putting up with it. Am I giving you the full Simpson view?"

"My goodness! You are in a state. There's no need to shout at me."

"Sorry. I'm not shouting at you. I'm just shouting. But I didn't start this. Nobby did, via Gilly."

"Because he's worried about you. Can't you see that?"

"You mean he's worried about solving this case. Or cases. Whatever. I don't figure high on his worry list."

"That's unfair. Nobby has a lot of worries on his plate just now. Gilly says he's harassed to bits. The last thing he needed was another of your - your complications."

"Oh dear. Poor Nobby. Diddums did he not want any complications, den? Well, I didn't start all this, he did. With his all-too-easy assumptions. But I'll finish it. Have no fear; I'll finish it."

"Tim! That's not your business. Your business is to help. If you can. Not go taking umbrage and shouting and swearing at people."

"No one's bashed any of them on the head. More's the pity. Moira Bassington, me and Dorkie, we've taken all the bashing. I'm trying to think why, but I can't think why if self-satisfied policemen sit grinning at me and inferring things while expecting me to pay for their breakfast."

"That's another thing; Nobby was highly embarrassed by what you hooted at the waitress about paying before you went out, slamming the café door."

"I do not hoot. I did not slam the door."

"That's not what he says. Nearly took it clean off the frame, apparently."

"Rubbish. I left quietly."

There was a brief silence. "As a matter of interest, where did you go then? To the Bank?"

"Mecklenburgh Square."

"Ah. Now we're getting somewhere. Let's hear the rest. Come on, brown study boy, get it off your chest; this is me, remember?"

I told her. She listened carefully, shaking her head occasionally in wonder. The great thing about Sue is that you know when she's listening that she's taking it all in and won't forget any of it. She's got a mind like mine for storage and she puts another perspective on the information. I tend to agree with the great Duke of Wellington, who once said that a woman's conversation gave him much more than he could give her. There was a mature man for you; according to that Parisian bluestocking Madame de Staël, the Great Duke was an intellectual force, not just a moulded military face on a Staffordshire jug, waiting for William Nicholson to paint him. So there must be something in what he said.

"God," Sue said, when I'd finished. "Your instincts were right. Those photographs are dynamite. I must have a look through them when we get back home. Now I do believe there's a connection with you. What it is, and how it came about is the key. But it would be too much of a coincidence if there weren't. And I share your view of coincidences." Her face creased. "You're probably in danger again, you realise that?"

"Maybe."

"Only maybe? I think it's more dangerous than that. You may know something someone else wants. Or they think you do. Promise me you'll tell Nobby all this."

"What?"

"And Sam Johnson. Promise?"

I sighed.

"Tim!"

"All right. I promise."

"And you'll apologise to Nobby?"

"What?"

"You behaved badly. If others did the same, it's still no excuse. You must apologise."

"All right, all right. I'll apologise."

"Good. Even if still grumpy, good. And I'll look at those photographs. Oh gosh, we're arriving. Let's try to forget all this for the moment." She gave me an appealing look. "I know you're not keen on modern flower paintings. But do try to be enthusiastic, will you? For Janet's sake; she seems pretty keen on Jim."

"Yes, dear. Very good, dear."

She gave me a prod in the ribs, grinned, and got out. We had parked round the corner from Jim Stockdale's gallery and she led the way to the front entrance. I followed dutifully, striding up the wide granite steps to the classical front door of the typical borough style of public building. Inside, a printed notice with an arrow pointed our way to the opening and there, at the door, was Janet, who embraced Sue before pecking both my cheeks.

"Sue! Tim! Thanks a million for coming. Jim's inside talking to the local councillors who've funded part of the costs. It seems to be going well. I was terrified that no one'd come but there's quite a decent gathering. Here's a catalogue for you."

She handed us both a coloured booklet, entitled 'Flowers

then and now; a painterly perspective.' I turned the pages to see what looked like Victorian illustrations of flowers set opposite modern still lives of blooms in various styles. While Sue chatted to Janet I leafed through it. The art-writing text seemed more restrained than usual, and I wondered if Jim was responsible.

"I thought this was contemporary?" I queried, at a pause in the gossip.

"It is. But the gallery's got quite a few older paintings in its permanent collection and the idea was to trot them out and compare them with modern work. See how the approach has changed, that sort of thing. Actually, some of the permanent collection doesn't see the light that often so Jim thought it was a good excuse to give them an airing. The flower ones, anyway."

"Ah. I see. Did Jim organise it all?"

"Oh yes." Janet smiled proudly. "It's been a lot of work."

"These things always are. Did he write the catalogue copy, too?"

"How did you guess?"

"It seems less abstruse than usual. Much better. Bet it held up his Finch-Hatton volume?"

"Oh, sure. But he says he's making steady progress on that."

More arrivals approached, so Sue said we'd see her later. We entered the main rooms and wandered from painting to painting as we mixed with a reasonable crowd including a group in wheelchairs. Soon, inside the rooms, we came across Jim Stockdale.

"Tim! Sue. Hi. Good of you both to come. Thanks very much."

"Our pleasure. Congratulations on the catalogue. Well written and researched."

He blushed just a little. "Thank you, Tim. I'm afraid there's nothing for your art fund in this modest assembly but we do like to support local talent and trot out our own collection."

"You never know, Jim. You might have a future Hockney hanging unknown on these walls."

He smiled. "Unlikely. But have a dekko and let me know if there is one. Some of the older things from the permanent collection might appeal to you, though. Might give you an idea for your next acquisition, eh?"

"You never know. I'll acknowledge the source of inspiration if one does."

"Thanks. I'll keep you to that promise. All publicity gratefully received. Oh, there's Councillor Morris. Excuse me, must butter him up."

"See you later, Jim."

We progressed through the exhibition. There was a blend of watercolours, gouache, oils and even tempera. Some were very good, others depended on botched impressionism to hide poor structure or weak drawing. On the whole it was colourful and easy to take in; these were pleasant things to live with. I thought of William Nicholson, a master of still lives, many with flowers, as I went round. What was it Rothenstein had said? Something about Marguerite Steen being wrong to call him the greatest still-life painter of his or any age? A dandy, Rothenstein called him, not a great master, as little original as a man of high gifts and undeviating independence could be. A small but perfect talent, painstakingly worked and made, with anguished effort, to look effortless? Kenneth Clark had said much the same. How condescending can you get? He would leave everyone I was looking at standing.

But then, of course, he should. He was a major figure in his day, despite those Rothenstein remarks about the modern public preferring the heroic failure like van Gogh to the completely achieved but minor success. Or similarly valuing the vehement but unstudied utterance above the polished epigram.

The polished epigram; that was a speciality of Saki's. *To have reached thirty is to have failed in life*. That wasn't from *The*

Unbearable Bassington, as far as I remembered. It was from another story. The Bassington story had plenty of other polished epigrams, or were they aphorisms -

Could she really be called Bassington? Bassington according to Sam Johnson, is a fairly rare name. Only two in the London telephone book. If not genuine, why choose that one?

"Tim?"

Sue had seemed preoccupied as she moved from picture to picture, replying very briefly to my occasional comment. Something that was troubling her had caused her now, to take my arm.

"What's up?" I asked, as we moved out of the main gallery into a side room, where more new and older paintings confronted us.

She took my arm. "Finch-Hatton," she murmured. "It was you, mentioning his Finch-Hatton book. And all these flower still-lives."

"What about it?"

"Marguerite Steen. That book you bought from Mr Goodston on the life of William Nicholson. You haven't read it yet?"

"Haven't had much time."

"I dipped into it yesterday - you left it on the dressing table. Right at the beginning there's an account of the 1880 Newark political elections. Nicholson's father, William Newzam Nicholson, became MP for Newark. In those days towns returned two MPs each. In this case, William Newzam Nicholson stood with a Finch-Hatton. Nicholson, who was a local manufacturer, was elected. Finch-Hatton wasn't; the other successful candidate was the Liberal."

I frowned. "Finch-Hatton? Stood for Newark with Nicholson's father?"

"Yes. Murray Finch-Hatton. You remember Jim's story about Lady Muriel's mother Edith, turning away the doctor because she was too ill to see him? Edith was Murray's wife. If Jim's writing a book about the Finch-Hattons, he must know that Murray, who became the twelfth Earl of Winchilsea, was at the Nicholsons house during the 1880 election. Young William remembered it all vividly because a Liberal mob attacked the house."

I stopped. "I don't quite see - "

"It's a strange coincidence, isn't it?"

"Yes, but - "

"And we both think coincidences are, well, unpleasant."

"All the same, I don't quite see - "

My voice trailed off. I was standing in front of one of the older paintings, a watercolour in a style of maybe a century ago. Bluish-purple hills in the background were set behind large green stalks of plants bearing lush red flowers on them. I looked at the title on the card by the picture. C.S Groves, it said, was the artist. Date c1910. The title was *Flowering Aloes near Port Elizabeth*.

"Tim? You don't quite see what?"

I hardly heard her. "Port Elizabeth," I murmured. "Flowering aloes. Those are the very same. Red blooms. In the photograph."

"Photograph?"

"Bassington. If she really was Bassington. She wasn't in Kew or Devon. Or Spain. She was in South Africa."

Chapter Nineteen

"This," said Sue, once were back at the flat and William's sitter had left, "could all be a load of red herrings."

"True."

"I mean, the connection between Jim Stockdale's genealogical research and the Nicholsons is tenuous, to put it mildly. So Sir William Nicholson's father, back in 1880, stood for parliament with the then Murray Finch-Hatton. Who inherited Haverholme Priory near Ewerby and became the twelfth Earl of Winchilsea. So what? I may simply be getting biographically paranoid." She gave me a meaning look. "I'm having suspicions which are the occupational hazard of being married to you."

I put down Marguerite Steen's book and looked at her. "Thank you very much."

"It's true. You thrive on this sort of thing and it's probably infectious. All the same, I'm disturbed."

I waved the book. "Finch-Hatton dined at the Nicholsons' house in the London Road, Newark. Steen says they were flattered because they were 'in trade' and he was an aristocrat. During the meal, he stood up and helped himself from the sideboard. No one middle class would have done that. They took it as the naturally superior behaviour of a lord." I scratched my jaw. "Finch-Hatton probably forgot that he was in a private house and behaved as he might behave during a constituency lunch. He lost at the election, anyway. Newark is not far from Ewerby and Haverholme but Nicholson's father was an important local worthy. He and the Liberal got in, although the voting was very close. I don't suppose there was much contact after that. It is pretty tangential, Sue."

She sat down on her favourite bit of the settee in front of the mantelpiece and looked up at me. "Murray Finch-Hatton only got Haverholme because his cousin, Sir Jenison Gordon, was incensed by another cousin's remarks about silver-weed growing round the house, implying neglect. Jenison was a peppery, eccentric bachelor. After these doubtless casual remarks he promptly went indoors and changed his will in Murray's favour. The Finch-Hattons had lost all their estates at Kirby and Eastwell Park due to Murray's stepbrother, the eleventh earl, gambling everything away. They were very grand once and had sold Nottingham House, which is now Kensington Palace, to William the Third. Haverholme was a fortuitous consolation prize. They sold that in 1927 and there's nothing much left of the building, now."

I gaped at this exposition. "Good God, Sue. Where on earth did you get this massive contribution to the memory-bank for a game of Trivial Pursuit?"

She frowned at me. "From Jim Stockdale, of course. He told it to Janet and me while you were dealing with William the night they came to dinner."

"And I thought you were talking curator-talk whilst I was consoling the boy."

"We were, by the time you got back. The thing that bugs me is why didn't Jim mention the Nicholson connection?"

"Why should he? It wasn't relevant."

"He'd just been looking through the books over there. He saw and mentioned the Ben Nicholson references."

"True. I didn't have the William Nicholson stuff then, though. I went to Mr Goodston afterwards."

"Oh, come on, Tim. Jim is a Modern British art freak, like you. He'd just run the gamut of those books. Anyone who knows your Fund would know that you haven't got a Ben Nicholson in it. But you have got the others. You said to Jim this evening that his catalogue was well researched. Remember? He had Finch-Hatton stories oozing from him at the dinner table. To mention that William's father, or Ben's grandfather, was involved with his big research project

146

should have been irresistible. But he didn't. He clammed up on that as though the mention of it might be suspicious in some way."

"He had better anecdotes to tell. Besides, the story's not really relevant to Ben. Just to William."

"It's a Nicholson story and it's a Finch-Hatton story. Wherever he's sourcing his Finch-Hatton material, I bet it comes up. He's an art gallery curator with a yen for such stuff. I find his omission very strange."

"Strange it may be, Sue, but it's not incriminating. We all forget stories at times when we might have shone with them. Hence the *esprit de l'escalier*. The good story remembered just when it's too late." I shook my head slowly. "It's too much of a coincidence, Sue. We'd never met Jim before, there's no connection with us, and it was the first time he'd been here. Who initiated the invitation?"

"Janet, actually. That's what's bugging me. She particularly asked if she could bring him."

"How did she meet him?"

Sue smiled slightly and dropped her eyelids. "I think he picked her up. She hasn't admitted it, but it was at a curator's one-day course we were both at - on social inclusiveness. I got separated from her. She didn't say anything at the time, but he started to appear from then on."

"All very natural. I suppose."

An uneasy thought was creeping across my mind. Could Jim Stockdale have wooed Janet, known to be a friend of Sue's, solely for the purpose of getting into our flat? With what end in view? How would he gain from such a visit? Could he possibly be trying to reconnoitre my library with a view to finding out my next investment decision? Surely not; this was getting as paranoid a thought train as Sue had suggested earlier on.

She was watching my face. "It's still a strange coincidence. Did you speak to Jim again this evening?"

"Only very briefly. He was pretty occupied, doing his

curatorial bit with another bunch of local councillors. I just said great show and well done, we're off, that sort of thing."

"I hope Janet didn't mind our popping off early like that."

"'Course she didn't. She was delighted how busy things were. I may have been a bit distrait though, I must admit. That African thing." I picked up the photograph copy of Moira Bassington in bare shoulders, standing pleat-skirted and sandalled in front of the flowers. "The small yellow flowers you say are potentillas; they grow all over here, but they're South African originally. Those red flowers are aloes; no question. So I reckon she was in South Africa when this was taken."

Sue looked thoughtful. "Murray Finch-Hatton was in South Africa, Tim. Brought back a lion cub."

"Sue! Please."

She grinned broadly. "It's true, according to Jim. Finch-Hatton dived overboard to save it on the way home. It lived at Haverholme as a pet, lying on the drawing-room sofa and disconcerting visitors. But when the neighbours got a bit worried and armed their footmen to protect their children, he gave it to London Zoo. Took it to Regent's Park in a hansom cab, on the seat next to him. He used to visit it regularly."

I put a hand to my brow. "This is all Jim, again?"

"Where else would I get that story?"

"I must have been out quite a while."

"You were."

"The intellectual pressure of this conversation is starting to revive my headache."

"You should go to the doctor."

"I should go to bed early." I put the photograph down. Thoughts about Dorkie Collins were starting to blot out those of Jim Stockdale. "I have to go to Weybridge tomorrow to look at car films. I need a good night's sleep."

At that moment, William let out a howl.

Chapter Twenty

Sylvan Holme was one of the few big Victorian houses still standing on St. George's Avenue. Where other great domestic piles of late nineteenth and early twentieth century prosperity had stood along it, most sites were now filled with clumps of terraced, lesser, modern dwellings and even blocks of flats. The area was still leafy, woody, well-heeled and slightly self-conscious, caught between the sheer luxury of the gated estate at St.George's Hill and the economic lifeline of the station. Occasional rumbles of electric trains could be heard from the main London south-west line running parallel to St.George's Avenue in a deep cutting along the backs of gardens on the north side. The noise was a constant reminder of the artery which caused this once sleepy, inconsequential riverside village to develop into an exclusive dormitory suburb for stockbrokers, lawyers, businessmen and even the more distinguished members of the D'Oyly Carte Opera Company at the height of its Edwardian, Savoyard fame.

Out beyond the station, on what was once low-lying river heathland where stood a number of dignified country houses, in 1906 the late Mr H.F. Locke King outraged the locals by building Brooklands, the first banked motor racing track in Britain, on the estate his family had owned for generations. His wife Mrs. (later Dame) Ethel Locke King, was as avid a supporter of the great concrete circuit as he was. At the first 1906 project meeting it was agreed that Locke King would himself fund the fabulous sum required for construction; this was not questioned since he had, after all, built the Mena House Hotel in Cairo. A racing driver called S.F.Edge astounded the gathering by stating that when the track came into being he wished to book it in order to drive a car unaided for twenty-four hours at an average speed of sixty miles an hour. Most of the gathering regarded him as a madman.

Locke King's neighbours were incensed but were unable to stop the project; planning authorities as we know them were not there to prevent a gentleman doing what he liked on his own land. As the work progressed, illustrated magazines in droves recorded its incredible progress in breathless prose.

Contemporary ladies described the track, when it was finished, as perfectly horrid.

There's not much left of it, now. A bit of banking and a museum, as there is almost everywhere where anything happened in Britain. The Vickers aero sheds and factory no longer turn out aircraft. The landing strip, from which early planes staggered off into the air, their engines thrashing to enable the frail craft to clear the shallow Byfleet banking, is out of existence. Weybridge and Brooklands are no longer synonymous; Weybridge is known for golf, gin and tonics, big mortgages and suburban aspiration.

The man who opened the door of Sylvan Holme to us was puffy, wheezy and of poor colour. Gerry Watson had said that he was seventy-odd but I would have put him older. The modern style of gymnastic, stringy retirement had passed him by. His smile of recognition at Frank Cordwell, however, lit up his face into a more vigorous, anticipatory mode.

"Frank! Jessica! Nice to see you." He peered at me queryingly.

"This is Tim Simpson." Frank was quick to introduce me in the vague terms we had agreed by phone. "He's from our prospective finance side. Tim, this is Quentin Leybourne."

I got a clammy handshake. "Ah! The money man, eh? Very good, very good. How do you do? Welcome. Come in, come in."

I stepped back gallantly to allow Jessica Browne and Frank to go first into a caustic-tiled hall of generous proportions, from which a heavy brown staircase rose up towards a gloomy landing lit in dim harlequin fashion by a vast stained glass window. Houses like this, I reflected as I peered upwards, have elsewhere been turned into country hotels or geriatric institutions. Or simply knocked down, which was to be the fate of this one. A faintly musty, damp smell, mingled with which an even thicker aroma of unhealthy cooking could be detected, met my nostrils. Jessica Browne of the soft clear skin, who I had only just met at the door with Frank Cordwell, gave me a faint, knowing smile.

"It's all set up in the billiard room, as before," Leybourne waved a hand inwards, towards the back of the hall. "Everything ready and shipshape for inspection. Not quite all Sir Garnet, perhaps, but as near as I can get to it." He turned to me in explanatory vein. "I don't know if they've told you, but I'm here all on my own, now. Place is empty, fallin' to bits. As soon as I leave it'll come down."

"I'm sorry to hear that," I answered, courteously.

He chuckled wheezily. "I'm not. These houses were fine when you had lots of servants. Utterly impracticable, now. They were stoutly made, I'll say that - my grandfather had the place built in 1911, just after my father was born. Grandpa was in metals, did very well. Knew his onions on the supply side. Good materials, seasoned wood, that sort of thing. Within fifteen years, after the Great War, it was already becoming an anachronism, but my father loved it. Nurseries miles down attic passages, cold flagged pantries, frightful stone sinks an' all, he loved it. He could walk down to Brooklands, d'you see, although he rarely did; cars were his passion. Mad keen on the track. And photography. My father never worked. Lucky beggar. Wish I could say the same. Here we are, all set up."

We went into a long rectangular room with broad windows at the far end. They would have looked out onto a garden had heavy green velvet curtains not been drawn across them, although I wondered what state of jungle neglect the garden might be in. In the centre of the room was a huge billiard or snooker table, its top covered with dark wood panels to protect the baize and, on these panels, stacks of film cans, books, files, albums. Above the table, set in what was evidently a high, chapel-like, single-story roof, was a glass belvedere or claraboya window for skylighting, now dirty, cracked and badly draped in holed tatters by what had once been a set of drawstring curtains. More immediately over the surface was a set of ancient snooker lamps under chipped metal shades painted dark green. Around the room were the heavy shelves of an old library, these too stacked with cans, books, albums and old box files with the obligatory hole in the end binding. The chilly atmosphere struck my limbs and back.

On the table stood a big old cine projector, set up to face a screen on a tripod stand in the bay of the windows.

"My father," Leybourne spoke to me by way of explanation, since the others presumably had heard it all before, "got mad keen on car racin' and photography when he was fifteen. His first attempts were a bit shaky but my grandfather was a practical man and didn't think universities were anything but hotbeds of vice and communism. He was a City man, hated anything intellectual. He knew if he left it too late, pressure for Dad to matriculate would start. So he took him out of school, bought him a ticket to Hollywood - ship and train - gave him a couple of introductions to American metal-trading connections in case of emergency and told him to learn his movie stuff there, practically. Dad stayed over a year. 1926 to '27. He was mad keen and learnt quickly. Wasn't interested in acting or directing. Could have been a damn good movie cameraman if he hadn't been a gentleman. Loved the technical side of it."

I smiled. "Did he ever race cars?"

Leybourne beamed at the question. "Rileys, off and on, once he got back. Brooklands and road races. The TT and so on. Had one of the same cars as Mike Hawthorn started on. Met my mother at an Autumn Handicap. Had a smash or two and eventually my mother - that would be around 1933 or '34 - said he should stop and stick to photography. So he did." He waved at the material around him. "Here it is. Never been used as a billiard room. Unheated, it's a cold hole, but the film's kept well in it. Hasn't it, Frank?"

"It's in remarkably good condition," Cordwell nodded in agreement.

"Like to see something?" Without waiting for an answer, Leybourne moved briskly to the projector. "I watched *Top Gear* on TV last night, did you? BBC 2?"

We all shook our heads.

"Pity. It was all about Rolls-Royce and Bentley. Or BMW and Volkswagen respectively, if we're talking about owner-ship." He leered at me, as though I might be responsible. "Bloody tragic, it is. They showed some archive footage, of course. Bentleys at Le Mans, including the new one coming third this year. The usual thing. There was a brief shot of Barnato and Birkin sittin' on the winning car in 1929. I've got better stuff than they used. Here, have a look at Birkin in his single-seater blower, well up the banking, taking the lap speed record."

He clicked a rather elderly brass switch screwed to the dark tabletop and the projector sprang into life. On the screen a speckled grey image, but very well in focus, of a big low car with enormous spoked wheels, bonnet cowling and pointed tail, streaking along an equally grey banked track sprang into life as the projector hummed and rotated. The driver wore what looked like a leather helmet, goggles and white overalls. A spotted silk scarf, polka dots streaming in the wind, put me in mind of William Nicholson.

"Great stuff, eh?" Leybourne demanded. "That's 1932, tak-ing the lap record up to 137.96 miles an hour. Car must have been all over the place. Track was as bumpy as hell by then. Birkin knew every inch of it."

I glanced sideways quickly at my companions. Jessica Browne gave me another quick, knowing smile but Frank Cordwell was rapt, staring at the screen. I thought someone should say something.

"I've always been an admirer of Tim Birkin," I said. This was true; as a boy, I liked his nickname, the same as mine - his real name was Sir Henry Ralph Stuart Birkin, son of a

Nottingham lace manufacturer - and his dashing but tragic end, illustrated by Rowan Atkinson in a TV cameo. "I've got his book, *Full Throttle,* with that Maserati he had on the cover."

I'd said the right thing. Leybourne gave me another beam of appreciation. "I say Frank, you've brought the right money man along." He stopped the projector and waved at the bookshelves. "Got that in first edition over there. Tell you what: I'll put that Maserati on for you. With Birkin in it, then Whitney Straight. Great car. Still going somewhere. The story is, as I'm sure you know, that Birkin burnt his arm on the exhaust pipe in Morocco. Septicaemia set in and he died. But some people contest that. They say it was a mosquito bite and heartbreak over some woman. Or something like that. Ah, here we are." He was rummaging amongst his films cans. "No, I tell you what, can't find Birkin right now but here's Whitney Straight in it - he took it over from Birkin and bumped up the Mountain circuit record with it. They were trying to keep up with road racing by then, of course."

Another image of antiquated but elegant sports cars swerving up the high Members' banking at odd angles, Talbots and Bugattis and the Maserati, low and square-bonneted, came up on the screen. "Whitsun 1932. The Nottingham Lightning Mountain Handicap," Leybourne said, proudly. "Very appropriate. There he is; Straight came second. Earl Howe won in his Bugatti - there it goes. Marvellous stuff."

The film tickered on for a while then cut to a view of what looked like a paddock, with cars standing waiting and rather jerky figures gesticulating and smiling. The winning Bugatti rolled past with clustered admirers alongside waving in triumph. In the background I saw a smaller car in side view, waiting presumably for the next race.

A pang of recognition hit my nerves.

"Hang on." I tried to sound casual. "What's that little car in the background?"

Leybourne stopped the film. "What?"

"Sorry. There's a small sports or racing car in the paddock there. As Earl Howe and Straight went past. I wondered what it was."

He rewound the film and set it going again. The side view of the car came up and he chuckled his wheezy chuckle once more. "It's an Amilcar. French. Be someone like Humphreys' Amilcar Six. Sometimes didn't start."

Now Jessica spoke for the first time. Her voice was clear and quiet. "Are you a Jacques Tati fan, Tim?"

"I am, as a matter of fact."

She smiled. "I've got all his films. *Mr Hulot's Holiday*'s the one. That old car he drives is an Amilcar. You know, that scene where the dog won't move in the road. And the spare tyre sequence. Hilarious. Must have been where you've seen one before."

"Oh, yes. Of course. Amazing thing, the memory."

She turned to Frank Cordwell. "Pierre's got one in his collection, hasn't he, Frank?"

"He certainly has. It hasn't been out lately though."

Icicles, again. Cold spiky icicles prickled down my spine. Moira Bassington, standing by a sports car. An old, primitive sports car. A man with his back to the camera. I needed to look again at that photo; I needed to look again quickly, before the image faded.

Leybourne had gone back to Whitney Straight as another sight of the Maserati sped across the grainy screen. "Look at that. Great chap. American. Father was killed in the First War. Millionaire in his own right. His mother remarried; Elmhirst, the chap who founded Dartington Hall. Straight gave up racing when he married, bit like my dear old Dad. No comparison; Straight was a terrific winner. Wartime air ace, second war of course. Head of B.O.A.C., Deputy Chairman of Rolls Royce. He'd be heartbroken at the car part going to BMW. Wow, what a fellow. Got an M.C., D.F.C., all that sort of thing. Wrote articles, belonged to all the clubs." Suddenly, he seemed to become aware of the silence. "Sorry, am I banging on again? Bit of an old anorak these days. I'll miss this lot, but at least it'll be in good hands."

He switched the projector off and turned to look at me expectantly. I tried to sort out a seething brain, to calm the prickling icicles, and asked him the first question that came into my head. It came clean out of my breakfast with Nobby.

"Appropriate? Why did you say appropriate?"

"Sorry?"

"The Mountain Handicap. You said very appropriate. Why?"

Silly question, I thought almost as soon as I said it, Birkin and Nottingham lace -

His face cleared. "Oh, that. Trivial Pursuit stuff. It was the Nottingham Lightning Mountain Handicap." He grinned knowingly. "Nottingham. Whitney Straight gave up car racing when he married into the aristocracy. Daughter of the Earl of Nottingham. Well, to be precise, the fourteenth Earl of Winchilsea and Nottingham."

"*Who?* Whose daughter?"

"Winchilsea and Nottingham's. Lady Daphne Finch-Hatton, she was. One of the Lincolnshire Finch-Hattons, I think. Or maybe another branch. They were related to that chap in *Out of Africa*, you know." He looked back almost regretfully at the blank screen and then at me, with what looked like concern. "I say. I'm frightfully neglectful these days. Terrible host. You look a bit pale, Mr Simpson. Long journey here, I expect. Let me get some coffee. Then we can talk money, can we?"

Chapter Twenty-one

"What did I tell you?" The voice on the phone was triumphant. "What did I tell you? You've probably missed the boat. Jeremy was right. I never thought I'd hear myself say it, but Jeremy was right."

I brought my spare hand up to meet my fevered brow. I was back in my office. My mind was seething with Finch-Hattons, fluttering and chirping across my skull like so many alarmed little birds of the first half of the surname's eponymous variety when confined to an aviary containing a kestrel. I was not calm.

Especially since, in the photograph in front of me, Moira Bassington stood in front of an Amilcar. Definitely an Amilcar.

The voice on the telephone was that of Charles Massenaux, crowing from his cubicle at Christerby's.

"As far as my records go, it's a record," he babbled. "A hundred and seventy-five thousand for a William Nicholson. The last big price was a hundred and fifty-five thousand for *Flowers in a Glass Jug* back in the '99 to 2000 season. Not counting the *Woman in White* back in '98. That went for a hundred and fifty grand. It bears out everything I said. And what Jeremy said."

I kept the spare hand pressed to the brow. Moira Bassington and Pierre Champion was a pairing I was finding it hard to absorb.

"You are referring, I take it Charles, to the latest Modern British sale at Sotheby's, at which the painting *Le Débit de la Rue Montaigne, Sainte Geneviève*, painted by Sir William Nicholson in 1911, went to a private buyer for £175,000? Yes?"

"Yes." The triumph in his voice died a little. "You knew, then. You should have been in there, pitching, Tim."

"And run it up to over two hundred thousand, in the teeth of a determined private buyer? Where's the sense in that?"

The tone turned challenging. "Can you find one cheaper?"
"Possibly."

"And trick some poor devil out of the market price?"

I ignored the implied insult. "I can save the poor devil, and the Fund, the exorbitant auctioneer's margins, for a start."

"Ouch, you bastard. Whose side are you on?"

"I can also buy perhaps a more typical William Nicholson than a dark Paris street scene, excellent though it may be. I may have to pay more. I may have to pay less. It will be decided on the individual merits of the case. You also noticed, I take it, that Winifred sold rather well, both at Sotheby's and at Phillips, where she raised £52,000 for a work fresh to the market? Reports also say that Ben's work went well but there weren't any big numbers coming up. One must keep calm."

"I should have known you'd be *au fait* with the latest sales. But you agree that William seems to be in the ascendant?"

"I do agree. And one should sell on a rising market rather than buying on it. Which makes my argument for buying a Ben all the more cogent."

"If you can find one that's kosher."

"If I can find one that's kosher. Did you see, by the way Charles, that Stanhope Forbes is still on the wax? At Phillips yet again. Not a million this time, but nearly quarter of a million for a lesser painting. I always said we should buy the Newlyn School."

There was a silence. Then: "Do you know who bought the William Nicholson, Tim?"

"A private buyer." Not Pierre Champion, I thought to myself, not him because I've already checked.

Could that really be him with Moira Bassington?

"Be interesting to know if someone's trying to second-guess you on your next acquisitions, though, wouldn't it?"

"That is always a risk, Charles. On the other hand there is room for plenty of investment in Modern British art. Our figures are trifling compared with the Continentals."

"Oh well, if you're happy, you're happy. But my advice is not to leave William until it's too late."

"Thank you, Charles. Your advice and concern are, as always, deeply appreciated. Very deeply appreciated. We shall take your important advice into full consideration."

"Sod you too," he said.

"How coarse. Listen Charles, I promised Jeremy I'd ask you: how involved does Pierre Champion seem to be getting with your esteemed operation?"

There was a brief silence. Then: "Very involved, Tim. Too damned involved for comfort."

"In what way?"

"In what way? He buys here. His man Gerry Watson buys here. Art and furniture and furnishings. Champion is also buying shares, as I'm sure you know, often through nominees. It's like creeping ivy. I sometimes wonder whether it's he who is buying, or Gerry, or both, or a nominee. He's a manipulator."

"He hasn't got a significant shareholding. Yet."

"Not yet, no. But he's the sort of man who builds up a collection. When it's a dominating collection, he cashes in. At a huge profit. I fear he collects shares in the same way. He's into several other quoted auctioneers and, I believe, a big private one in France. He likes to play a kind of Monopoly game, you know? I'll swap my Bond Street for your Trafalgar Square or a railway station. It's not illegal but it is unnerving. Why?"

"Just a private interest he's expressed."

"What in?"

"Photographic archives."

"Oh God. *Et tu, brute?* Yet another? The whole world is assembling photographic archives. I put it down to Stephen Poliakoff myself. Join the stampede; it's like the Gold Rush."

"Those who made money on the Gold Rush are said to be those who sold picks, shovels, tents and services. Rather like fine art auctioneers."

"Or merchant bankers."

"Or whores."

"Sod you, too," he said.

And rang off.

Which, with impeccable timing, coincided with my door flying open.

Jeremy stood there with an art auction report in his hand. The William Nicholson painting of Paris sold for £175,000 was visible on the front page. Jeremy's hair was dishevelled. His eye was wild.

"What did I tell you?" I shouted, before he could say it first.

Chapter Twenty-two

"This kind of thing," I said to Nobby Roberts and Sam Johnson, "can lead to insanity. The mind becomes overloaded with random but seemingly-connected trivia." I gave them a suitably humble smile. "I need your trained, analytical approach."

It was lunchtime on the following day. We were sitting in the pub at which I had first met Sam Johnson. I had spent an evening at home running through the events of the past twenty-four hours with Sue until we were both thoroughly confused. In the end, she prompted me to phone Nobby and arrange a meeting with him and Sam Johnson. Despite a rather clipped reply to my call, he agreed readily.

Which meant that they were still stuck.

I had bought beer and apologised fulsomely to them both. They were relieved, as far as I could tell, and had waved the memory of my last outburst aside with generous disclaimers. I was, they said, clearly *hors de combat* at the time of the aborted breakfast. Almost certainly still concussed. Nobby said that he regretted being so opprobrious, and pleaded pressure of work, which was quite a climbdown for him. He peered at me anxiously, enquiring whether I had had my head looked at. I replied that anyone who ran an Art Fund the way I do had always needed his head looking at, regularly. They laughed. All in all, now that suitable excuses could be used, it was Prodigal's Return Time.

They were, however, expectant.

Taking it carefully, I had run through the photograph sequence with them, explaining the relevance of the sites. Nobby's face got longer and longer.

"You mean," he asked eventually, "that all these places she visited have something to do with William and, or, Ben Nicholson?"

161

"Yes. Except for the sports car shot and the flowering aloes. I can't place those in the Nicholson canon, except for William's visit to South Africa in 1931."

He frowned in concentration. "Just because Pierre Champion has got an Amilcar, it doesn't mean that she's standing in front of his."

"No."

"Could be any Amilcar at any race meeting. There are lots of vintage car rallies these days."

"Yes."

"You say he's gone off to the West Country somewhere. Probably to buy a Ben Nicholson painting?"

"I think so. St.Ives is a likely spot."

"There's nothing criminal in that. Even if he is pre-empting you in some way, it's only likely to upset you, not kill anyone. And actually, it's still only an assumption on your part. He might be buying a Munnings of that area or a Newlyn painting."

"He might, although it would have to be an exceptional Munnings. On the other hand, Stanhope Forbes might be a good bet."

"From what you say, he'd have to be pretty confident of provenance to buy a Ben Nicholson."

"Yes."

"And he's a bit odd if he thinks that he'll get you on board his particular business bandwagon by trumping your ace, or whatever the right analogy should be."

"Big cheeses tend to be odd. Some of them like to show monetary power. Some like to show how clever they are. Some like to pee on your patch, just to show precedence. It's part of a dominance pattern."

"He doesn't know you, then."

"I'm quite not sure what you mean by that."

He held up a conciliatory hand. "We won't quarrel again, Tim." Turning to Sam Johnson, he said, "You'd better just check with Champion about that Amilcar, though, when you can get hold of him. Ask him if he knows the Bassington woman. Show him the portrait photo in case she used another name. He'll probably deny anything to do with her, one way or the other, but if he's innocent he might just suggest who owns that car." He turned back to me. "What else have you got to tell us? This Finch-Hatton obsession; go through it again."

I did. He clutched at his brow. "Please. Forget it. Just forget it. Try, try to forget it. Please. As a policeman with some experience of leads, I beg you to discard it. Right?"

"If you say so, Chief Inspector."

"We have enough red herrings already. Enough to stock a fishmonger's. Drop that one. Or rather, those. It is all so circumstantial as to be ludicrous. You'll be reading the whole of Karen Blixen or Isak Dinesen or whatever she's called next, then heading off for Kenya."

"Not me."

"I wouldn't put it past you. The South African photo with the aloes: what do you make of that?"

I looked at Sam Johnson. "How is Dorkie Collins?"

"Getting better. He will be questionable, Foster says the hospital says, within two days. Or thereabouts. Right now, he seems to be rambling. Something about traps."

"Traps?"

"Whether he fell into one, or was trapped in some other way, I don't know. It's not anything to help. But they are optimistic about his making a reasonable recovery."

"Is anyone guarding him?"

Sam nodded. "Night and day. A constable on the ward. No one has tried to see him, though."

"Thank goodness for that. He's the key to a lot of it, I think."

"You mean, because of South Africa, and the photo of the Bassington woman there, a direct connection exists?"

"It's a strong probability."

Nobby cleared his throat. "The name Bassington; you reckon it's a pseudonym of some sort, don't you?"

I stared gloomily at my beer. "I can't be sure. It's just that it's so unusual. And you, Sam, gave me the idea when you said that her flat seemed like a hidey-hole rather than a real residence. As though it was used for a specific purpose, a role of some sort."

A vision of Dorkie Collins and his remarks about Edie Nicholson came to me. Four names used at various times, like Laura Riding. Women with roles to play, disguises to be put on. Was Dorkie thinking of Moira Bassington when he said it?

"Why Bassington, do you think?" Nobby was waiting.

I cleared my throat. "*The Unbearable Bassington* is a bitter story. The mother, Francesca Bassington, lives on an economic knife-edge and wants her wayward son Comus, the self-absorbed shit of the title, to marry well so as to save both of them. In sheer petulance he torpedoes his chance with a pretty heiress who loves him. His mother owns some furniture and a valuable Dutch painting by an artist called Van Der Meulen which are her only, precious assets. After the heiress disaster the only job available to Comus is in West Africa, the white man's grave, far from the witty social world he loves. He has a premonition of his death if he goes to West Africa. He wants his mother to sell the Van Der Meulen to save him from his fate and buy him an English position, but she won't do it. Her possessions are too important to her. He goes to West Africa, which is described in desolate terms, and soon dies in utter misery. At the end of the story, while Francesca is walking in St James's Park, tormented by guilt about his death, she receives the news that the Van Der Meulen is a fake."

"Cheerful chap, your Saki."

"The cruelty of the story is that the mother has to live on, economically crushed, knowing what she has done. If the painting had been genuine, it might have been worse. But it is a fake; the story is ironic tragedy at its highest level."

"I'll remember to keep that one off my list."

"It's a brilliant read. Munro was a polished writer, full of quotable epigrammatic stuff. He had a Wildean wit but it was a bit short on pity, is the verdict on him. A master of his technique but limited in breadth of scope. He was, in a way, to fiction, what William Nicholson was to painting."

"What happened to this great wit?"

"He died in the trenches, as a corporal. The last words he uttered were 'Put that bloody cigarette out'."

There was a silence for a moment. You can not critically shade the memory of anyone who died in the trenches.

"The terrible effect of a fake painting and a fatal exile to Africa. West rather than South, but near enough?" Nobby queried, after a decent interval. "Something in that which we should look for?"

I looked at Sam Johnson. "*Addresses are given to us to conceal our whereabouts.* That's one of Saki's. There must be another address somewhere."

He shook his head, sadly. "I'm stymied. We seem to be getting nowhere. The flat was cleared of anything that might have helped, if it ever contained anything."

"The notebook? The diary that had my name in it? You had cryptographers looking at it, you said."

He shook his head. "They've come up with very little so far. Conjectures as abstruse as your Finch-Hatton material. We did find one more thing. She made a note about some sort of support group for female researchers. It must sometimes be a lonely and tough life. All very clandestine, still. I can't find any evidence of one, so far. Her little book has a Latin reference to a flower and some bloke, or Wales, maybe."

"What flower?"

"An *iridacea*."

"What is that?"

Sam Johnson smiled. "I grow them at home. The Latin is the name for the common iris. The other name, the bloke, or maybe a reference to Wales, was Barry. With a query beside it."

The great icy prickles returned, redoubled.

"Iris Barry?"

"You've swallowed a wasp again." Nobby was as sharp as a knife. "What are you - "

But I was already punching numbers into my mobile phone. I pointed at Sam Johnson. "You'd better come with me, quick. Now."

"Where to?"

"Outer Essex. Mangate. To see a lady called Jessica Browne."

Chapter Twenty-three

We went in Sam's car. He drove fast, straight up the M11. The receptionist at Mangate said in answer to my call that Jessica Browne had gone home to lunch but would be back by two-thirty. I didn't query whether she regularly went home to lunch or whether this was for something special. A deep inner voice just told me to get there and get there quick, providing she wasn't away with Frank Cordwell looking at archival material somewhere. The receptionist said no she wasn't booked out, she was down as being in the office all day today. But had I got an appointment -

I'd rung off, then.

Iris Barry: it would be a good name for a women film researchers' support group. Symbolic, covering an icon of a victim of male persecution from Wyndham Lewis, other relationships and marriages, a long lonely struggle, the establishment of an expertise in the face of a male-dominated industry, enormous courage, an international reputation, personal familiarity with major American film moguls, curatorship of an entirely new form of museum and archive.

She sat for *Praxitella* in 1921, providing Lewis with his mask-like and monumental portrait image now in the Leeds Art Gallery. During that time she worked for the Ministry of Munitions, ordering machine guns, and as a librarian at the School for Oriental Studies.

Quite apart from being a poet, novelist and film critic.

She started from illegitimate roots; her real name was Crump, the daughter of a diseased brassfounder and a gypsy fortune teller. There was wealth in the brassfounder's family but, coming from the wrong side of the blanket, she never got any of it.

Was Bassington similar? Did she identify with Iris Barry in some way because of parallels in her own life?

"William Nicholson," I said to Sam Johnson, as the speedo needle flickered into the higher nineties, "had an illegitimate child, you know. Maybe two. There's a story in Bruce Arnold's *Orpen* about Nicholson sharing a model with Albert Rutherston - William Rothenstein's brother - and Alvaro Guevara. The model became pregnant and they all worried who was responsible until they worked out that it was Nicholson. I wonder what happened to the child."

"It would be rather dead by now, I should think. We are talking of pre-1910, are we?"

"We are. So it could conceivably be alive, even if in its nineties. There could be grandchildren, possibly. They could be around fortyish, given the usual sort of quarter-century generation spread."

"Could, could, might. Very hypothetical. In those days, Tim, illegitimate children tended to get farmed out like Edgar Wallace or stuck in orphanages. Few knew who their parents were."

"Some got sent to the colonies, Sam. Or went there themselves. Like Edgar Wallace, to South Africa."

"Some didn't. It's a theory, but this case has too many theories. Do I turn left here?"

"You do."

We shot into the car park of Champion's big agricultural complex. The same dusty silos stood in tall tubular columns. Conveyors were running between buildings. There was a line of unremarkable vehicles where the employees parked; no DB7 this time. We strode quickly into the foyer and fronted up to the receptionist.

"Jessica Browne," I said. "Please tell her Tim Simpson is here to see her."

The receptionist was a middle-aged, defensive chatelaine. "I'm afraid Miss Browne isn't back yet," she said, triumphantly. "She's obviously been detained. You didn't have an appointment, did you?"

"Drat. Would you call her at home, please? It's urgent."

"I - I don't think - "

Sam Johnson stuck his warrant card under her nose. "I am Detective Inspector Johnson of Chelsea CID," he snapped. "We need to talk to Miss Browne urgently about an important matter. Kindly call her at home. It's nearby, is it?"

"Yes." The receptionist's eyes had opened wide. "I'll call for you now."

There was a silence while she dialled and waited, her slim earpiece in place. I could hear the dial tone ringing at the other end. Ringing and ringing.

The receptionist looked up at us. "There seems to be no reply. Perhaps she's on her way."

I looked at my watch. Nearly half-past three. A long time to be at lunch. "Is Frank Cordwell in?"

"No. He's out all day, today."

"Gerry Watson?"

"He's not based here. He's at Hammersmith today, I believe."

Sam leant forward impatiently. "Has Jessica Browne got a mobile?"

"Yes, she has."

"Try it. Please." He was still pretty short.

Another round of dialling and waiting. And waiting. Another shake of the head. "No answer."

Anxiety began to well up in me.

"Where does she live?" Sam's voice was beginning to produce an anxious edge, too.

"I - we're not allowed to give personal - "

"*Where does she live?*"

The address came forth. It was in a village five miles away. We left the reception area almost at a trot and piled into the car. I navigated, Sam drove briskly. We found the village but five miles seems to take an eternity when your heart is up in your throat, pounding. We needed Jessica Browne; we needed to know the details of the Iris Barry Support Group; we needed to show Jessica the photo of Moira Bassington and find out

169

if she had attended, was even a member, what her name was, anything. If anyone could be connected with the Group, it had to be Jessica Browne.

She lived in a smart modern bungalow with a freshly-planted front garden. A car was still parked in the driveway. Relief flooded through me.

"She's still here," I said.

But there was no answer to the doorbell. Sam Johnson and I looked at each other, seeing lines of worry etched into our faces.

"You stay here," he said, shortly. "I'll go round the back."

He disappeared round the pathway that went down the side of the bungalow. I stood like a prune at the silent front door, thinking of Dorkie, thinking of Moira Bassington, trying to keep calm as relentless time ticked by.

The front door opened. Sam Johnson stood there, holding his mobile phone at the ready.

"Don't go in," he said, shortly.

"You mean - you mean she's - "

"She's dead, yes. Murdered. Hit on the head. The body's lying by a projector. Looks like she was watching a film. The back door was unlocked. This is recent, Tim, very recent. I'm afraid we're going to be here for quite a while."

He looked away from my expression and started to talk rapidly into his mobile phone.

Chapter Twenty-four

"Film," I said to Sue that evening. "It has to be to do with film."

She sat in her usual place on the settee. William was fast asleep. I had got back to London, eventually, by train from Stansted, to which an obliging Essex bobby ran me in his patrol car. I reflected that it was a good job that Sam had been with me and made the discovery of Jessica Browne's body, otherwise I'd have been in an Essex police station all night.

"A woman researcher in Pimlico, behind the Tate Gallery. A dealing man in Hastings Old Town. Now a woman film archivist in Essex." Sue cocked her head to one side. "What can the connection be?"

"South Africa, films and archives. I'm starting to think about Dorkie's Boer War archive."

"And not the Nicholson angle? Nothing to do with the Art Fund? All those photos of her standing in Nicholson places?"

"La Bassington was apparently tracking Nicholsons sources. She hadn't visited by any means all of them. There's Llys Bach up in Harlech, for example; no sign of that. My feeling is that's unfinished business. Let's try the other line of enquiry; she was a film researcher. Jessica Browne had been running some film on her own projector. Apparently she had a library of films. They haven't seen anything relevant so far, though. So whatever it was, maybe the killer took the film with him."

"Him?"

"It's got to be Champion, Frank Cordwell or Gerry Watson. One of those three. They're the prime suspects. Who else? Sam Johnson is blue-arsing about grabbing them for a grilling. If there's a chink in the alibi of any one of them for yesterday lunchtime, he's had it."

"But what's the motive? What has any of them got to gain?"

I had to admit that the motive aspect worried me. If Bassington had been after blackmail over, say, an affair, there was little to be gained in the cases of Frank Cordwell and Gerry Watson because they weren't married. Pierre Champion was married, with a family over in Paris, but he had been the unconcerned subject of one or two rumoured high-profile affairs in the gossip columns already. These he simply shrugged off. His money seemed to insulate him from damage from any speculation of that sort.

On the other hand, if the film was pornographic there was a lot to play for. Very violent emotions might be aroused.

"I don't know," I said. "I think it's a film. Either valuable in its own right or showing something important. Sam Johnson and a team of experts are working on it. The trouble is that all three of those men have probably visited Jessica Browne at home fairly recently, so forensic evidence of their presence, by DNA, won't necessarily mean anything. He says he's looking through all her papers to find anything he can about an Iris Barry Support Group and maybe a list of members, but it will take time. I was put properly in my place on the sidelines. Kept outside until someone amongst all the teams of people present decided I was purely supernumerary, non-combatant, superfluous to requirements, whatever, and allowed me to go home. Without much thanks for giving them at least a quick start on a murder. She'd only been dead about an hour."

Sue was quiet. I knew what she was thinking. Maybe if I hadn't walked out of breakfast in a huff, the Iris Barry clue might have come up earlier and maybe Jessica Browne would still be alive. Maybe. *Could, could, might*, as Sam had said about my musings on illegitimacy. Too many threads to follow: the last thing I would have imagined when I started looking for an investment in the Nicholsons was a hangover from the acquisition of Wyndham Lewis's *Kermesse* in the form of Iris Barry. The very last thing.

The phone rang.

I picked up the receiver, relieved at the interruption.

"Tim? Is that you?" A clear voice, deep, with a marked South African accent, came over the line.

"Hello? Yes, this is Tim Simpson. Who is that?"

"It's Harry here. Harry Hannibal. Remember me?"

"No, Harry - oh, Alpie! Of course I do. What a surprise! Christ! How are you?"

A deep chuckle. "I'm fine Tim, man. They don't call me Alpie any more now. I'm Harry these days. Old and respectable, like you, I imagine."

"Some chance. Never say die, Alpie. But where are you?"

"I'm in Port Elizabeth. I hear you're not just married but you're a dad as well, now."

"I am. You?"

"Two, Tim. Boy and a girl. Listen, to business: I just heard that poor old Dorkie's in a bad way, eh?"

"He's in hospital, yes. How did you know? I haven't heard from you for yonks."

"Hell, man, he didn't turn up at an Old Rhodian dinner in London the other day. He used to go regularly. Hundreds of them over there, now. So Crod Codrington - remember he used to play lock for Richmond sometimes - he's ex-Rhodes University too, called around Hastings to find out where Dorkie was. They said he'd been badly injured by some burglars and was laid up. Crod's a Grahamstown man as well as ex-Rhodes so he talked to the police and they said a guy called Simpson arrived in the nick of time to bale Dorkie out. I knew it would be you. I got your address from the old college rugby club secretary. Is it true about Dorkie? They say no one is allowed to see him."

"Yes, I'm afraid it is, but they think he'll be OK, Alp - sorry, Harry. In the long run, I mean."

Another chuckle. "You can still call me Alpie, Tim. Thank heaven Dorkie's not too bad then. It's terrible, eh? Things are rough here but we don't think of England as having violence like that. Was it you who pitched up to save him?"

"A bit late, yes, I did. Look, I'm going to see him as soon as the hospital say it's OK. I'll give him your love if you like."

"Good. Please do that. I've got a soft spot for old Dorkie. Blood is thicker than water, you know?"

"Sure."

"How's that pal of yours that used to play on the wing with the girls? Nobby? Went to the bad, didn't he? Became a toffee-nosed policeman, I hear."

"Nobby's well. I'll tell him you asked after him."

Another chuckle. "Tactful boy, you are. Well, let me know how Dorkie shapes up. He's my second uncle twice removed or something like that."

"OK." A thought struck me. "Alpie? Did you ever know a lady called Moira Bassington?"

"Nope. You can't pin any paternity on me, Tim."

"Think. She was in South Africa sometime. Had herself photographed in front of flowering aloes and potentillas."

"That covers a lot of ground. And a lot of girls."

"She may have changed her name. She'd be about forty now. Darkish, good-looking. It's important, Alpie."

Silence. Then: "Did you say Moira? Not Myra?"

"Moira's the name here."

"But Bassington?"

"Yes."

"You're not by any chance thinking of Myra Headington, are you? Hell, Tim, you're not mixed up with her?"

"Who's Myra Headington?"

"Bad news. But she's related to Dorkie, eh? And so, I suppose, to me. Hell, she left for England a long time ago. After she'd got through several rugby sides over here. She had a terrible reputation. Came from Trappes Valley."

"Traps? Dorkie's been raving about traps or being trapped."

"No, not traps. Trappes." He spelt it out. "It's near Bathurst. Named after a British Army captain during settler days. Hicksville, man. No paved roads. Prickly pear and thorn

174

bushes. Cattle and pines. Pineapples, that is. 1820 Settler country. Terrible. She married a poor mutt called Headington who came from a farm way away, over near Cradock somewhere. Dropped him in no time. She was born a Broadbent. Myra Nicole Broadbent. Gee, she caused havoc, man. She moved here to P.E. and was practically a tart. Then she up sticks and went to England. Trying for white, as they say here. Not that she wasn't white already, but you know what I mean. Upping herself a grade. Her mother was always banging on that her family was superior in some way. Superior hell, they lived in a tin shack with a long drop at the bottom of the garden. They were English, though, originally. Probably came out with pith helmets and long khaki shorts. The farm went bust and her father died. Don't know what happened to the mother. Why am I telling you all this?"

"You say she was related to Dorkie?"

"Was?"

"She's dead, Alpie. Murdered by someone she probably knew. Or picked up."

"Jeez. Murdered? Picked up is probably more like it. She visited Dorkie from time to time. Mainly to borrow money. He didn't like her but we whites have got to stick together, you know?"

"That's local humour, is it?"

"Hell, don't take it to heart, Tim. We're in multiracial societies all of us now, aren't we? We have eleven official languages here. Shit, eh?"

"Any other names this delightfully generous lady might have used?"

"She lived with a guy called Jannie van Rooyen for a while. A big rough *kerel* with a short temper, but I think she was too much even for him. I think he followed her to England. And she may have called herself Mrs van Rooyen for a while. But they never lasted long, eh? None of them lasted long with Myra. I haven't heard of her for a long, long time. But I can ask around. Someone will know. It's a small world."

175

Alpie

"Please do, Dorkie. Please ask. This call is costing you. Give me your number, just in case, and I'll call you back in a couple of days."

We exchanged information carefully and finished with suitable, valdictory expressions. Sue was watching me intently.

"Quite the old South African chum network, is it? There's always a new dimension to you, Tim."

I tapped the bit of paper I'd been writing on. "Rugby is multinational these days. And multiracial. But now we have four names, Sue. She could have used four different names: Broadbent, Headington, Van Rooyen and Bassington. Four, just like Edie Nicholson and Laura Riding. No wonder poor Dorkie had that on his mind. But Alpie says she had a big rough boy friend called Jannie van Rooyen, who came over here with her, or after her. That might put the Balaclava brigade into an entirely different context."

"Aha. I couldn't see any of the other three doing that sort of heavies' work. My goodness, she does seem to have played the field, in one way or another."

I smiled down at her. "One girl in her time warms many beds. And maybe plays many parts while doing it. No - don't throw that; you'll wake the boy."

Chapter Twenty-five

Next morning, heading for Hastings, I was seething. There are times when life, to put it mildly, is absolutely bloody.

"I gave Sam Johnson all Alpie's information," I said to Sue, reassuring her once more as we sped along the winding farther section of the road. It was emptier in the fresh mid-morning of a weekday and we were making better progress than I had before. "He is going to check with any information that comes up in Jessica Browne's house about the Iris Barry Group. Under Broadbent, Headington, van Rooyen or Bassington. So I did my duty. I have also told him to look for van Rooyen. Which is what the police are good at. Or are supposed to be good at. I must say it won't be easy."

We were on our way to see Dorkie Collins, having received official approval that morning from Sam Johnson via Foster of Hastings CID. Dorkie was, apparently, sitting up and making a bit of sense. He had asked specifically to see me. Sue immediately called the babysitter, cancelled her Tate schedule, and insisted on coming with me. I had no objection; a hospital visit is all the better for the presence of a sympathetic female. Quite apart from that, I needed Sue to talk to.

My telephone conversations had not induced calm.

According to Sam Johnson, who was not initially in a mood to impart very much confidential police information, there was no reason to detain Pierre Champion, Gerry Watson or Frank Cordwell. Which, reading between the lines, meant that they all must have alibis that were satisfactory or satisfactory enough for them to be at liberty while they were checked.

Frank Cordwell was, according to Sam, deeply upset by Jessica's death. The other two were shocked but Cordwell had showed the most obvious distress. He had had to abandon his interview, emotionally upset, after explaining that he had been away from the Mangate complex in London, visiting a prospective client. Sam's men would be checking on his story.

He said that Jessica Browne was irreplaceable to him. She was an essential part of his operation and had been for a long time.

A vision of Frank Cordwell in his original baggy outfit, shyly but firmly explaining himself to me and Sir Hamish Lang in the City, persisted in my mind. Since then he seemed to have become more relaxed, to wear clothes that suited him better, to be more in control of himself and events. He was pleasant to me without seeming to be very engaged, or concerned, about the future finance question. There was no doubt of the preoccupation with material mentioned by Gerry Watson, I'd seen that in Weybridge, and he certainly seemed to be able to unearth it, which was a quality more important than administrative ability. Pierre Champion must have appreciated that. And yet, and yet; it was Mark Twain who said, in an essay on autobiography of which Jim Stockdale would have approved, that people's acts and words are but the thin visible crust of their lives. Real life is lived in the head; the brain grinds all day long. Their thoughts, seething with fire, are people's history, and these can not be guessed at. Biographies which chart events and actions are but the surface, the clothes and buttons of the man; the biography of the man himself cannot be written down. Frank Cordwell was deeply absorbed in his vocation; his brain was entirely his own province, unrevealed to me. I had little real grasp of him at all.

Why was I suddenly thinking of Mark Twain? Of course; Sir William Nicholson's portrait of him, executed in New York for a woodcut in 1900, was in the book I bought from Mr Goodston.

Once you start these strong muscular hares, they run for miles.

Gerry Watson claimed to have been in Hammersmith until early afternoon. His secretary, however, had left before eleven o' clock to go to a dentist appointment and had been given the afternoon off to visit her mother, who was unwell. Watson had no need of her because he intended to go up to Essex later on. He was adamant that he was in his office until about three. He had then driven up to Mangate to check on some furniture which had been returned at the end of a hire, so as to make sure it was in good nick. The security man at Mangate confirmed that he arrived at about five o' clock. There were possible ways in which his story could be further corroborated and these were being looked into.

Pierre Champion was in Paris. Sam Johnson talked to him on the phone. He had returned from the West Country the day before Jessica's death and gone to Mangate to deliver a film he wanted preserved for safekeeping. Jessica Browne had taken charge of it. After that, he had driven to Stansted and caught a flight to Paris, around seven in the evening. He was in Paris, no question, on the day of her death.

Sam, instinctively reacting to the mention of a film, asked what it was. Pierre Champion replied that it was just a can of old film which he wanted putting in a safe place. Sam, undeterred, demanded to know what was the subject of the film. Champion tried to demur, but when Sam, getting a bit peremptory, told him that a film was probably not just relevant but crucial to his enquiries, and that this might be it, Champion had to buckle under, especially since he had admitted knowing a woman called Moira Bassington as well as, indirectly, employing Jessica Browne. Sam, finding this new connection between the two, was a bit taken aback by his frankness. It was a brief affair, according to Champion, nothing very serious. He met her at a magazine's publicity reception; she was one of the researchers for the issue in question and they had clicked. Yes, he had taken her to vintage car rallies. In his Amilcar. He would be happy to make a statement on his return to England. He had not seen her for several weeks, actually now he thought about it, months. He was in France during the week she was killed.

So what about this film, asked Sam.

Champion demanded reassurance that the information he was about to provide would be treated in absolute confidence. Sam gave that assurance provided that the information did not need to be imparted in the course of solving a crime.

It was an unusual and unique film, Champion said, of an artist painting a picture in his studio in 1949. It served as corroboration of the authenticity of a painting which he, Champion, had bought for a large sum. He was, therefore, anxious to preserve the film and had taken it straight to Mangate for safe-keeping. He had phoned Mangate when the terrible news about Jessica came to him. The film was still safely in place. This had been checked by a junior archivist.

"Christ," I said to Sam, icicles starting to form down my back. "This painting - did he say how much is a large sum?"

"Six figures, apparently," said Sam.

"And who was the artist? Of the painting and, presumably, in the film?"

There was a silence. Then: "I gave an assurance," Sam muttered. "We have to be very careful about these things."

"Sam!" I yelled at him. "I gave you the Iris Barry lead! I've just given you the crucial lead on Bassington and her other names! You can unravel her life now. Do you want me to help or not? Do you?"

"All the same - "

"Sam!"

"Confidential. This is absolutely confidential. You are not to reveal it or make any commercial use of it. Right?"

"Right! All right. I promise to keep stumm."

"Nicholson," he almost muttered again. "The painting is by Ben Nicholson. Sorry, but Champion seems to have upstaged you, Tim."

Chapter Twenty-six

"What a bastard," I said to Sue, as we sped down the last fast bit of road round Pembury. "What an utter, smarmy, half-frog, ruthless Clever Dick. How did he know? Eh? How did he know that Ben Nicholson was next on the agenda?"

"Tim, keep calm. Calm. It may not have been beyond his wit to guess that there was a major painter you haven't got in the Fund yet and have a go at him. He's a risk-taker, a bit of a gambler. He has his own sources. He may just fancy a flutter. Why not?"

"I don't believe it. You've said it all about coincidences yourself. He's been sniffing round the bloody Bank for ages. He likes to bet on certainties. I just don't see how he found out, though. None of us would let on, none of us, and that includes Charles."

"Maybe those two thugs drummed it out of Dorkie Collins."

I scratched my jaw whilst overtaking a lorry loaded with gypsum plasterboard on the hill down to Lamberhurst. "You think those two were working for Champion?"

"I don't know. But I do think they were hirelings of some sort. You need money and connections to employ men like that. None of the others is in that league. So my first thought is of Pierre Champion. He must have all sorts working for him."

"Jim Stockdale might have guessed," I murmured, thoughtfully. "He ran through the books over there with a very intense interest. And turned the conversation that way when we went to his floral opening night."

Sue's voice went thoughtful. "It's really hard to imagine that Jim would be involved in such a thing. I know I've been suspicious but I'm worried that we might be becoming totally paranoid. Even a boyfriend of Janet's isn't safe from our suspicions. Didn't Nobby tell you to drop that line of thought?"

"He did, but you never know. Scanning those books would give Jim Stockdale a good clue. Yet there's no evidence of his having any connection with Champion. It is possible that poor old Dorkie, with the fakes staring at him and his attackers from the wall, might have had to cough it up. But they took something, and I think that something was more important to them than anything else."

"He'll soon be able to tell us what it was, thank heavens."

"Yes, but it's a bit late." I gestured reminiscently as we passed the Royal Oak inn at Whatlington. "What really bugs me is what happens now. If I buy a Ben Nicholson for the Fund, that slick bastard Champion will probably double his money. He'll be waiting for me to go ahead before letting the world know he's got one, too. If I don't, he'll eventually announce his purchase, with this bloody film, to the same world, and leave us behind. We'll look as though we are too dumb or timid to keep up. In some respects I feel I am being driven to buy a Ben Nicholson, yet either way, he'll upstage me."

"Good heavens, it isn't personal, is it? There's surely enough room in the collecting world for both of you, isn't there? Think of everyone else who's got Ben Nicholson in their collection. What about all of them? Besides, you're supposed to be pitching for his business at Mangate, aren't you? You can't afford to let this get in the way of business that the Bank urgently needs and for which they're depending on you."

I chuckled. "Oh, boy. I can just see Hamish Lang's face if he finds out I've told that frog-eating chancer Pierre Champion to sod off. Especially after his careful introductions and dubious looks in my direction, as though Freddy Harbledown wasn't all there when he appointed me."

"Well you can't tell Champion to sod off, can you? You don't *know*, Tim, officially you don't know. You promised Sam Johnson to keep it to yourself. You promised. It will have to remain a secret as long as Champion wants it to. You can't behave like a spoilt kid who's annoyed because another kid's got his new toy before you have. This male territorial business is so childish."

"I agree. Absolutely, Sue. It's typical of Pierre Champion. Utterly childish. He wants to rub my nose in the fact that he's peed on my tree at the same time as I've got to truckle to him for his business. It's typical of the man. I must not give him the satisfaction of reacting to it."

"Well, there you are, then. I'm glad you see it for what it is. A mature view of these things is essential."

"Absolutely. A mature view is what I need to take. Calm, mature and rational. The archive project is very important. I must smile and behave like a diplomat. Show no resentment."

"Right."

"Then I'll break his bloody nose."

"Tim!"

I grinned. "Well, there are more ways of killing a cat than by stuffing it with cream, Sue. Ah, we're coming into Hastings. From the Ridge where the hospital stands we can look at the sea, sparkling with distant promise. Poor old Dorkie is waiting for us. Fear naught, and all may yet be well."

Chapter Twenty-seven

Dorkie had a strange thing about ha-de-das. He said, quite rightly, that anyone who has sat at twilight listening to them as they wing home back over the bush to roost never forgets the sound. The harsh cries are plaintive, sardonic and raucous but oddly appealing, like a child you know is only making a dreadful noise because it needs you. It is the cry of something that feels excluded and alone.

As though the cry were not enough, the ha-de-da ibis is an ungainly grey-brown bird with a squat body, frayed wide wings, almost no tail and a down-curving beak like the spout-tube on a melting oil can. Its ground behaviour looks clumsy yet it has a charm you cannot help liking. As it lumbers along on its two scaly legs its head seems always half-cocked, alert for worms or crickets while it pretends to ignore you; Dorkie said he always felt that a ha-de-da was waiting to see which way you, an intruder, would jump.

Dorkie was like many exiles, seizing upon small symbolic things that twist the knife of poignant regret rather than dwelling on the major reason for their expatriation.

When really disturbed the ha-de-da makes its loud, nerve-jarring, startling squawk and flaps gawkily off to avoid attack, taking a mate or two with it. You often see two or three of them stumping about together in irregular, inexplicable combinations. Which is odd because although they're gregarious enough to congregate in trees at night, they are supposed to be solitary when nesting. Something that ha-de-das and Moira Bassington seemed to have in common. According to Sam Johnson, her flat in Pimlico gave little clue as to her irregular, inexplicable combinations. Evidence of the circles in which she had moved, from post-colonial to vintage cars, had been eradicated from the perch in which she congregated at night.

Addresses are given to us to conceal our whereabouts. There had to be another one, somewhere.

The ha-de-da used to be wild but nowadays a lot of them potter grumpily around suburbia, pecking at this and that in disappointment, as though empty, thorny Africa once fed them better. The bird is a great survivor of domestic encroachment without being in any way tame. Unlike the guinea fowl, which has two-legged predators to cope with as well as the rest, the ha-de-da doesn't have to worry very much about humans. Africans regard it as unlucky, spooked in some way, carrying spells as puckish as a tokolosh. No Xhosa disturbs the ha-de-da and precious few of his dogs.

I've no idea what it tastes like, anyway.

The ha-de-da doesn't have a nice tourist image like a springbok or a koala. It isn't gaudy and exotic or spotted and violent, or shaped like a squashed handbag. You won't find craft models of ha-de-das in the new curio and craft shops along the Cape routes like you will guinea fowls or hippos or ostriches or swarms of carved elephants. The Xhosa boys don't make clever wire models like they do eagles, artesian windmills and Harley Davidsons to offer as you speed by like a flash lad in your German or Japanese car. They don't sculpt ha-de-das or print pictures of them on tea towels. To the Africans, ha-de-das won't sell.

Dorkie liked them and so do a lot of Eastern Province whites, but you don't come across them much elsewhere. For instance, I've never seen any ha-de-da souvenirs of South Africa. No paintings or drawings or pottery or stuffed children's toys. The only memory people take of them is perhaps those wild cries, ringing in their ears.

Or maybe a set of holiday snaps.

He sat upright on his hospital bed, looking straight ahead rather blankly, as though his thoughts were elsewhere. We were expected; his guardian policeman let us through to him with a cheerful remark and the news that Inspector Foster had had a talk to him. Foster sent us his regards and apologies that he had been called elsewhere, to another crisis of some sort. Dorkie was, the attendant nurse said, much better but still frail. We should try not to tire him too much. She looked with approval at Sue as she spoke; it is always a good idea to bring a woman to a hospital bedside.

There were bandages round his head and one hand was completely wrapped in white, but his face wasn't skew or an eye dropped, for all that he'd had a stroke. His features were still lined but leathery, like a colonial whose skin has been exposed to more sunlight and wind than we would normally get. According to the nurse, he had been more concussed than anything else and the stroke was, mercifully, mild. His mind was not affected.

As soon as he saw us, Dorkie perked up. The gaze became focused; a smile moved his lips.

"Tim. Sue. Great to see you." He accepted a brief embrace from Sue and a handshake from me. "I owe you Tim, man. Foster told me. Hell, I owe you."

"Nothing. You owe me nothing."

"Just my life, eh? You're probably right."

"That's not what I meant, you old buzzard."

"No, of course not. I know that. But if you hadn't turned up, I'd have been a goner, for sure."

We sat down beside him, handing over the flowers and a bunch of grapes so standard, but often so appreciated, to hospital visits. "What did they want, Dorkie?" I asked, as Sue put the flowers in an empty vase. "Those two thugs?"

He looked cautiously towards the police guard and seemed reassured that he had moved tactfully out of earshot. "I told them - the police - that they wanted cash and valuables. Which is strictly speaking true, because they did. They took what spare cash I had."

"Were they after your Boer War stuff as well?"

He shook his head. "No. They wanted the film. And they got it."

"Film? What film?"

His gaze fell and he didn't answer. I opened my mouth, but Sue gave me a surreptitious shake of the head to indicate that he needed time.

Eventually, he looked up at us. "It was hers. Myra's. She left it with me for safe keeping."

"Myra? That's Moira Bassington, as I know of her?"

He nodded dumbly and then spoke. "She's dead, isn't she?"

"Yes. I'm sorry, Dorkie. When did you hear?"

"Inspector Foster told me. I still haven't quite taken it in. I hadn't heard, you see. She lived such a clandestine life. I suppose I tried to tell you about her, in a way, when we talked about the Nicholsons. The four names that Edie used. I was thinking about Myra then."

"Alpie Hannibal called," I said, gently. "He sent you his best, Dorkie. He told me she came from your neck of the woods."

"Yes. Trappes Valley. We were distantly related. We were closer than the blood relationship might seem, but it was a family thing." He shook his head very slightly, as though the movement hurt him. "She used to think I was a sort of Dutch Uncle, I suppose. She needed someone, you see, someone she could trust. She lived a lonely yet exploited life. There were so many men - so many - "

He stopped, and bit his lip. I waited while he composed himself, then asked, "Why did she pick on the name Bassington?"

He smiled faintly. "She was self-educated. Old books from junk shops. She saw that story as symbolic. She was exiled to this country - she didn't like it, she thought it was awful here - because there was nothing left for her in Trappes Valley. She fell out with her mother. She said her mother wouldn't help her. She tried P.E. for a while but she realised she was sliding into squalor and decided to make a clean break. And now she's died here, away from home, like Bassington in the story. She was trying to make enough money to go back. It's ironic, isn't it?"

I nodded, thinking sadly of her bare-shouldered, sunny image in the photograph before the flowering aloes. "What was the Nicholson connection? Why did she go to all those places?"

"That was her stupid mother's fault." A little animation came back into his tones. "Stupid woman. There was a story that her grandmother, who came from London, was an illegitimate Nicholson. They even had a painting they said was by William, passed down the family. A sort of gift from the artist in compensation for making his model pregnant. I told them how silly it was as soon as I saw it. You only had to go to a gallery and look at a real one to see that it was daub, an imitation of that style. Lots of families have things like that up in an attic; people invent histories for them. There was probably no truth in the story but they called her Myra Nicole, the Nicole being a sort of gesture to it." He frowned ruefully. "I didn't know that Myra had pinned some sort of hope on the painting. I destroyed that hope as soon as I saw it and opened my big mouth. But the Nicholson thing was still important to her. She spent a lot of time with different boyfriends, getting them to take her round this country. She was still working on that, the last time I saw her."

"She hadn't finished visiting all those Nicholson places?"

"No. There were a lot, you know."

"Quite an effort, it must have been."

He nodded sadly. "It was an identity thing, important, to be a descendant of Sir William Nicholson, not just a nobody from a tin shack in Trappes Valley without a flush toilet to its name."

Sue leant forward. "Was it as bad as all that? Her background, I mean?"

Dorkie made a small gesture with his unbandaged hand. "That's another irony. In some ways, she had an idyllic childhood. It was safe. The Africans used to be very friendly there because they all lived off the land together and though they could see the whites were better off than them, they weren't that much. There were justifiable resentments but on the whole, relations were good. She could run free and barefoot in a way no town child can. She loved the flora and fauna of the area. In the past, the Boers didn't dispute the place, you know. They knew it wasn't worth anything like the Free State or the Karoo or the Transvaal. Just rocks and thorns, stone-faced krantzes, floods and droughts and crop failure. But now that their northern territories have gone to hell in an armoured car the Afrikaners rather like Eastern Province. Those dismal farms up roadless prickly kloofs and beside drifts are being bought by Jo'burgers and Vaalies and done up as holiday homes. The Broadbents got nothing for their place; in fact the bank repossessed it. But now things are changing. In pound sterling terms, they're still cheap but they may not be for ever. She might have made it back home. She dreamed of it all the time. I'm too old now, I've settled here, but with a bit more money, Myra could have done it."

"Did you know a guy called van Rooyen? Jannie van Rooyen?"

Dorkie shook his head. "Never met him. She spoke of him, briefly. I'd left South Africa long before she lived with him in P.E. A big *ou* with a bad temper, I heard."

"Alpie thought he'd come over here. I wondered if he was one of the two who attacked you. He'd have an accent, I assume."

Dorkie shook his head. "I'd have known the accent at once. Although, come to think of it, only the smaller one spoke. He had the usual sort of sub-Cockney voice. I think I recognised him. I've told Inspector Foster. I think it was Danny Mahoney, but I can't be certain. They hit me, which dazed me, and he was muffled by his balaclava."

"What was on the film they wanted? South African stuff?"

"No, not at all. It was Nicholson, Ben Nicholson, painting, in his studio around 1949. Myra was nearly frantic with delight when she found it. She was a good researcher, you know, but the pay was poor. She looked hard and came across it in some fellow's collection of ex-British Council stuff. After the war, they were promoting British culture and Ben Nicholson was one of their favourites. The film wasn't considered good enough to use - something duff about the sound track - but this chap kept it. He let Myra have it for nothing, she said." He frowned and another sad look came into his face. "I didn't ask in return for what favours."

I looked at Sue, whose eyes were saying you have knowledge but you can't use it, you promised Sam Johnson.

"Did you always keep it for her?"

"Oh no, she only brought it over to Hastings quite recently. I hadn't seen her for a long time. She'd been living with some fellow on and off but she kept a flat in Pimlico she rented cheap, she said. For business purposes. She wanted me to keep the film for safety. She said something about it being a form of insurance and I mustn't lose it. So I agreed."

"If the two thugs got what they wanted, why were they still tormenting you?"

"They wanted to know if it was the only copy."

"Well it was, wasn't it?"

He hesitated, then shook his head. "There are one or two studios in Hastings who do good copy work very reasonably. I got one to copy Myra's film just to be on the safe side. Made a video of it, actually. When those two asked if this was the only copy, I was already confused. I said it was but I must have been unconvincing; they didn't believe me. They wanted to be certain, I think. They turned nasty. That was when, thank God, you arrived."

"So there is another copy?"

He nodded.

"Can I see it?"

"Of course you can. But it's nothing to do with the Nicholsons I've got for your Art Fund. The ones I phoned you about."

"No?"

191

"No." He looked at me anxiously. "Our agreement still stands, does it?"

I didn't hesitate, despite an image of Pierre Champion's face, triumphant, coming to me. "Of course it does, Dorkie. One thing, though: did you ever tell Moira - Myra - about me?"

"No. Absolutely not. I always promised complete confidentiality with you. As I did for her."

"OK. Our agreement stands."

He beamed. At last, he actually beamed. "Great, Tim. Got a pen and a bit of paper?"

"Yes." I felt Sue, beside me, starting to tense with anticipation as I took a pen and a business card out of my pocket. This was what she'd really come with me for; she has the sense of the chase as highly developed as anyone.

"You haven't got far to go. Write down this address. Right here in Hastings. Well, St. Leonards actually. You can go round as soon as you leave the hospital and after you pick up the video." Dorkie gave me an intense, appealing stare. "You will take it for me, won't you? I want that kind of bad luck out of the house. Before I have to come home to it."

Chapter Twenty-eight

In the dark print in the dark hall, Buller's troops were still crossing the Tugela river, caught forever urging themselves forward with limbers, horses, guns and ammunition. Outside, the bicycle was still chained to the railings. Some things seem to get stuck.

In the downstairs front showroom the same ugly images in bitter prints hung on the walls. Sue looked at them curiously without comment. I crossed to the shelves on the wall opposite the door, where jugs and other pottery and memorabilia mingled with each other. There among them, put at the back since otherwise it would have stuck out like a sore thumb, was a pottery jug with the upper torso of a man in red uniform and dark cocked hat moulded on it. His epaulettes gleamed with silver lustre. Nothing to do with the Boer War; this was earlier. I looked at the caption incised under the beaky face.

"The Marquis Wellington jug," I said, picking it up. "Dorkie said he couldn't have the William Nicholson painting but he had one of the jugs. Something nearly as good for a man with a thing about William. Here it is. A wonder Moira Bassington didn't want it."

Sue shivered. "Let's not waste time, Tim. In the kitchen, is where he said."

"OK, Sue." I put the jug back on the shelf.

We went into the kitchen, where the blue and white pottery from T G Green adorned the dresser shelves. Even the rolling pin I'd broken was still there. Next to them, innocuous and plain white, was a rectangular pottery jar with a slightly domed lid. On the side was printed a simple caption.

Gebruik Smit's Tee.

"Meant to be a tea caddy," I said, picking up the lid. "I wonder who Smit was. Ah, here we are."

The video fitted neatly into the rectangular shape, covered by a couple of bills. As normal and as unremarkable a hiding place as any. I took the flat cassette out reverently and slid it into my jacket pocket.

"Safe and sound," I said. "But let's see if it brings bad luck with it."

"Tim." Sue's voice was cautious. "Don't tempt the gods."

"I'm not superstitious. Let's go, Sue."

Technically, Dorkie was correct. The household to which he had directed us was not in Hastings. You crossed the unmarked divide somewhere before going west of the London Road which arrows down the centre of St.Leonards to the sea. Then you entered an area more salubrious, settled and suburban than the great cliffed terraces of old houses jumbled along the border between the two indistinguishable boroughs of Hastings to the east and St.Leonards to the west. Due to previous experience, Sue and I had little difficulty in finding our way to the residential road we sought. We moved with speed and anticipation, since I had phoned in advance from Dorkie's bedside and let him confirm who I was.

The door of the unremarkable, modern detached house, made of red brick and gardened with, amongst other things, potentillas and African lilies, swung open almost at once to my pressure on the bell.

The Barboroughs were in their late sixties. He was bald, a bit of fair hair remaining round the edges, with a large stomach retained by a sky-blue shirt above khaki trousers and suede shoes. She was carefully coiffed with neat white hair and wore a fawn suit of modern, synthetic fabric. A gold brooch was pinned to her lapel. Both were much cleaner, brighter coloured and more carefully tended than English equivalents might have been. They stood ranged almost in formation in their carpeted hall, he to the front, she slightly behind, like a District Officer and his lady receiving guests at an official reception.

"Welcome," he said, shaking my hand. "I'm Sandy Barborough. This is my wife Betty. Thank you for phoning in advance. Dawson told us to expect you - how is he, by the way?"

"Dawson?"

He smiled. "Dawson Collins. I expect you call him Dorkie. That's what we all called him in P.E."

"Oh." I smiled back. "I've never thought about where the name came from. Now I know. How do you do?"

Introductions over, we were ushered into a modern living room with a Shepherd print of an elephant waving its ears prominent on one wall and a green Tretchikoff siren pouting on another. There was no sign of any Nicholsons. African reproduction was the order of the décor; I took in an ebony elephant and a carved warthog on side tables as Sue and I sat on a sensible, Dralon-covered settee.

"Dorkie's much better," I said, by way of a belated answer. "Sitting up and taking nourishment at last."

"Thank heavens." Betty Barborough had a stronger accent than her husband. "We were really worried about him when we heard." She made a vague gesture round the room. "We haven't been here all that long, although we came back to England a while ago. Our main things are still packed, so it's still a bit of a *gemors* in here. It's been a very anxious time for us and the news of his attack was a terrible shock. We thought we would be absolutely safe in this country."

"You've left South Africa for good?"

"We still have a small cottage at Kenton on Sea." She made it sound like Essex. "We hope to go back for holidays. But after we were held up and robbed three times at home - that was in Johannesburg - we decided enough was enough. The third time we were both beaten up." She hesitated for a moment, searching for words. "I thought they would kill us. Our neighbours were killed after they'd raped both mother and daughter. Then we were carjacked by a man with a gun. Sandy still has a British passport, so we were lucky. We were able to leave. There's been no problem about living here. Just money, of course."

"I'm very sorry. It must be a dreadful upheaval and experience."

She smiled slightly. "It's over, now."

Yet Moira Bassington, I thought to myself, hated it here. She wanted nothing more than to go back. It must be a question of age. The younger you are, the less you worry about yourself.

"Can we offer you some refreshment? Coffee? Tea?"

We accepted coffee and Betty Barborough disappeared towards the kitchen. Her husband gave me a careful stare.

"I've heard all about you from Dorkie. He says that you can be relied upon to be absolutely discreet."

"Yes, certainly. About our sources, if requested."

"Look, we've lost a hell of a lot in leaving. With the rand at sixteen to the pound, this place is hellishly expensive for us. I'm not sure if we won't end up in Spain or maybe France. Somewhere warm where food and wine are much cheaper. We were wealthy in South Africa but all I could afford here was this house and some small savings in the bank. That was all open and above board, eh? We were allowed to bring that much out. But there are limits, as I'm sure you know. The SA Government is strict about exchange control."

"I understand," I said, feeling Sue shift uncomfortably on the sofa beside me.

"We were allowed to bring our household possessions." He looked round him without enthusiasm. "Not much, but domestic furniture et cetera was OK. I had all our paintings packed by Pickfords and shipped with the furniture just as though they were normal decoration. We had a couple of good South African paintings: Tinus De Jongh and a Joss Nell. They muttered about those a bit but white painters are out of fashion now, so in the end we weren't penalised. Actually, we had one or two British paintings like Russell Flint and a Bernard Dunstan; they didn't reckon anything to those. Nor the Nicholsons." He put on a wry expression. "My heart was in my mouth, I can tell you, when Pickfords packed the lot and put them in a wardrobe that went into a container. Six weeks to deliver them here, counting time at sea. I didn't dare insure them for their real value. We've been on tenterhooks. Just when they were due, there was another delay, here at British customs. A further week or two of nail biting."

"There's been a bit of a *komplikasie* I remember Dorkie saying, a bit of a *gemors*. I suppose that must have been it?"

"For sure. Anyway, to cut a long story short, eventually everything was released, no problem. The paintings are safely in our bank vault in London. I've got good photographs here to show you. If you're interested you can of course see the real thing up in town."

"That would be essential."

He leant forward as his wife came into the room, carrying a loaded tray. "The most important thing to us is discretion. We are reluctant to do the obvious and give them to one of the famous auctioneers to sell. There's a chance the SA Government people will find out and there could be repercussions. Even though there shouldn't be and it's all been done openly, you never can tell when they might change their minds."

"We still have family in South Africa," Betty Barborough said, putting her tray down. "They could be penalised financially. Or worse. And we do want to go back. To visit."

"They're your paintings, I take it? You have full title to them?"

Her husband nodded sadly. "My grandfather had a real love of art. And a good eye. He bought from established galleries and kept receipts. I've got the documentation, of course. Including his will and my father's. It's a blow to have to sell them, but we have no alternative."

"I'm sorry."

"Look, it's our problem. I mustn't bore you with it. Here, let me get the photos for you."

He heaved himself up and went across to a bureau while his wife served us coffee. A sense of unreality began to seep into my mind. After everything that had happened, was this mundane suburban living room to provide the culmination of my chase?

"These are the ones by Sir William Nicholson."

"Ones. You mean you have more than one?"

"Oh, yes. Two of each."

Ignoring my open mouth, he handed me two colour photographic prints, quite professional by the look of them, and Sue took my arm, nails digging in, as I received them from him, letting her breath fall warm and moist on my cheek.

I found myself looking at an Impressionistic painting of a Cape Dutch house, white, with trees and colourful garden vegetation round it. A shock of recognition shook me.

"This is Vergelegen," I said, struggling with the pronunciation. "I've eaten in the restaurant there. It belongs to Anglo-American, doesn't it?"

"Well done." Betty Barborough was thoroughly approving. "Yes, it is. Painted in 1931. It was still a private house, then."

I sat holding the picture, remembering that the seventeenth century house, home of an early Dutch pioneer called van der Stel, was mentioned by William Nicholson in his letters to his daughter Liza sometime in 1939.

"I'd no idea he painted it," I said.

"He left this in South Africa. Probably with Lady Phillips. Somehow it found its way to a gallery in Cape Town. Sandy's grandfather bought it there. The other one he bought in England. He came over regularly."

The other photograph showed a still life of a pottery jug with flowers in it, blue and pink, with a green dish beside the jug. A knife and fork were laid on the tabletop between the flowers and the dish. It was signed and dated 1928.

"A classic William Nicholson," Sue said, almost in my ear. "Not bordering on abstract and more decorative than many."

"Here are the Ben Nicholsons." Sandy Barborough held up

two more photos. "I shan't worry too much about selling them. My grandfather took to Modernism and abstraction, particularly in the fifties, but I've never been keen. My father wasn't either; he thought Grandpa was wasting his money. One of them is better than the other, though, I think."

"At least you can see something normal in that one," his wife agreed pointing at one photo. "The other's meaningless to me."

He handed me the two photos. I heard Sue suck in her breath as she saw the top one.

"A white relief," she said, softly. "Like the one in the Tate, bought by the Contemporary Art Society. Nineteen thirties?"

"Nineteen thirty-five," nodded Betty Barborough.

I stared at the photo. The relief, of the kind which had incensed Jeremy, reminded me of the Nicholson Wall installed by Sir Geoffrey Jellicoe at Sutton Place. The way the square areas were built up, with circles inset into them, was very similar. At Sutton Place the wall is seen head-on with a reflection in Jellicoe's pond, doubly accented as it were, so that Jellicoe, who was a keen enthusiast, could expound upon its effect on the subconscious. Here the work looked modest, as though the building up of depth by card and board was easily achieved, familiar now that it has been so often done. But the use of building board was novel in the thirties, and the painting with white oil paint misunderstood. Since then all sorts of speculation, encompassing expressions of the concept of the infinite, have dogged the constant motifs of square and circle Ben Nicholson used.

Given his and his father's love lives, triangles might have been more appropriate.

The second painting was a nineteen forties window number, like his famous Mousehole painting.

"Nineteen forty-nine?" Sue's query drew another approving nod from both Barboroughs. "A sill life-landscape, he called this type of work. Oil on canvas?"

More nods.

I stared at the arrangement. A view out of a window over what might have been St.Ives was interrupted by a still group of objects in post-Cubist style, with perspectives flattened and confusing, so that the Cubist objects seemed to be suspended somewhere rather than located on the window sill. The colours were greens, browns, black, dull yellow or buff and blue for some harbour water and sky. 1949 was the year he and Barbara Hepworth took to working well apart, in studios across the town, and she often stayed overnight in hers. There was a strange feeling to the mixture of realism and abstraction, as though the viewer, like the artist, was caught between the two.

"What do you think?" Sandy Barborough's voice was anxious.

"Can you just answer a couple of questions for me?"

"Of course."

I looked up at him. "Have you ever met or been approached by, a man called Pierre Champion?"

He frowned. "I've heard that name somewhere. But no, I haven't. I've kept this very confidential. I trust Dorkie and he says I can trust you. And your wife, if you'll excuse me, who Dorkie says is an important member of the Tate staff."

"Thanks. She is. What about Jannie van Rooyen?'

A shake of the head. "No. Never heard of him. Van Rooyen's a common name but I don't know a Jannie."

"Moira Bassington?"

"No." He was getting uneasy.

"Sorry. She might have called herself Myra Headington. Or Broadbent."

A slight smile now came to his face and he glanced slyly at his wife. "I've heard of Myra Headington. Not in Jo'burg though. She was a scandal in P.E. years ago."

"More than a scandal," his wife said.

He still looked amused. "She bothered poor Dorkie. I mean, he's her uncle, isn't he? Or something like that. I thought she came over here a long time ago."

"She did. But she hasn't contacted you recently?"

"No. Definitely not."

"I should hope not." His wife was much firmer.

I blinked. I wasn't going to get answers I was seeking here.

They were looking at me anxiously still, waiting. A pang of remorse went through me for torturing them with suspense.

"They look marvellous," I said. "All four of them. Don't you think so, Sue?"

"Yes," she said, in a tone that meant it.

I looked at Sandy Barborough. "Your grandfather was a remarkable man. He obviously had taste and the courage of his own eye. The William paintings weren't hard to like and buy, but Ben was a very peculiar taste in his time. It wasn't until late in his life, and after many international awards, and a torrent of publicity, that his stuff took off. Never mind that, though. Subject to examination and verification, I think my board would approve their purchase." I paused, feeling that maybe I was coming over as a bit evasive. "The decision is largely with me, but it does have to be approved."

"How much?" Sandy Barborough blurted out the question, then held up his hand. "Sorry, I realise there are caveats you have to issue at this stage, but can you give us an idea? Just an estimate? Without obligation?"

I braced myself. Sue had gone deadly quiet. "The William Nicholsons would have been about fifty thousand each, maximum, a year ago. Since then, things have changed, as I'm sure you know. The view of Vergelegen is less desirable here than the still life although South African stuff does seem to have its specialist buyers. I'd say between a hundred and fifty and two hundred thousand for those two. The Ben Nicholsons are more difficult in view of all the trouble in recent years but I'd say about three hundred thousand for the one and nearly half a million for the other." I waited, watching their faces, white and tense and frozen. "We save you the odd twenty percent commission of course, by buying directly off you. So putting all four together, and assuming all is correct and so on, I'd say we are talking of something approaching a million pounds."

Sandy Barborough unfroze his expression.

"For something approaching a million pounds," he said, "they are yours."

Chapter Twenty-nine

When you take a gamble, you take a gamble: no crying once the chips are down. I drove back in a state of high adrenalin. If those paintings were kosher, and my gut feeling was positive, then the gamble was a good one: fair to the Barboroughs but with plenty of upward potential for the Fund. Of course art is about illusions; an art dealer sells illusions the same way as a Ferrari salesman; they are not retailing nice pictures or useful transport. Inspiration and therapy are the business of art.

We talked a lot on the way home. I don't remember much of what we said, not in terms of the actual words; we were too excited. Adrenalin pumped through my system; Sue shifted from side to side in her seat the whole way.

In my jacket pocket, the video made a flat rectangular lump which seemed to push against my hip with insistent, self-contained energy.

As soon as we were back in Onslow Gardens, I got us both a gin and tonic, put the video in the machine and switched on. We sat in front of the monitor screen together, glasses in hand, staring.

"This is it," I said. "This must be what the whole thing is about. We've got Dorkie and Moira Bassington's bad luck charm in front of us. Let's hope it answers all our questions."

Sue didn't answer. A shiver went through her and she took a sip of her drink.

The screen lit up. There was no sound. A run-in of rather speckled blank film suddenly gave way, in grainy black and white, to a shot of a studio with battened walls painted white. In the corner there was a motor bike. Against one wall was a large geometric abstract painting with a central square panel, slightly skew, containing a circle. Further away could be seen another, similar painting, also against the wall. There was a wooden table with jars containing brushes and a bottle of some necessary artistic liquid like turpentine or varnish or perhaps something alcoholic standing on it. The focus moved slowly, showing other paintings on the walls. The floor was boarded and spotted with what must be assumed to be paint.

"Those big panels," Sue said, suddenly, "must be the ones he did for a shipping line in Glasgow. For a new vessel they were commissioning, I think. This must be around 1949, Tim. They were obviously so big that they had to stand on the floor."

I was looking at the motor bike. There was an idea in my head that Ben Nicholson had an old car, which he drove erratically, but I couldn't quite remember. Just as I was thinking about it, and cars like Amilcars, he appeared on this silent screen.

He was small, alert, rather neat-featured, with not much chin. His hair had receded quite a long way, which is perhaps why he often wore a beret in that thirties-artistic or Spanish Republican style, but it was not on here. He wore a short-sleeved shirt and his arms were strong, with competent hands. They were sporting and artistic arms, capable of producing parabolas, lines, circles and squares. He looked somewhat like his father, with the same large forehead and strong eyebrows which quirked easily into what seemed like a frown.

I sat quite still. This was Ben Nicholson: the man who in his time even the most hostile critics of abstract art admitted to be the most committed and consistent abstract artist in Britain. If to some he was a great man and to others he was of no significance, there was at least agreement on this point. Either this was a genius I was looking at or someone leading art up a blind alley. There seems to be no middle ground to occupy.

In front of my eyes he turned and moved to gesture at the first large painting standing on the floor. Considering that he would have been around fifty-five years old at the time of this film, if it was made when Sue thought, and that he suffered from asthma, he didn't look too bad. His eyes looked piercingly at the camera. All his life he took anti-asthma drugs, of which ephedrine had effects he probably didn't understand. He was also plagued by insomnia, for which he tied a spotted silk handkerchief - his father's style again - over his head at night. But on the screen he looked well-kept and keen.

Now he was pointing at a painting on the wall and talking to the camera.

"What on earth happened to the soundtrack?" Sue sounded tense and irritable. "God, it would be fantastic if we could hear him speaking."

"Maybe that was why the film wasn't used by the British Council."

"All those influences," she murmured. "From Wyndham Lewis and Picasso to Mondrian. Miro, as well."

"What about Barbara Hepworth?"

"Of course. She was the intellectual to his instinctive art. What a relationship that was. And how tragic her death."

"Burnt in bed when the worse for wear."

"Yes. But that's not the way she should be remembered."

Now the focus was back on the big panel. Nicholson stood beside it, perhaps to show how big it was, certainly taller than him. He wore light coloured trousers and these seemed to emphasise his wiry figure. The film moved to the table with brushes and paints, then to the paintings on the walls. I noticed one with a whorled design, rather like the fake Dorkie had.

Nicholson commanded the centre of the screen once again. It was hard to believe that this confident- looking, physically sinuous man received an allowance from his father until he was forty-five and was in recurrent financial difficulties until the period we were looking at. Or that he suffered from constant ill health, although that does not seem to have diminished an amorous disposition as active as his father's. There were years of struggle but, after 1945, Ben Nicholson played the British Council card brilliantly. Active in his own promotion, he kept himself as much as possible in the mind of everyone influential in the art world. Travel and movement were essential to his scheme. His work was exhibited all over Europe. By some, he was hailed as the first British artist of international significance, despite Henry Moore, Barbara Hepworth and Graham Sutherland having rival claims. Even Sir - as he was by then - Kenneth Clark at last took him up. Nicholson turned down a knighthood and the offer of other honours. He said, despite his promotion of his work, that he didn't believe in the culture of the individual. He destroyed letters and personal memorabilia almost obsessively. It was a public and triumphal climax, set against a background of infidelity, strife and domestic discord. But on the film, he looked calm. On the film everything in the studio was ordered, under control; a pattern was being created.

That's what films are for.

Janet Heath's remarks about *Out of Africa* came to me. Was the scene I was watching a fiction as well?

The focus moved away again, as though the cameraman had lost his sense of place in the programme of events. There was another traverse of the paintings on the walls, then the screen went blank.

"Show seems to be over," I said, stopping the machine and putting it on to rewind. "Want to see it again?"

"Of course." Sue took another sip of her drink. "I don't understand."

"What?"

"Why is it so important? Why kill, or torture, for it? It's not worth that much in itself, is it? I mean, it's a valuable archive or record. No one would dispute that. I felt quite in awe looking at him like that, although there must be other, better films of him in existence. Why is this one so important? Just a fragment like this?"

"Something to do with Moira Bassington's life. And probably Jessica Browne's."

"But what? I mean where did she get it?"

"You heard what Dorkie said. Presumably its origins are kosher. Here we are; it's rewound again."

We sat through another screening without speaking. I watched the same views come up on the screen, like enduring one of those forties Government documentaries that the comedian Harry Enfield loves to parody. The style brought rationing, coupons, earnest and condescending domestic advice from clipped-vowel commentators, if there had been any, to mind. Here was a man who belonged to that era. An era, before and after the deprivations of war, of serious social concern, egalitarian principles, anti-establishment movements of high principle and stewed tea. Ben was not a drinker. His father liked a glass of the right wine to accompany a fastidious meal. Ben was all the pi-jawed things Mr Goodston had deplored when compared with the *fin-de-siecle*, Naughty Nineties, hedonistic anarchism of his father. Could that be why his art is so unpopular with many people? Is its subconscious message actually one of order and conformity and responsibility rather than the imaginative capture and wondering observation of humanity and nature?

I remembered Mr Goodston once musing that people who believe in the structure of society can cock elaborate snooks at it and its morals for their enjoyment. That is the pure, safe devilment of the schoolboy who has no scope to alter the rules: William? Those, more adult, who have no faith in the rules espouse new structures and orders to impose: Ben?

"It's to do with provenance, isn't it?" Sue said, breaking my thoughts.

"Yes. It must be."

"This film is verification. That's why it's so important."

"I agree, Sue."

She put her drink down, abruptly. "It sounds dangerous to me. What are you going to do, now?"

I smiled at her. "Don't worry. I'm a great believer in self-preservation." I looked at Ben Nicholson, still on the screen in front of his controversial, geometric work, and the saying slipped straight out from my subconscious. "Never be a pioneer; the Early Christian gets the fattest lion."

She frowned. "Who said that?"

"Saki. Who else?"

Chapter Thirty

"Well, well," Jeremy White said, staring at me across the hard mahogany shine of his Georgian table, on which the Barboroughs' photographs were placed. "Well, well. Well."

Between us, Geoffrey Price had written something, slowly and deliberately, on the fresh, lined block of paper in front of him. He used a rather fat fountain pen of a dated and expensive type, which used ink, real old liquid ink, from a bottle. Probably a glass bottle. I couldn't quite see his notes but I could guess pretty accurately what he had written.

One million pounds?

Jeremy cleared his throat. "You are an astounding fellow, Tim."

"Thank you."

"I take my hat off to you. There has been violence, admittedly, but these seem to be quite exceptional paintings. More important, new to the market. Fresh goods."

"Yes."

"You - um - you are sure that - "

"Would you like me to run through the reasoning in detail for you?"

"If you wouldn't mind."

I had run through it pretty comprehensively with Sue on our way back from Hastings and St.Leonards. Her view oscillated wildly between worry that I might have offered too little and worry that I might have offered too much. She was quite firm about the ethics of the transaction. The paintings had been bought fair and square and belonged to the Barboroughs. No government had any right to prevent them from selling, wherever they might want to sell. They'd had a terrible set of experiences, they were old, and they had a right to retire in peace. No one was going to pay them a pension. Now that we

209

have a son of our own, Sue's more idealistic views on society have been changing.

I had also, swearing them both to silence, revealed Sam Johnson's secret news about Pierre Champion's acquisition to Jeremy and Geoffrey. It seemed only fair in view of what I was proposing. Coming as it did after the recent record sale of a William Nicholson, their shocked faces told of fears, doubts and anxieties about my proposed purchase as much as similar feelings about the nature of the man they were proposing to deal with. At the same time, I could sense suppressed excitement. They felt there was a rush on, like hunters at a bargain sale or sprinters towards a Klondike. Such times engender their own precipitate stampedes.

"Let's take William first," I said. "He's perhaps the easiest. When he died, his reputation went into eclipse. People wrote of him as Ben's father rather than an artist in his own right. Rothenstein and Kenneth Clark were condescending. But people like his work. You particularly, Jeremy. Charles Massenaux too. There is a solid phalanx of collectors who ignore advanced critical opinion, just like people who buy Munnings for big money. They like what they see and they're prepared to pay for it. Who are we to say that they're wrong?"

"They're not." Jeremy was emphatic.

"So, quite recently, someone paid over £90,000 for a lustre mug painting from John Gielgud's collection."

"It did have that Gielgud cachet," Geoffrey piped up for the first time. "This hasn't - "

"The papers say that Gielgud bought it in 1998 for £38,000. Quite an appreciation in three years, isn't it, just for the owner's name? I think we have to move fast, particularly now that someone has paid £175,000 for a Paris street scene."

"I agree," Jeremy was still emphatic. "Although this South African house isn't perhaps what the market most appreciates."

"I think that there are South Africans who'd give their eye

teeth for that painting. Maybe Anglo-American, the owners of Vergelegen, among them. They are not short of a bob or two. The house is part of the country's history. It may be a superior tourist attraction now, and a damned good restaurant plus vineyard, but van der Stel built a Dutch palace there originally, one which made his fellow burghers deeply jealous. It has emotional overtones. I checked: Lionel Phillips spent a fortune restoring the place. He must have been delighted that William painted it during his stay there."

"I suppose - "

"It's a painting not unlike ones Nicholson did at Sutton Veny. He was good at buildings, like his brother-in-law, the shiftless Jamie Pryde, but less stark and depressing. This painting says a lot about him and the Phillips and Edie. I'm surprised he left it behind. Maybe Florence Phillips, his mother-in-law, of whom he was not fond, wangled it out of him. His portrait of her wasn't altogether satisfactory. This could have been a consolation prize."

"You've convinced me. What about Ben?"

"Ah, Ben. Take the white relief first. You may hate it, Jeremy, but architects of the period raved about that part of Ben Nicholson's work. If you look at the *Arena* TV programme on the life of Sir Geoffrey Jellicoe, who was our greatest landscape architect until his death, you can see him walking along the Nicholson Wall at Sutton Place - once Paul Getty's house. Jellicoe is running his hands over the surface and clucking to himself in sheer joy. These reliefs brought massive inspiration to him, to architect friends of his like Freddie Gibberd, and his ilk. The Tate has one. There were all sorts of schemes to do more architectural walls, which didn't come off. Ben was bashful about them but the reliefs set the scene for his post-1945 celebrity. They are important to any record of design."

Jeremy picked up the photograph, scowled at it, shook his head slightly, and smiled. "I must confess to cross checking on you, Tim. I talked to an architect friend about the Modern

Movement. He said that you were right. What about this other one? The 'sill still-life' as you called it?"

"It's probably not going to be as highly rated as his earlier work but it's a classic example of his sort of return to figurative work from abstraction. It should be seen in the context of a chronological series. Both works have their place in his story." I looked at Jeremy, preparing for his fondness for publicity. "We'll almost certainly be asked to loan these to various exhibitions."

"Ah. Very good. But one thing does worry me; you say the Barboroughs wish to avoid publicity?"

"Yes, but I've thought about that. When we announce the purchase we can say we have acquired them from a private source which wishes to remain anonymous. The documentation supporting authenticity can be shown to the expert we'll pay to vet them before we hand over the cash but from there on any papers shown will have their names erased."

"Which expert will you use?" Geoffrey demanded.

I grinned. "Not one from the Tate, to Sue's chagrin. In view of past history I think it would be wise to seek someone objective. There are two or three independents I can think of."

"The money? You think we should pay that much? In view of John Drewe and the upsets?"

"Look, there are fake Picassos and fake Monets, Mondrians, Braques, Van Goghs, you name them. It doesn't stop the real ones from hitting the high numbers, does it? I don't think my assessment is wrong. It's fair to the Barboroughs and it's fair to us. It won't take long for Ben to accelerate. I think we'll set off a landslide. It's now or never."

Jeremy flushed. The word landslide always excites him. The idea of setting one off is irresistible to him.

"Tim. Really. You are a terrible fellow. Aren't you worried about Pierre Champion? A Ben Nicholson landslide will put a fortune into his pocket, won't it?"

"It might. If he has a real one. So what? It won't be a bigger fortune than ours."

212

"How sanguine a view you take. How unlike you that is. I am suspicious. Freddy Harbledown has been asking about you. Did you see Watson? What progress are you making on the archive finance?"

"We have a meeting tomorrow at Mangate."

"Would it be a good idea if I came, too?"

I looked at him in surprise. In his face there was a genuine appeal. Whether he wanted to show support for me in view of my earlier grousing, or whether there was another motive was impossible to tell. I was inclined to give him the benefit of the doubt.

"Of course you are most welcome, Jeremy. We can go up together. Champion, Gerry Watson and Frank Cordwell will all be present"

A look of gratification spread across his face. "Excellent. Thank you, Tim. I hope we can bring matters to a conclusion?"

"I hope so too. I have asked another friend, and his assistants, to join us. It should be a very interesting meeting."

Chapter Thirty-one

Back in Onslow Gardens, on my return from work that evening, I sensed that there was something of a drama in the air.

"Janet," answered Sue, when I made tentative queries as to the reason for her distraction.

"Janet?"

"Floods of tears all afternoon. I've had her all over me. That scoundrel Jim Stockdale has dropped her."

I raised my eyebrows. "Dropped? He's hardly had time to pick her up yet."

"She was setting such store by the relationship. Got frightfully keen on him. He's behaved abominably. What really pisses her off is that she worked like a dog on that exhibition for him. She's absolutely livid. Hours of work, apparently. Quite apart from being generally, well, obliging is I suppose the word to use. He's had his fun and now he's dumped her. It really is a bad business."

I kept my eyebrows back in a level position. It is a feature of the female love ledger that being obliging, in the sense used by Sue, goes down as a female credit entry and is matched by an equivalent male debit. This is despite any female encouragement or enjoyment that may have taken place. Mere men may wish to argue about this odd imbalance of the account, particularly in view of modern attitudes to partnership, but I am too cowardly to bring it up.

"Oh dear. It certainly doesn't seem to have lasted very long."

"She's really upset. She's had bad luck with her boyfriends, really she has. But this rekindles all those paranoid suspicions I had about him."

"Maybe she's fishing in the wrong pool. To someone who is not involved in the art world in any way, Janet might seem an exotic, mysterious creature. To a fellow curator she perhaps seems to be just another dusty academic. It's a case of familiarity and all that."

Sue's eyes widened in surprise. "You know, Tim, you may have something there."

This was a gratifying response on a subject on which I am considered, by Sue, to be something of a tyro. I strolled across to the bookcase, thinking carefully. "If she tried a more physical type, a fireman say, or a stoker in a hot pie factory, she might do better."

I lost credibility immediately.

"Oh, Tim, really! Janet is highly educated. A bit of rough may be all right for a night, but hardly for a more permanent relationship."

"Right, then, that argues for an accountant or a maths master or a lecturer on economics. Someone as far removed from art as possible, but mentally competent."

"God, how dull."

"A banker then, perhaps?"

"I wouldn't recommend a banker to anyone."

"Thanks."

"I still feel he had an ulterior motive. She said this afternoon that he asked to be invited here."

I stood in front of the bookcase. The two Ben Nicholson books, the big 1993 catalogue and Sarah Jane Checkland, were still there, as they had been the night Janet brought Jim Stockdale to dinner. They were joined now by the Marguerite Steen and Andrew Nicholson books on Sir William I had bought from Mr Goodston after this whole thing started.

"Timing," I said out loud. "As in the theatre, timing is everything."

"What?" Sue demanded. "What timing? What are you talking about?"

But fortunately, at that moment, with superb timing, our very own William let out a howl.

So I didn't have to explain.

Chapter Thirty-two

We assembled in the same Essex conference room we had met in before. This time Mangate fielded Pierre Champion, Gerry Watson and Frank Cordwell. Champion looked his normal self, fit and brushed, eyes speculative and keen. He'd flown in from Paris then driven from Stansted. Gerry Watson was as always the urbane, suited London man, unruffled by having to leave Hammersmith early. Frank Cordwell was in his blue jacket and grey trousers, which were badly creased. He looked tired and drawn.

We didn't mention Jessica Browne.

Jeremy and I were met at the door by Sam Johnson, who had been waiting outside in his own car, together with someone I didn't know who stayed in the front passenger's seat. Sam looked at me, looked at my briefcase, and didn't say much.

"I thought we were meeting to discuss the Visual Records project," Champion said, frowning as Sam came into the conference room with us. He initially had a sort of satisfied air as he looked at me, as though he knew something I didn't, but as soon as he saw Sam he looked put out. "I'm waiting for White's proposals. I'm glad to see you've stirred your stumps to be here, Jeremy."

"My pleasure." Jeremy was unperturbed.

"Why have you brought Inspector Johnson?"

"We haven't. He has come of his own volition."

This was not quite true, since I'd persuaded him to come, but technically it was his volition. Jeremy was being economical with the actuality in his own style.

"Inspector?"

"There are matters to clarify, Mr.Champion." Sam was unperturbed, too.

"We are all here about Visual Records, in a sense." I moved

into place on the opposite side of the conference table from Champion and his managers. "Visual records play an important part in what we have to discuss." I gestured for Jeremy and Sam to sit beside me. "I'm glad you have all the necessary projection and video equipment here, and the screen still set up, because there is something we need to watch."

Champion was still disconcerted by Sam's presence. "Oh? What's that?"

"The film you gave Jessica Browne for safe keeping."

He frowned. "That is a private matter. The film is not available for public showing."

Sam Johnson leant forward. "I must insist on seeing it."

"Why?"

"It is material evidence in the investigation I am conducting into the murders of Jessica Browne and Moira Bassington. Also known as Myra Broadbent, Myra Headington and Myra van Rooyen."

Champion blinked.

Sam still leant forward. "You have admitted to me in an earlier discussion that you knew her and that she accompanied you to vintage car race meetings."

Champion glanced about him, having the grace to look slightly embarrassed, but not much. "Yes I have. There is no crime in that."

"Of course not. But you conducted an affair with her?"

"Yes. For a short time. So what? I am not suspected of her murder, surely?"

Sam turned to Frank Cordwell. "Do you still maintain that you did not know her? Remember, I phoned and asked you at the start on my enquiry."

Cordwell gave him a tired look. "I never met her."

"But your assistant, Jessica Browne, was a member of the Iris Barry support group? She must have known her. Bassington belonged to that. Under the name Headington."

"Look, I have better things to do than chat about hen gatherings. If Jessica belonged, she didn't talk about their

217

meetings to me. I knew she was an Iris Barry fan, that's all. Names like Headington wouldn't have meant anything. The whole thing was a girly get-together."

Sam turned to Gerry Watson. "Did you know Moira Bassington? By that or any other name?"

Gerry cleared his throat. "Yes. I met her in company with Pierre. At a car rally. That's all."

Sam paused, then looked at Champion. "May we see the film, please?"

There was a silent moment as he and Champion stared at each other. Then Sam said: "I can take it, and you, all of you, to the local police station to view it if you wish. An Essex police car will be here by now. In your car park."

"Is it really necessary?"

"I insist."

Champion looked at Frank Cordwell and nodded. "You can get it, Frank."

We sat in silence while Cordwell disappeared, came back, and set the film up. It was an old type and he used a cine projector for it.

"I take it," I said to Champion,"that this is a film of Ben Nicholson, in his studio, in 1949? Made for the British Council?"

He stared at me before answering, shortly. "Yes. It is."

Cordwell clicked a switch and the film began slowly to rotate. On the screen in front of us came an image of Ben Nicholson, wiry, alert, small and balding, standing in a white-painted room with battens on the walls. A motor bike stood in one corner. He wore a dark short-sleeved shirt and lighter trousers, like someone going to a summer tennis match. As the reel turned he moved about in front of a huge panel, about seven feet by six. The film was black and white and did not have a sound track. The big panel had circles and squares overlaid with sloping lines, dark and light patches providing some sort of perspective. Without colour, it was difficult to get a proper idea of the depth.

"That's one of two panels for the *Rangitane*," I said. "For the New Zealand Shipping Company. This has to be 1949. You've got a historic record."

No one responded but Champion shot me a look of satisfaction. There were other paintings on the battened walls: a large Cubist-abstract thing and smaller more complex compositions. The film focused on Nicholson, pointing at one of them, then to the big panel. It re-focused on an abstract painting with whorled shapes to the centre. After holding still on this for what seemed quite a while, it moved off again. A table with an old-fashioned kettle amongst pots of brushes came into view. More paintings passed the camera. The film went out of focus, then got it back again. Nicholson gestured briskly. The whorled painting on which the film had dwelt for those long moments could be seen once again, hanging on the battened wall behind him as he spoke soundlessly.

"Enough," I said.

Frank Cordwell switched off. Everyone looked at me.

"You bought a Ben Nicholson painting mostly on the basis of that film. And presumably some documentation," I said to Champion, making it a statement, not a question. "Probably from a man called Danny Mahoney, though he may be using a pseudonym."

He glared at Sam Johnson. "I told you my purchase was strictly a confidential matter. How dare you breach my confidence? I'll have you demoted for this."

"You bought a fake." I made that a statement, too.

"What?"

"You bought the painting the film focused on, the one with whorled shapes, didn't you? The film is black and white. The design you bought is similar to the one on the wall. It is not the same, however. The focusing was cut in to the film to fool you. Someone painted a new Ben Nicholson, like the one on the wall, and had it added to the film. Quite convincing, I'm sure. Danny was good in his day. What colours did he use?"

"Rubbish. You are talking rubbish."

"But you did buy that painting?"

"Yes. It is absolutely genuine."

I opened my briefcase and took out the video I'd got from Dorkie Collins. I put it on the table. "Moira Bassington came across the 1949 film by complete chance during her normal researches. A bit of luck for someone unlucky. Recently, she deposited it with Dorkie Collins in Hastings. This was after your new one was made. She left it with Dorkie as an insurance. She had an accomplice who had arranged to make a new, doctored film but she was fearful of the results. The fake painting sequence was inserted into the doctored film. By keeping the original she kept the evidence. Actually, she had two, or even three accomplices. There was the guy who produced the fake painting, probably Danny. There was a big lug called Jannie van Rooyen who came to grab the original film back from Dorkie after her death, and there was the guy who put up the idea of selling the fake to you in the first place."

"This is fantastic. Pure speculation."

"You deposited this film here after you bought the painting down in the West Country. Jessica Browne, who was curious, looked at it on this very projector. She realised right away that it wasn't as old as it should be and that the sequence didn't quite fit. Those close-ups had been added to an earlier film. To convince you that the Ben Nicholson was genuine. You were in a bit of a hurry. Haste and greed always make a mug for a con man. You thought I was going to invest in Nicholson for the Fund and you had to get in quick."

I paused. Champion stared at me, his face setting. I picked up the video.

"Dorkie was cautious, too. He had his own copy made of the original film. On video. He did it because he didn't trust Myra, or rather the men she consorted with. Which was wise, because they broke in and took her original. They might have killed him if I hadn't arrived by chance. This is Dorkie's copy. Let's put it on, shall we?"

Frank Cordwell stood up, picked up the video and slid it

into the slot of a recorder under a monitor screen. We sat solemnly watching while the same film played through. This time it didn't have the close-up sequence in it. The whorled painting could be seen in the distant background as Nicholson gesticulated. But no detail came up.

"Christ," Pierre Champion said. Then he glared at me. "You've cut the detail out deliberately to discredit my painting."

"I don't need to do that. Dorkie Collins will testify that this is a true copy of Moira Bassington's original film."

He sat still, his eyes widened in tension.

I looked at Frank Cordwell. "She took the doctored film home at lunchtime to have a closer look on her own equipment. I think she phoned you, on your mobile, to tell you her suspicions."

He looked back at me. "She tried to phone me. Her number was on my mobile but I was out of range. By the time I had signal back, it was about four o' clock. There was no answer. She was dead by then."

"Why would she have been suspicious?"

He gestured at the screen. "My guess would be the jump. The jump isn't quite right. From looking at Nicholson, then the big painting, then to focusing on the painting meant to be on the wall. If it wasn't on the wall, as you are inferring, the close-up was done in another studio. When the focus moves off the whorled painting to the table with pots on, there's a cut-in on the movement. It's perfectly normal editing if you're not alert. Jessica could have picked either of those up."

"If she couldn't get you to tell you about it, who would she have phoned?"

"She wouldn't have phoned Pierre until she was dead certain there was a criminal reason for tampering with the film. Until she'd discussed it with me. Showed it to me. The implications were too serious."

I looked at Gerry Watson. "But she might have phoned you if she couldn't get through to Frank. You are a director of

Mangate Visual Records, you understand film technically and you know Pierre better than they did. She'd have asked you what to do."

"She didn't. I received no such call."

Sam Johnson leant forward again. "There was a call to you from her office at ten forty-three that morning."

"So what? The office call me all the time, about all sorts of things."

"This was from her personal line."

"Look here, am I being accused of something? I've accounted for my movements that day."

"I'm afraid you haven't. There's a big gap between the time of your secretary leaving your Hammersmith office and you arriving here at Mangate. A gap in which you could have gone to her house, silenced her forever and brought the film back to its place here in the archives."

"Could. But didn't."

"I think you did."

"What possible motive could I have?"

I gestured at Pierre Champion. "How long before Mangate Solutions makes a profit, Pierre?"

He grimaced. "Four years, maybe five. It's a long-term investment. Same as the photo archives will be."

"You said you had a share in the profits," I said to Gerry Watson. "Not much of a share if there aren't any. I think you took up with Moira when Pierre was finished with her. I think you needed money, or were excited by the prospect of it. When she told you she had that film you had a brilliant idea."

"Crazy. You're crazy."

He looked sideways. Champion was staring at him, narrowing his eyes.

"You told Moira about me. She wrote my name down as a possible mug, too. Or at least as the stimulus to Pierre Champion. Sooner or later, you thought, I'd be bound to get round to looking at Ben Nicholson. You sold the idea of investing in Ben Nicholson to Pierre Champion for much the same reasons as I had. If White's Art Fund were going to invest as well though, it was irresistible. All he had to do was to buy an authentic painting and wait for me to get round to it. You could get a man down in the West Country - Danny Mahoney - to produce the painting, fake up the film and contact Pierre, apparently independently. Bob's your uncle."

"He did." Champion was white, now. "He did give me the idea."

"And bingo, you bit."

"This is crazy." Gerry Watson's mouth was in a set line. "Mad. There is no evidence that I colluded with the dealer, Danny Mahoney in St.Ives, over this."

"No? That's not what Jannie van Rooyen will say."

"Don't bluff. You'll never see Jannie van Rooyen or Danny Mahoney. They'll be long gone."

I looked at Champion. "How much did you pay?"

He hesitated. Then: "Three hundred and sixty thousand pounds."

"By bank transfer, I imagine. On the Continent?"

"Yes."

"To an external account that will have been cleared out by now. Not bad; originally four of them with ninety thousand apiece, now only three with a hundred and twenty each. You didn't go for Sir William as well, as I did?"

He frowned. "Sir William? Sir William Nicholson?"

"It was all a question of timing. Gerry here gave you the idea. Danny Mahoney provided the painting and the documentation. Gerry arranged for the doctored film to go to Mahoney. But the scheme needed confirmation that I was going for a Ben Nicholson. Once that was given the green light, there was no stopping you from snapping one up. And Jim Stockdale gave it to you, either via Gerry here or someone else. I don't know how the connection works, but Sam's men are questioning him now. I have a feeling he belongs to the same film club as Gerry. Stockwell, or South London

223

somewhere. He only saw my Ben Nicholson books. I bought the William Nicholson ones after his visit. Otherwise you'd have been after a William too."

"You have bought both a William Nicholson and a Ben Nicholson?'

"Two of each, actually."

There was a brief silence. Champion stared at me fixedly, still white of face. Then Sam Johnson was back on the trail, directing himself at Gerry Watson. "You killed Jessica Browne because she saw through your film. It was bad luck, really. If she hadn't been curious it might have stayed in store for years. Why did you kill Moira Bassington?"

"I didn't. I had nothing to do with either death."

"Blackmail, was it? Did she want more than her share?"

Gerry Watson didn't reply. He stared fixedly at the table top.

"Mr Watson? Did you hear my question? It is only a matter of time, you know, before we assemble sufficient forensic, documentary and material evidence of your collusion in con-spiracy to defraud and your collusion and direct involvement in murder. Your relationship with Bassington, Headington, Broadbent, van Rooyen, whatever, will come to light in its entirety. It will not take us long to find, in your flat where she lived with you on and off, evidence of her presence."

"She was a tart! It could have been anyone."

"You haven't answered my question."

Gerry Watson glared at him. "Am I under arrest?"

Sam didn't hesitate. "Yes, you are. Gerald Watson, I am arresting you on suspicion of the murders of - "

And then he went through it, the whole necessary official routine, while we sat there, numb and tense as high wires. His companion from the car, as though to a signal, came in to the conference room to listen while he did it. Then they led Gerry Watson away.

We sat alone for a dumb minute.

"Christ," said Pierre Champion, eventually.

"Excuse me," said Frank Cordwell. "This has been horribly upsetting. I'm going back to my office."

He didn't wait for a response. He just got up and left.

"We had better leave, too," I said to Jeremy, whose face was a picture. "I think any questions of finance need to be postponed in view of the circumstances."

I stood up.

"Just a minute," Champion said. He looked quite controlled for a man who's just lost three hundred and sixty thousand pounds and seen his faithful manager arrested for the murder of his ex-mistress, as well as another woman, and conspiracy to defraud him. "I'd like a word with you, Simpson." He avoided looking at Jeremy. "Two minutes, that's all."

Jeremy stood up too. "I'll see you outside, at the car, Tim."

I didn't sit down again. I had no intention of staying longer than Champion's two minutes.

Jeremy left. Champion stood up and moved closer to me.

"How much?" he demanded.

"Sorry?"

"How much do you want? To run this whole show? Frank's obviously a technician. Gerry will get life. You've pulled off a double for your Fund. Name your price. Just name your price and I'll meet it."

"Sorry. I'm not in the market for another job."

An angry tic twitched his mouth. "You'd be better to move now. I'll get White's and Christerby's myself, eventually, you know. The lot."

"I don't think so," I answered. "Not while I'm part of them."

Then I left.

Chapter Thirty-three

There was silence for a while as we motored steadily southwards, then Jeremy spoke.

"I really must come out with you more often, you know," he said. "I really must. I keep forgetting how much I'm missing, stuck there in my office. Life is really dull in the City these days."

"You are most welcome, Jeremy."

"How kind. I shall make a point of it. That was really quite a performance."

"Thank you."

"God, what a shit that man is. Champion, I mean. The whole thing is his fault, really. And what is more I expect he had the insolence to offer you a job, did he? In luxurious terms?"

"Yes he did."

"Utterly unscrupulous. There is simply no limit to the treachery of people like that. The City used to winnow them out sharpish but the old understandings have long gone."

It is an endearing feature of Jeremy that he did not ask me whether I had considered the offer. He just made his perfectly correct assumption that I had not. He and I go back a long way.

After another silent minute or two, he spoke again.

"You'll be telling Freddy Harbledown not to get involved with Champion's project, I suppose?" he queried.

"I rather thought you would want to do that."

"Good heavens, no. I wouldn't intrude on your moment of glory for all the tea in China. I shall come to the meeting, of course. I can't wait to see Freddy's face when you tell him this story."

"He may regret the missed investment opportunity, mayn't he?"

"Indeed. The Bank exists to invest money, not to leave it lying in the safe."

"I've been thinking about that. If it was valid for Pierre Champion to invest in a photo and film archive, why shouldn't we?"

He sat up sharply. "Us?"

"Sure. Our very selves. We have the administrative and financial systems in place. We even have an Art Fund, which has parallels. All we need is the right expertise. I think that Frank Cordwell will be having severe doubts about staying with Champion. I think he's very good at what he does. He might be very susceptible to an offer. Then Bob's your uncle. The White Film Archive. With you, me and Geoffrey at his elbow, Frank Cordwell might do us proud."

"Good God, do you know I sometimes think you are one of the most Machiavellian devils I've ever come across, Tim. You mean you'd swipe Champion's man, just as he tried to swipe you?"

"Let us just say that once we decided to run an archive ourselves, our headhunting consultants approached suitable candidates, amongst whom Frank Cordwell would be obvious. It would follow a decision by the main Board, of course, with Freddy to the fore."

"Fiendish. Absolutely fiendish. I love it. I love it."

"Shall I raise it at our meeting with Freddy, or will you?"

"It's all yours, Tim. All yours. You can rely on my absolute support."

"Thank you, Jeremy." I smiled sideways at his beaming face. "You're happy about the Nicholson paintings? For the Fund?"

He smiled happily. "Rapturous. I've no doubt your expert will be quite emphatic about them. It is a coup. I can just imagine what a field day we're going to have, when we launch the news of this acquisition."

"We won't mention Pierre Champion's duff purchase, will we?"

His smile broadened. "Indeed not. Not at this stage. There is no need for us to say anything. We can leave the police, and the criminal court reporters, to do all of that for us. By the time they've finished, his reputation will be so severely dented that the City will think twice, if not three times, about backing him."

"I feel quite sorry for him, in a way. He's about to join the list of those distinguished unfortunates who've been skinned in the pursuit of a Ben Nicholson. I can hear them all saying 'join the club, Pierre' when this news breaks."

"Save your sympathy." He looked at his watch. "Good heavens do you see what time it is? I wondered why I was feeling peckish. Round here we should be able to find somewhere decent, and I really mean decent, for lunch. Shouldn't we?"

"Of course we can."

"Oh, good." He sat back in his seat and sighed contentedly. "I really must come out with you more often, Tim."

"How about seeing Hamish Lang with me? To tell him the story as well? His face should be worth an outing."

"Heavens. What a wonderful suggestion. Thank you, I shall not miss the occasion." He smiled wolfishly as I turned off the motorway to head for a village restaurant of excellent, if expensive cuisine. "You must admit that, these days, you are having all the fun."

Chapter Thirty-four

"I shall be paying for this breakfast," Nobby Roberts said, after we'd ordered the full works.

"Oh?"

"Yes. I realise that you'll say that it is my turn to pay anyway, but I'm buying this one regardless of turns."

"Really?"

"Yes, really. It has to do with withdrawing that unfortunate remark I made about being corrupted. Lamentable. I apologise."

"Ah. That had been forgotten, Nobby. Entirely forgotten. Like Good Queen Bess, we had forgot the fart, my Lord."

He stared out of the window at the traffic passing on Victoria Street for a moment as though, once again, preparing what he had to say. "As long as events work out the way these have worked out, I feel that these breakfasts bring more of a sense of obligation than anything else."

"Oh, steady on, lad. If they bring feelings of obligation you'll want to discontinue them. Which would be terrible. There is no worse debt than one of gratitude. It works in reverse though, you'll be pleased to hear. If you had not brought up the matter of the lady Bassington, I wouldn't have had the joy of watching Pierre Champion's face go white at the news that he'd been sold a massively expensive fake. More than a couple of Aston Martins' worth. It made the whole thing a delight. The publicity will be worth watching, too."

"I'm glad you see it that way. I'll pay, all the same."

"Handsome of you. I gather Sam Johnson and his resources have assembled a pretty tight case against Gerry Watson?"

"Yes. He declined my invitation to join us today by the way, not because of your performance last time, but due to pressure of work. The CPS seem to think the case is strong. Your dashing curator Jim Stockdale was promised a hefty fee in return for confirming your interest in Ben Nicholson after a visit to your flat. He buckled very quickly under pressure, naming Watson, who was a member of the same film club. But that is minor stuff. The forensic and other evidence in the Jessica Browne case is quite strong."

"What about the money?"

"We found a receipt for one hundred and twenty thousand pounds from a Swiss bank account in Watson's flat. People don't realise what we can find out about Swiss accounts these days."

"Careless of him."

"I'm only sorry we haven't found Mahoney and van Rooyen yet. Mahoney will surface sometime. I expect we'll have to use extradition from South Africa in van Rooyen's case."

"I wouldn't bank on it. If he's got any sense he'll keep his money and himself out of South Africa. What about the Moira Bassington murder? Is it down to him?"

"Watson still denies it vehemently. He says van Rooyen has a hot temper. I think that either he got jealous or maybe she tried to blackmail him. That has yet to come out in the wash; my feeling is that Watson cleaned out her flat, so he was at least an accomplice once the deed was done. He was almost certainly the principal photographer for all those holiday snaps of hers. He admits taking the one in front of the Amilcar. That's when he met her, with Pierre Champion. My gut feeling is that it was him, not van Rooyen; the MOs in both cases are very similar."

I pursed my lips. "Poor Moira Bassington and her belief in her Nicholson heritage. I think she would have gone back to the Eastern Cape with the film and her money. Don't ask me under what name. With the equivalent of a million rand deposited offshore she could have lived well back in South Africa. She could have given the Saki story an entirely different ending. She didn't manage it; Pimlico was her West Africa."

"She doesn't deserve your pity. She was party to conspiracy to defraud."

"She might have argued that she didn't alter the film, fake the painting or forge supporting documents. It was all done by others."

"Try that on Pierre Champion. I think he dropped her and she took up with Watson's suggestion for revenge."

"Hell hath no fury." I was thinking of Janet Heath, whose comments on Jim Stockdale, once she learnt of his real motivation, wouldn't bear repeating.

"You've gone through with your purchase off these Barborough people?"

"Oh yes. All clear and above board. But discreetly, Nobby."

"Understood. And Dorkie Collins?"

"Is back home. Much better. With three percent of a million in his bank account."

He raised his eyebrows. "Three?"

"Yes. In view of the circumstances, Jeremy was happy to agree with my suggestion, despite an original agreement of two and three quarters. He felt, like me, that for coming up with four paintings, Dorkie deserved it."

"Generous of him."

"A rather good lunch on the way back from Essex helped to prepare him for the suggestion. It's a pity lunches are so few and far between these days. It just helped to make me feel that all's well that ends well. I would have hated being a director of a Champion company."

He smiled as our breakfasts were put down in front of us.

"What does Sue think?"

"Oh, she says it was her revelation of the Finch-Hatton connection with the Nicholsons, and hence Jim Stockdale's duplicity, that was crucial to solving the whole case."

"I bet you dispute that."

I shook my head. "Not me, Nobby. It would be foolish to argue such a point. I like the ladies to think that their credit balance is well in the black." I looked down with appreciation at the fried eggs, the bacon, the sausages, fried bread, mushrooms and other delicacies fragrantly steaming under my nose. "That way, they're inclined to be much more - how shall I put it - obliging?"

He frowned humorously. "That's a disgraceful attitude to take. Particularly with someone as fragrant as Sue. She is your wife and the mother of your son, remember?"

"I sit reproved. Nice of you to remind me. I gather Jim Stockdale will not be using his spare time to finish his book, anyway. An American woman has got in front of him."

He looked at me thoughtfully. "That Finch-Hatton business was confusing. There were references coming up all over the place."

"Yes. Too many. I had them going round and round in my head along with all the Nicholson material."

"Thank heavens your head keeps so many facts in it, no matter how abstruse. But I'm sure there are times when it's too full." He raised his head to quote. *"In baiting a mousetrap with cheese, always leave room for the mouse."*

"Oh no. Don't tell me - "

"Yes. It is. Saki." He speared some breakfast goodies and smiled at me. "I'm getting the hang of it, Tim."